TONY EVANS was born was forced out of the city of the Thatcher years and United States in his early eventually became Football

These days he is a freelance writer and broadcaster, specialising in the crossovers between sport and politics. He lives in London with his wife and daughter.

Follow Tony on Twitter: @TonyEvans92a

GOOD GUYS LOST

TONY EVANS

Northodox Press Ltd
Maiden Greve, Malton,
North Yorkshire, YO17 7BE

This edition 2022

1
First published in Great Britain by
Northodox Press Ltd 2022

Copyright © Tony Evans 2022

Tony Evans asserts the moral right to
be identified as the author of this work.

ISBN: 9781915179159

This book is set in Caslon Pro Std

For Grace, whose response to adversity has been
breathtaking for one so young.

And Alisa, whose love and strength keeps us going.

CHARISMA

'There has never been a better time to be poor,' the youth said, catching the attention of the group of boys sitting or squatting around him on the stairs on their tenement block. They ceased their game of pontoon to listen. Silence in such a gathering was unusual, and as the spitting and swearing subsided, the nine teenagers found themselves tuned in onto the same wavelength.

Billy paused just long enough, perhaps too long, so that the tension almost broke. When he spoke again, there was a surge of belief in his voice, a tone that captures an audience.

Two flights above, in an identical concrete stairwell, which the sun never reached, a four-year-old felt the thrill of the words as much as the group below. It was the first time the child had consciously experienced charisma and, like the youths downstairs, he felt captivated.

'There has never been a better time to be young and working class. For the first time, we have money in our pockets. The world knows who we are. Everyone wants to talk like us. Our accents open doors. We can do exactly what we want and we don't have to be like our mams and dads.'

Somewhere in his oration, Billy's charisma had gone awry. When he'd spoken of parents, his mates had begun to snort, then curse, and finally deal their cards. The authentic conviction of his opening gambit drifted away, and then he was just another kid fighting to make his voice heard over the flippant upsurge.

The clamour grew gaudier until the neighbour, Mrs Ashton, appeared with a bucket of water to flush the group out of the gloom and into the sun. They laughed and jeered at each other and indirectly at their neighbour.

The group mooched off to find another block to lay out their cigarettes, tanners, and cards. The flats, running in long rows between Vauxhall and Scotland Road, spewed out the meat that fed the factories and docks.

Billy looked back and spotted the boy peering through the railings on the third landing. He winked extravagantly and skipped off at the rear of the little gang, bouncing along with the happy- threatening strut young men assume in groups.

He was wrong, of course. This was 1965 and the doors that appeared to be ajar to Billy and his friends were illusionary. The accent was no longer opening escape routes. Those who rode The Beatles' coattails had already done so, often with faux versions of the Liverpool dialect.

But his charisma lingered in the air as it does when it leaves an imprint, however fleeting its presence. The young boy sat on the stairs and savoured its feeling, repeating the words and trying to feed in the crackle of relevance with no success. 'There has never been a better time to be poor,' the child said. 'Never.'

The eavesdropping boy was me, of course. I realise, when I look back, that this was the instant that I became properly sentient and became aware of the world. There were earlier memories; they were a tableau of fleeting significance with little substance.

He had not thought about being poor before that moment. After this, it became clear what it meant. It was the day I joined the great war against patronage, the crusade against vulgarism. Or am I recounting history backwards?

Things are so different now, so much change has occurred, that I don't recognise that child. He lived in a different world than the one I now inhabit. I can only recall his story as if it happened to someone else. His growth into adulthood and the struggles that came along the way feel like a tale told to me by someone else, someone I distrust. The dismantling of the fabric of his society somehow broke the narrative chain between me and him.

Perhaps none of the subsequent battles involved me at all. So why am I so certain I was on the losing side?

Billy's story is easier to tell, but it throws up many questions. Some are difficult to answer. It is best to start with the hardest.

What generates charisma? Separates one man from another and allows a politician or entertainer to stand before an audience and immediately, instinctively, grasp their attention? What is it that speaks and spells, coruscating brilliance to the world?

Billy had it. Sometimes. Where did it come from? It is simpler to explain where he came from.

He was born on a January night in 1950, making his grand entrance with an unexpected, though typical, flourish. His mother, Lilly, still had a month to grow when she sat on a misplaced knitting needle. The unexpected enema forced a sudden and premature labour. There was barely time for the midwife to arrive before a squalling boy popped out, born at home in Burlington Street and nonetheless healthy for it.

Billy caused a fuss right from the start. Few households were so divided by a choice of name. Mickey, Lilly's husband, was away at sea at the time of birth. He was still a week from port when the needle precipitated his son's early entrance.

The new father was outraged when presented with little William. He was expecting a boy to be given the names James Larkin, in homage to the great labour leader and republican. That honour would have to wait for his second son, two years later. His wife used Mickey's absence to register the child with a forename of her choice.

It wasn't a simple matter of taste that enraged her husband. William was just another name across most of England, but on the

Celtic fringe - and in the tenements of Liverpool's Catholic North End - it was imbued with politics, triumphalism and humiliation.

Billy's mother had grown up a mile inland, on the Protestant slopes of Everton Brow. It was a parallel, orange-tinted universe to the dockside community in which she gave birth.

In the terraces off Netherfield Road, fidelity to the crown was instinctive and William of Orange a symbol of Protestant domination. The loyalty of the residents was unshakeable. They often decorated the fanlight windows above the front doors with crude depictions of King Billy on his white charger at the battle of the Boyne or beautifully composed photographs of George VI displaying sombre regality. Respect for the monarchy was ingrained in Everton's heights.

From the scrubbed steps of their terraced houses, the Protestant occupants could look down the steep streets all the way to the Mersey and beyond. What they saw was alien territory. The demarcation line was clear. England as they knew it ended at Great Homer Street, the home to the ragged bazaar known as Paddy's Market, where the North End's poorest shopped.

Three hundred yards west of the market was St Anthony's church, perched on Scotland Road like a beacon for the disposed. Squeezed between here and the river were the cramped, pinched tenements where Catholics lived, still rife with rancid courts and leaky cellar dwellings. More than a century had passed since the Famine, but the folk memory of division persisted. Lilly's childhood Protestant neighbours despised "the Irish" of the docklands. The Papists refused to assimilate and produced throngs of feral children, they told each other. Her father was in the Orange Lodge and proud of his staunchness.

Marrying someone from the other side of the religious divide was still anathema in the 1940s, but Lilly crossed the line for love. It could have been a dangerous adventure.

The sectarian riots that Lilly's parents remembered in the early part of the century were largely a thing of the past, but there were enough flashpoints during the marching season to make life uncomfortable for interlopers in the other community. Lilly moved into an overwhelmingly Catholic and republican area. It had sent an Irish Nationalist MP to Westminster less than two decades before she married Mickey. Down in Liverpool 3, even the most meagre slums were decorated with pictures of Popes. No one wore orange.

She would never deny her background, though. Billy might have been born under the gaze of a pontiff, but his mother used him to assert her identity.

So, it was with a certain amount of satisfaction that Lilly watched the Irish parish priest scowl at young William's name over the baptism font. You don't have to be a bigot to enjoy annoying priests– or husbands, for that matter.

For all that, Billy grew up in a happy home. In the tight-knit tenements, Lilly could've been seen as an outsider– especially with a husband away at sea for long periods. But, right from the start, she embraced the complex network of insular, extended family relationships that characterise ghetto life. She had a forthright honesty that defied exclusion. People liked her. She had something about her.

It would have been easy for others to resent the family. By the standards of the neigbourhood, they were well off. Mickey was a 'Cunard Yank,' a seaman who made the Liverpool-New York run in the summer on the Britannic, leaving the bomb-craters and austerity of a land fit for heroes for cities that were filled with luxuries and pleasure. In an era when few men of any social background knew their wife's dress size, Mickey and his friends would shop for their womenfolk in Macy's and Bloomingdales, stopping by at Sears and Brooks Brothers for their own suits. When the stores are 3,000 miles away, you'd better get the right fit.

They strutted home from the docks carrying bags full of food and clothes, but that was the least of it. Fridges, record players and washing machines were bought cheaply in the second-hand shops of Manhattan, manhandled up the gangplank and, with a little help from the ship's electrician, made workable– if not safe– on the National Grid.

So Billy, when he wasn't clambering over the adventure playgrounds the Luftwaffe had created, stealing lead and committing the casual vandalism that comes naturally to young boys, came home to clothes and toys that his school friends could only dream about. 'They dress him like a little prince,' the old women would say admiringly after church on Sunday.

Then there was the music. Mickey's younger shipmates, sharp in kid mohair suits and Tony Curtis haircuts, would bring home records fresh from Birdland or the Metronome. They blared out of the tenements, echoing across the concrete valleys and bouncing off factory walls.

The young bucks bought instruments, too, imagining that in their idle hours in the cabins they would learn to play and– maybe– one day make recordings themselves. It was from one such dreamer who had quickly grown bored with his instrument that Mickey bought a Gretsch semi-acoustic guitar for his eldest son. For a couple of years, it was of little interest to Billy and lay unused in the flat. Then, when he was ten, he picked it up and studied it with intent for the first time. Rock 'n' roll had arrived. Times had changed. He'd never had it so good.

The once stringless and unloved guitar took over Billy's life. At first, the pads of his fingers hurt, but with persistence, he learned to strum and fingerpick a tune. Instinctively, his brain could unravel the mathematical formulae behind a variety of songs and recompute them for a voice more suited to the sea shanty. The sound was plaintive, nasal, and cheaply moving. It could hold an audience, however briefly, to silence. It granted Billy charisma.

He began to entertain. Initially, it was just family and friends who came together after Sunday dinner, bottles of Mackesen cracked for women, whiskey poured for men primed by the pub for a singalong. Billy would roughly duplicate the hits of the day– Smoke Gets In Your Eyes, Cathy's Clown– earning coos and generous nods.

Capturing the audience and keeping it were different problems. The diet of chart toppers soon lost the wavering attention. This was family activity, not a concert. Everyone wanted to sing. What Do You Want To Make Those Eyes At Me For? would get things going but, invariably, he was forced to play the 'old songs,' even though they were of no great vintage: If You're Irish, Come Into My Parlour and Come Round Any Old Time.

On Sundays, with the reek of carrot, turnip, and cabbage still lingering after a robust dinner, a dozen or more people would cram into the tiny living room and talk, smoke, drink, and sing. At teatime, two white, square boxes of cakes and jelly cremes from Sayers were produced. The young minstrel was well rewarded with treats as well as threepenny bits, tanners, and shillings.

When Billy was thirteen, the Sunday afternoon venue changed. He started taking his guitar to the parish club after the lock in. He would be indulged in a song or two of his own choice and half a bitter before drink gave his neighbours a voice. Then, he would strum Your Cheating Heart while a local woman poured what feelings she had left after producing half a dozen or more children into a wobbly yodel that encapsulated the pub-singer's pain. The drinkers loved country and western, the descendent of rhythms that had, like these people, left Ireland in a time of famine. The music had journeyed on to the Americas, to be made richer and more powerful, and had returned to touch the lives of the fellow travellers who had been beached in Liverpool. Soon the songs of the stranded were to sweep the world, but no one could imagine that when Billy initially took to the stage. Soon, though, he was adding Beatles' tunes to his repertoire and dreaming that he could follow in their footsteps. For the time being, he had to be content to duet with drunks, dream of Nashville and show off his beer breath to his mates as they shuffled along to six o'clock mass.

One Sunday afternoon, after he had been entertaining drinkers in the big club, Billy was packing up his guitar when a woman called him over to her table.

'You were good, lad,' she said, over a forest of Mackeson bottles. 'You should let Sissy tell your fortune. She'll tell you whether you're going to be the next Gerry Marsden.'

Billy looked at the women with suspicion. Was he being mocked? But Sissy Campbell, who was in her thirties but could have been nearing double that age, grabbed his wrist and began examining his palm.

'I see a future for you on the stage,' she said with great seriousness. Despite his misgivings, he wanted to know more.

'The Landing Stage!'

The women cackled, and Billy felt foolish. 'The Lanny' was at the Pier Head, a dock that rose and fell with the tides of the Mersey. It was the world's first floating platform for servicing ships and a source of civic pride. It was also a site of tragedy.

Billy's grandfather had been a porter there thirty years earlier, waiting for liners to land so he could earn a pittance by hauling the trunks of the wealthy from the river to the Adelphi Hotel. When he was thirty-one, a seagull pecked him in the eye and the wound became infected. He did not live to see thirty-two.

The crones guffawing around the table knew that a mesh of tight-knit communities was frequently barbed, but the easy joke couldn't be resisted.

Trying not to show how severely the malevolent gibe had

affected him, the young man took his guitar case, went down the stairs, and pushed open the exit. Outside, he breathed in the afternoon air and made a momentous decision. That would be the last time he would entertain for free. He would never again perform merely to give pleasure to an ungrateful audience. If he was to be humiliated after performing in the future, he would be paid for his art.

Across Burlington Street, from one of the perverse courtyards that gave Portland Gardens its name, came the sound of boys playing. There was a thirty-a-side football match going on, and Billy went across and looked over the wall at the mayhem. Jimmy, his brother, spotted him and trotted across.

'Come'ed, Tommy's waiting. Go pudding and beef.'

If someone turned up and the sides had equal numbers, the newcomer had to remain a spectator until someone else arrived to even up the teams. The pair would confer and decide who would be the designated 'pudding' or 'beef.' The choice would generally be made by the toughest kid in the game; the 'cock' of his street or block, who called whichever word came to mind. It was a coin toss for kids who had no coins and randomised the selection, so that all the best players didn't congregate on the same team. But Billy didn't want to get involved. 'Nah, I'm fed up,' he said. 'I feel like a pudding, anyway.'

He told his younger brother about the incident in the club. 'They're soft,' Jimmy said dismissively. 'Come'ed, play. Tommy's been waiting ages.' The other boy looked on in disappointment. His hopes were raised by Billy's arrival, but now he went and sat on the wall, frustrated.

Billy was not interested. He went home and sat spreading chords slowly as the twilight deepened.

When darkness fell and the squares were quiet during mass, Billy headed towards the church. Sissy Campbell lived on the ground floor of the Bond Street flats and her back windows looked across Eldon Street at Our Lady's. Billy had not come to pray. He launched a fragment of brick through the woman's window and scampered through the arch back into Bond Street before the glass had stopped tinkling. He slipped into the deserted stairwell of the next block and sat down, hidden just beyond the first turn on the stairs. 'Predict that,' he said before strolling down to Vauxhall Road, where his mates were lurking around the doorway to The Black Dog pub.

'Why shouldn't working-class men dress well? Why shouldn't working-class men wear nice suits?'

The boy would hear the phrase again almost two decades later, as a declaration of class war. But this was the first time it reached his ears. The speaker was his uncle, Bobby Moran, responding to a barmaid's flirtatious suggestion that he was a bit 'flash.' Uncle and nephew had been to Anfield together for the match and had stopped at the Honky Tonk on Scotland Road because Bobby wanted to see someone. Nobody called him by his real name, though. He had long been known as 'Duke' because of a childhood obsession with John Wayne.

Everything is connected. Duke was Billy's cousin, too. The way the boy looked up at Billy, Billy looked up to Duke. The nickname suited him. He had something special about him. Perhaps it was the smell.

Duke smelled of the gym, sweat, and power. Yet, all the pungency that drove people away was absent. An odour of distilled masculinity, a heady, magnetic scent with the merest undercurrent of threat that needed no cosmetic overlay.

Duke wore midnight blue kid mohair suits and had an aura of confidence that seemed borrowed from a different social class. Stolen would be a more accurate word, for he was a thief.

'My name's crime,' he would say, while selecting whatever he wanted in a shop. 'And crime doesn't pay.' Shoplifting was just the beginning.

The age of the Cunard Yank had passed, and the likes of

Duke assumed the succession and the glamour, although their only voyaging came on the Seacombe ferry. Yet these were men who were also travelling beyond the limit of their horizons.

This was a time when gangsters and footballers lived among the communities that bred and revered them. Their income was maybe three times that of the average wage, and they lived in tenements, terraces, and semis in the suburbs. Some even felt responsibilities to those around them.

Most people thought Duke could've been either. Both of the city's football clubs had given him trials, but the distinct and discrete mindsets of the gangster and sportsman were mutually exclusive, and Duke's talents pushed him towards darker games than passing and shooting.

He was a natural athlete and boxed almost as well as he headed the ball. Early on, though, he knew he was not belt-winning quality. In the ring at Lee Jones, better boxers were scared of him. They knew that in the less subtle arts of street fighting, Duke was championship material. The head that drove caseballs towards the net crushed noses and shut down senses quicker than his punches.

By night, he donned the tuxedo of a doorman. By day he stole, progressing from the shoplifting of his youth to breaking into bonded warehouses. By the mid-1960s, he was branching out to sub-post offices and dreaming of a lucrative bank job. His friends and accomplices had dangerous nicknames: The Gasman, the Panther, the Dog. They were feared figures.

Duke was born on December 21st, 1940, as German bombs rained down on the city. Just before the raid started, his mother went into labour with her fourth child, sirens howling their warning. The pregnant woman was rushed to Mill Road Hospital from the family flat in Blackstock Gardens. Neighbours ushered the other three kids down to the air-raid shelter in the block.

While Mrs Moran screamed in agony at Duke's prolonged entry, a German bomb scored a direct hit on the flimsy shelter back home. There were hundreds of people inside: not only had locals flooded down the tenement staircases to find protection, two trains on the nearby line had been stopped and their passengers directed to apparent safety.

They lost count of the bodies after the two hundred mark because rescuers could not jigsaw the mass of limbs and trunks together in a verifiable manner. Two of the Moran children were never identified nor found. The eldest, Joey, was at the top end of the shelter, playing with a mate. When he recovered consciousness, ten-year-old Joey was trapped between his dead friend and an avalanche of rubble. It was not the end of the family's anguish over that grim holiday season.

Their father, in the Merchant Navy, would never hear about his children's deaths or the birth of his son. He was in the engine room of the SS British Premier off the coast of Africa on Christmas Day when U-65's torpedoes sunk the tanker. His body was never found. The Morans were one of the many families in the area whose lives were destroyed during that dreadful December.

The sense of drama and tragedy which greeted Duke's arrival into the world never left him. He followed in his big brother's footsteps, working as a bouncer. Men feared Joey Moran. During his adolescence, he became an expert fist fighter, honing his violent skills while on National Service; and after his discharge, Joey was recruited to man the doors of the more upmarket clubs in town.

Duke was different, even though he was almost as dangerous. He had a swagger his brother would never carry off. At twenty-six, the younger was widely admired and the Tate and Lyle's swooned when he walked along Vauxhall Road dressed, with no exaggeration, to kill.

Wiser women, like his mother, despaired. Any wife he took would have to live dangerously. In love, like everything else, Duke did his finest work outside the rules, beyond the law.

Duke had an eye for trouble. He sensed it first and dealt with it; some said prematurely. Initially he avoided becoming a doorman, working in St John's market, humping crates of produce on and off trucks before dawn for paltry wages and the odd box of unsold fruit. It didn't take long for him to recognise his more unsavoury skills were worth being paid for. His older brother had forged a reputation as a hard man, and the youngster followed the family trade.

When Duke dropped the child at home after leaving the Honky Tonk, his sister-in-law told him that Billy was looking for him. 'He said he wanted a word.' The boy was sent to run down the block to see if Billy was home.

Before phones, kids often acted as couriers. 'Will you go on a message for me?' was a regular question asked of them by adults and it could mean going to the shops or passing on information. It usually came with a reward of a tanner or a shilling.

Billy wasn't at home. The child left word that Duke was heading to town and would be about for the next few hours.

It took Billy a while to locate his cousin; starting off in Ma Moores, before looking in the Pieshop and later about the Mitre. There was no sign, just the faint aftersmell of Duke's presence overriding the tobacco, body odour and the stench of ale. He was directed across Dale Street to the Manchester Street Wine Lodge, where he found his quarry untangling from a conversation with a half-drunk middle-aged neighbour. Surreptitiously, Duke gave the man a brown ten-bob note and turned his attention to his relative.

They stood at the long narrow bar and talked football for a while, Billy basking in the reflected glory, until he felt brave enough to get to his point.

'I need a job,' he said. 'Can I do anything with you?'

'You play guitar, I sing,' Duke laughed.

'On the door of the club?'

Duke smiled. 'You look just about hard enough to collect

glasses. What do you want me to do? If some buck kicks off, hold him while you hit him?'

Billy shrugged. 'Go to sea,' Duke said. 'Your Dad will sort you out. Get your ticket. Get out of here for a while. Take your guitar, see the world, and practice in your cabin. You don't want to be like me. Look at my nose.' It was flattened at the bridge. Billy thought it suited Duke's face perfectly.

'Besides, what would your Dad do to me if you started running round the club playing the hard man? Get on a liner. Go around the globe. Get to know some exotic girls. If I was your age and had a chance to get out, I would.'

It did not take second sight to see that Billy was destined for at least a spell on the ships and the landing stage beckoned. Within weeks of the meeting in the wine lodge, he disappeared. People often did in these parts, for months and sometimes years. Inquiries about whereabouts were often met with the answer: 'Gone to sea.' Occasionally, it was true.

There's a photograph of Billy's wedding day that tells the story better than any words but to show it here would be a betrayal. It would prove that this is not mere fiction, and some fictions must be maintained. So all that is left is description.

Billy captures the eye. Ever the showman, he is trying to make the best of it. His hair is parted far on the right and has a lacquered stiffness. It would take prolonged shaking to make it Beatleish.

He is wearing a suit, modishly cut but without the flamboyance of Duke's two-piecers. A carnation is angled across the narrow lapel, the petals dangerously close to a handkerchief fluffed out of the breast pocket. The shirt is white, basic and the tie thin and striped. He looks like a grammar schoolboy playing at being a grown up.

There is a discernible gap between Billy and his new wife. They are not a couple: they are still too young to show intimacy in public. Marie – pronounced, ironically, as 'Marry' - has her head angled slightly towards the groom, her charcoal hair under a lace veil. The face is bowed, with her chin sucked in. The initial impression is that she is trying to avoid the scrutiny of the camera. Her dress is lacy at the sides with a plain front panel. It is flared at the waist. The shapelessness is deliberate. The hem stops two or three inches above the knee. It would make a fine communion dress.

Billy's hand rests on a little boy's shoulder. The child is wearing short pants, as if to give Billy's grown-up demeanour a frame of reference. Under a V-neck jumper, the boy has a white shirt and an elasticated bowtie. Like Marie, the youngster has that timid, embarrassed smirk of someone feeling uncomfortable.

Looking again, it is not Billy that stands out, but a chain of hands, a train of contact that runs across the centre of this photograph. Billy's fingers grasp the boy's right shoulder, seeming to propel the little arm across the child's body to where it meets Marie's gloved hand. That is the path of touch on this sad little snapshot. A young couple forced into marriage while incapable of showing direct affection in public. You could write a novel about this picture. It would not be a book about love.

It was a registry office wedding. That itself signified shame. Afterwards, a strange little celebratory dinner was held at The Mons, a new pub on Breeze Hill in Bootle. There were less than twenty people present; it was for immediate family and the very close. There were no friends of the couple invited. Even Duke was excluded.

Everything had been arranged quickly.

Less than two months earlier, Billy had returned from his travels. His tan and newfound confidence made it clear that he had really been away to sea. He was a boiler-room man on the Canberra, transporting ten-pound Poms to freedom in Australia. Friends were beguiled with tales of exotic beauties from Suez to Sydney. Hometown girls were entranced by his apparent sophistication and freespending attitude. His contemporaries saw a new worldliness about Billy, but his mother was less easily fooled.

'Hey, you, dirty ticket,' she said as he admired himself in the mirror before heading out for a night in town. 'You be careful.' Billy just laughed.

She was particularly concerned about Marie, a plain but flighty little thing from Burroughs Gardens. Lilly began counting off the days until her son was back on the high seas. It could not come quickly enough.

Disaster came sooner. It takes many forms, but this calamity began with a knock on the door at 4.30 on a Tuesday afternoon. Lilly opened up to find a woman on the landing, headscarf pinched under her chin and a determined expression on her face. It was Marie's mother. The two women knew each other by sight, but had never spoken.

'Mrs Green, I need to talk to you about our Marie and your William.' Immediately, Lilly knew her worst fears had come to fruition. 'You'd better come in,' she said. It was not how she had imagined finding out she was going to be a grandmother.

Billy could not believe how fast the world changed. It was a matter of weeks from the rather unsatisfactory premature ejaculation that precipitated the crisis to the hasty legalities that tied him into a loveless marriage. This was no way to lose your virginity.

The ostensibly childlike Marie was more experienced than her husband but no less bewildered by the whirlwind wedding. She looked even more of a lost adolescent than the boy she had married. One waitress at the reception asked Marie if she had enjoyed her day as a bridesmaid. 'I'm the bride,' the young girl replied haughtily. The server guffawed at what appeared to be a joke. No one else was laughing. There were no tips that afternoon.

This slight was the only memorable part of the day. There were no speeches. At the end of the meal, the group split up. There would be no long night of singing in Burly; no guitar playing; no old songs. There were none of the usual rituals of union and celebration. Billy went back to his in-laws and a different life. Any drinking was mournful. This had not been a marriage. It had been a public disowning. Things would never be quite the same again.

The phrase "gone away to sea" was often a euphemism for jail. For Billy, work was a release. It was a relief to be away from his in-laws. Home and family were the prison. He was used to being in cramped quarters with people he would not choose for roommates, but life in his new home made the existence below decks feel like a holiday cruise.

This trip did not have the carefree nature of his previous voyage. He did little socialising when in port. He was reluctant to spend as before. With the money he saved, he was hoping to rent a place of his own when he got home.

He also worried that, like his father, he would be at sea when the baby arrived, although his older crewmates averred it might be for the better if he missed the drama of birth. And so, with history repeating itself, he arrived back in Liverpool to be welcomed by a son and a wife. Neither seemed particularly happy to see him. His new wife was resentful at his presence and experience. Billy had not shared her life for long enough to make any sort of imprint; and while she grew and groaned, he had surely been exploiting the full potential of the glamorous fleshpots of the east, at least in her hormone-fuelled imagination.

There had been friction between the families, too. Marie, heavily pregnant and heavily indignant, had loudly complained at bingo that Billy had not sent her any money for weeks and that life was a cakewalk for seamen compared to her lot. Gossip like this spread widely and rapidly and, two days later, the young wife emerged from the same bingo venue to find her mother-in-law waiting. Billy might be in disgrace in Lilly's household, but no one – not even his spouse – was going to badmouth him in public. A short, intense exchange took place, and Marie departed in tears. The women never spoke again. In the space of a year, Billy's future had gone from one of endless horizons to being at the centre of a domestic conflict he could not control.

Home was no longer welcoming. So, this is how it feels to be a man, he thought: claustrophobic, powerless, and terrified. He would have taken solace in his guitar, but he had already been shouted down by his in-laws for attempting to strum a lullaby for his baby son. For the first time, he understood the urge to run away to sea. He was eighteen, and the Sixties had ended for him two years early.

It might have been easier if the mutual antipathy with his young wife didn't stop at the bedroom door. Sex was the only time they came together. The mistake that led to the shotgun wedding was compounded by two more errors. In 1969, another boy was born and in 1970 a girl came along.

Life was getting more difficult. The liner trade was dying as aeroplanes made international travel quicker and easier. Now Billy waited to be allocated a ship from 'the pool', the list of sailors looking for work. While he mooched about Liverpool, the money started to run low and the already strained relations with his young wife – now almost old enough to get the key to the door – grew worse.

Shortly after his third child was born, Billy sailed on the Axina. The relative luxury of the Canberra was gone, and the future would consist of grittier vessels and voyages. The age of the tanker was arriving.

It was a perilous career. Transporting highly flammable material is always a risk. Two years earlier, three tankers exploded while their storage areas were being cleaned. Oil carriers on the Vietnam run had been shelled by the Viet Cong.

Going away to sea for long periods is fraught with different kinds of danger, too. While Billy was moving slowly south from the Persian Gulf, happily strumming his guitar, something hit the rocks: his marriage.

The crisis was provoked by fears that he was dead. The Axina's radio officer had a breakdown mid-voyage and failed to maintain contact with the outside world. He ignored all attempts to communicate with the ship. Concern mounted across the maritime industry for more than a week. Meanwhile, Axina steamed on, oblivious to the growing panic ashore.

Newspaper reports tried to play down the seriousness of the situation. 'It is possible that they may have some engine problems,' a Shell company spokesman said. The lack of radio contact told its own story to the experienced sea salts in the dockland pubs of Liverpool. One of Billy's old school friends listened in to the downbeat conversations in the bar of the Glass House. He decided to visit Marie that night to console her. She welcomed the attention. It felt like this was the first man to show her any interest since her marriage – and that included her husband. In the next few doom-laden days, Mike Larty was almost an ever-present in Marie's life. He gave her the sort of emotional support she had never felt from her absent spouse. He was different, too, from many of the men from the area. Larty was studying for a degree at the Polytechnic and hoped to become a teacher. He was mockingly nicknamed Bamber, after the presenter of University Challenge, a TV quiz show. She was smitten. For the first time in her life, Marie was in love. She was secretly delighted Billy was dead.

Then the good news came through that the Axina was safe. The ship's first officer had been relaxing on Sunday and had tuned in to the BBC World Service. He almost choked on a cup of tea when he heard the grim report about his missing ship. He charged up to the bridge to inform the captain, and the pair stormed to the radio room. Nearly ten days' worth of messages had been unsent and desperate attempts to make contact had been left unacknowledged. The emergency on the high seas was over.

Back in Liverpool, the crisis was just beginning. Billy would not know. He was a month away from being paid off. His wife's new romance still had plenty of time to germinate.

Duke was used to starting dialogues that other people did not want. Now he had to instigate a conversation he dreaded. Again, he met Billy in the Manchester Street Wine Lodge. It was quiet there in the first hour after opening and they were unlikely to be interrupted. They embraced in the long, brown, smoky bar. A drunk sat nursing a glass of Aussie Whites. Other than that, there were just the two of them and the barman. The older man ordered two whiskeys with the pints. His companion raised his eyebrows. It was only just gone five in the evening.

Billy had returned home the night before to a very strained reception. He knew something was wrong – it always had been difficult, but now it was worse. The married couple barely spoke.

When Billy complained about his rather sour welcome, Duke was relieved. He had feared an explosion of violence if Marie had admitted her new relationship. People were talking, though, and it was only a matter of time before Billy heard the gossip.

'Bamber?' the cuckolded husband said, aghast, when the news of the affair was relayed. 'Are you sure?' Duke nodded.

'He's my mate. I went to school with him.' They moved on to Bismarck, a fortified port, to supplement the pints of Guinness. 'Well, not my mate. He was in our class, though. I'll kill the fucker.'

'If anyone does any killing, it'll be me,' Duke said sternly. 'I wanted to wait until you got home before doing anything serious. I warned him off. I spoke to Marie. Go home and make it up with her. She's only a kid. You're only a kid.'

'I'm going back to my mam's tonight,' Billy said. 'I'll come to the club first.'

They left the Wine Lodge heading for the Hotsy Totsy in North Street. It was only three hundred yards or so away. Duke was on the door that night. They were passing the Mitre as Mike Larty emerged laughing with four mates. Everyone froze except Larty, who ran back into the pub followed by Billy. Duke said nothing but scanned the faces of the adulterer's three mates, who he knew fancied themselves as hardcases, catching the eye of each. They had the good sense to know when to back off. 'Stay out of it,' Duke said. No one argued.

Larty exited the Mitre on Dale Street and crossed the road. It was a mistake. He was not quick enough, and Billy caught him after about forty yards and sent him skidding with a blow to the back of the head. Larty scrambled on all fours, reached the wall guarding the approaches to the Queensway tunnel, and tried to use it to stand up. Billy kicked his legs away and began punching, blow after blow, raining on to the victim's head. The attacker felt his knuckles break and the power begin to leave his fists, so he picked up a short length of wood that was on the floor and used it to beat his quarry. The stick became bloody and Larty lapsed into semi-consciousness.

Duke took his time following. He walked through the Mitre slowly, poised. He had an image to maintain. It became clear that the chase had exited the pub and his pace quickened as he went back on to Dale Street. A small crowd of people were standing watching the beating. Immediately, Duke could see things had spiralled out of control. A woman was yelling, 'Where's the police? We need a policeman.'

'Enough,' Duke shouted. Billy looked over his shoulder, turned back to the lifeless body he had been hitting, and seemed to relax. 'We've got to go, Billy,' Duke said.

Instead of turning to leave, Billy picked Larty up. Duke was confused for a moment. Then he saw his cousin lift the man and haul him to the crest of the wall. 'No!'

Billy got the body to the top and pushed him over. Even with the traffic noises, Duke could hear the thud when Larty landed. Beyond the wall, ten feet below, was one of the exit lanes of the Mersey tunnel.

'Fuck,' Duke said, grabbing Billy and pulling him away. 'He'd better be dead.' Then he looked at the watching crowd and changed his mind. 'He'd better not be dead.' Duke leapt up on the wall and peered over. No car had hit Larty, and he was moaning and moving. Tunnel police were swarming towards the victim. 'You need to get out of here, Billy. Let me see what I can do.'

'I'm going to jail,' Billy said, walking back towards the Mitre. 'It can't be worse than my life now. I'll have another drink or two. I'll be off the ale for a while. You go the club. You don't want to get nicked as well.'

Duke shrugged sadly. It was all so obvious and public that no one would be able to claim Billy was back at sea.

GIRL POWER

'Just say the word, please. Just say it. Please. Just give me this one chance. I'll be better, I promise. I'll do anything. All I want is one chance. I'll change. Everything will change. Please, please, please... Just say the word. I'm not asking for much... I'll do anything... please. It means so much.'

And as her forbearers had mumbled in desperation to deities, the young girl implored a woman on judgment day to intercede for her. Her hands instinctively formed a prayer shape as she wept with the agony of growing hopelessness.

'She was good,' said the man on the left, in an angelic Welsh lilt. 'I like her.'

'Thank you, thank you, please, please, please,' the girl said, momentarily shifting her focus from the centre of her attention. From the right came a growl.

'Why? What's she got? She's boring.'

'No, she can sing.'

'She can hit the right notes.' The men argued while the woman watched the pleading with an unbroken stare, not even stopping to blink.

'But so can a million people. Where's the star quality? Where's the charisma? Just say no and let's move on.'

A nondescript pop star from a 1990s boy band looked on, semi-detached and not sure how to manage his role as a judge. He shrugged and said, 'I like her.' That was two votes. She needed a third.

The girl gibbered, mumbling a simplified rosary of pleases

and chances and change. Until the woman spoke.

'No, not much there…' and the girl wilted visibly. 'But I can see something. I can see something… Yes, there's something I recognise. When I'm finished with her, millions will see it.'

Now the girl fell to her knees as the man on the right snorted.

'I'm going to say… I'm going to give you a chance,' the woman said. 'You're through, Baby Lamb.'

The girl leapt to her feet, bounced about, and ran to the table. 'Thank you, thank you, thank you. You've changed my life. You've changed my life.'

The woman smiled, the Welshman smiled, but they were not smiles of belief, merely indications that it was time to move on. There were more, many more, to be weighed and accounted for, and time was short. The other man scowled.

'I'll prove you wrong,' the girl said to him. 'I'll prove you wrong.' The gift-granted bravado began to rise. 'I'll be better next time.'

'You'd better be,' he said before turning to the woman. 'I don't know what you saw, but it wasn't charisma. Isn't that what we're looking for? This is a joke.'

Outside the room, the girl whooped and yelled and screamed. Hundreds looked on with envy and hate, dreaming that they would come hopping from those doors, howling with joy before the day was out.

They sat there, a congregation craving the same thing, all mumbling the same words in their minds and under their breath: 'Please let it be me. I'll do anything. I promise. I'll change. I'll be better. Just let me be the one. Please.'

So the vast mantra, something like prayer, rose from the convention centre where they queued and stood and waited. It was vaguely like prayer, but prayer needs common cause and humility. This was a million shards of prayer, sharpened and made dangerous by ambition, spinning uncontrollably and invisibly with slashing brutality, damaging all those who came into contact with it.

And the cameras rolled on. Redemption is entertainment, and entertainment is redemption. The girl skipped on, loudly lauding herself as she set off on the journey of discovery. 'I'm in heaven,' she said. 'Heaven.'

'Why do they call you Missy?' the interviewer asked. She smirked. 'Because I'm in charge. Because I've always been a bossy little miss. You don't do what I say, then I'll punish you.'

Suggestive, flirty, with an undercurrent of steel that gave delicious substance to the threat, Missy accepted without question the stardom that had come to her. She was warm and funny, that much was clear, and seemed to have a core of humanity that the other judges on the show did not possess. She was a natural. She could switch from mother figure to dominatrix before the victim had realised that they were bound and gagged. She carried a riding crop as a prop to enhance the effect. The public loved her.

'What makes you such a good judge on the show?' Missy mused a moment, as if reflecting on the question, but she didn't need to think. 'I can see something,' she answered, and the image of the girl flashed in her mind again, unexpectedly. 'I can see what the people are going to love before they can.'

And she could. She had an unerring instinct about what touched and moved the British public. The superficialities of the toneless, nervous, and gauche wanabees did not register with Missy; she could see beyond that, to the solid ore of marketability. It was not always talent she saw, but that something, that unquantifiable element that would get people off their backsides and drive them to the shops.

This flair enraged her enemies because they could not even identify it, never mind emulate it. But this skill is not what drew people – men especially – to Missy.

In an industry where beautiful women are commonplace, she was often overlooked in the first scan of a room. Her entry to a party went undetected – at least until the television show brought instant recognition.

It was certainly not her intellect that got her noticed, either. She was sharp rather than clever and people who can grasp reality immediately have no need to philosophise.

No, Missy was able to make people gasp and laugh in a single instant. She had the knack of turning danger into comedy and controlling the situation, while others were still trying to understand what was developing. Men, powerful, handsome men, found this seductive, though Missy understood their thought processes, too, and ultimately kept her aloofness even during and after the sexual act. They came back for more, but Missy was the boss. She was in control. She had learned early on that men in the entertainment business could not be relied upon, and she refused to be compromised.

But few who had been exposed to Missy would ever forget her. Now the nation was exposed to her every Saturday night.

By the 1950s, Irish emigrants were no longer heading for Liverpool. They were driven by economic opportunities rather than desperation. The south of England was their preferred destination.

Missy's parents were among this new influx. They were simple, unsophisticated people whose desire for a modest life should have kept them a long way from London, but their urge to give their child a good start forced them away from the depressed west coast of the twenty-six counties. They arrived in the capital and headed along the Thames, where the ragged east end had worn away and begun bleeding into Essex. Missy was born in… can anyone be sure of the year? It was definitely in the sixties. No, that is wrong, too. Missy was created much later. Someone quite different from the television personality arrived, kicking and squealing somewhere near Barking while Kennedy was still alive.

One of her enemies once said that Missy had 'risen without trace'. It was not quite true, but when the evil spotlight of publicity fell upon her in early middle age, it found little sensation to illuminate. Her previous success was all behind the scenes, and she appeared to come from nowhere to her vast body of fans. She seemed like living proof that history was over.

So, what did the nation know about her?

The News of the World was first to recognise her potential for putting on sales and gave her a double-page spread, headlined: A man's world? Not while I'm here, says Charisma's dominatrix.

The woman with the power to create stars last night laughed off suggestions that she is a puppet of the show's producers. 'They brought me in because they know I can see talent,' said Missy, the Charisma judge who has become the nation's favourite flighty aunt. 'Those boys on the panel haven't got my eye for potential. They need me to point them in the right direction. Men do.'

Viewers of the No 1 television show have voted Missy the star of the series and love her mix of shrewdness and sympathy. But while crowds flock towards her in public, she lives a solitary private life at her Essex mansion. Is she, like many fortysomething single women, looking for love?

'You must be joking,' she laughed, producing the cackle that has become her catchphrase. 'I work in showbusiness. I learnt early on not to trust men in this profession. They're all vain and self-centred. Have fun, but do it on your own terms. Men want me, I don't want them. At least not full-time.'

T2 in The Times was even less revealing.

You can see what's attractive about Missy. She is not beautiful, but her vivacity enchants even the most curmudgeonry of interviewers. She makes wide-eyed eye contact and flatters constantly. 'That is a superb question, Baby Lamb,' she says and then thinks about it before answering. It is not a good question, but you are won over.

Yet, by then, she is already secure. She has seen – quickly – that this will not be a hatchet job. And, knowing that, she turns the interlocutor into a confidante. It is heady for an interviewer and the seduction is impossible to avoid.

The Mirror loved her. Its approval of working-class achievement jumped out of the page as the paper's prized female columnist was let loose with characteristic ballsy boorishness.

They laugh at Essex girls, but who would snigger at Missy, the queen of British entertainment? The Eastender has all the qualities that made the people from that corner of London famous. She shoots down the theory that Charisma, the talent show that made her a household name, is lowering standards in the entertainment world.

'It's about giving people a chance,' she said. 'People whose lives are difficult and who have the talent but have never had the opportunity. We give them the platform to show how good they are. Not everyone can go to stage school or afford to work their way up the ladder. We give those with no chance a chance.'

Yet none of the millions of column inches added a shred of insight to the image on the television screen.

Popbitch, the scurrilous email, was able to hint at a darker aspect of her personality. Its readership was hip, showbizzy and addicted to gossip. There was plenty of chatter about Missy around the Groucho, Soho House, and The Ivy. Those in the know knew who this snippet was about.

Which TV judge picked up some male talent at a boutique hotel in the West End and handed down a stern sentence? On finding the beau was married and his wife out of town, the nation's darling tied the man to the bed and, instead of performing the acts she'd promised, invited her friends up to the suite to torture the unlucky seducer. After ordering nearly a grand's worth of champagne on room service, the coven of harpies cut up their victim's credit cards and left a message on his wife's answering machine telling her that hubby was a cheat and to check his swollen and bruised balls if she believed otherwise.

But nothing written had any real solidity. Facts were few, and no one was able – or willing - to capture the essence of his oddly overpowering woman. A couple of things were agreed and easily checked on Wikipedia: that she worked her way up from the most humble beginnings to become one of the foremost A&R operators in London. That's it. Detail was thin. None of the pieces even used her real name.

After the girl passed the audition, she was taken aside by a researcher who was clearly a level up from the minions she'd dealt with before. He was extremely camp and supercilious.

'OK darling, this doesn't mean you've made it. What number are you?'

'2063.' He ticked her name off the list on a clipboard.

'Got you. Now Julie, where are you from? You've got a nice northern accent.' It was not a compliment.

'Warrington.'

'Oooh, nice. Do you have a story?'

'A story?'

'A back story. Troubles in your life. It's almost as important as your talent. The viewers like a story.'

She sat and thought. No, there was no story. 'No.'

'Mmmm,' he mewed. 'Well, you'll be hearing from us. Have a think. Everyone has a story. You won't get far if you leave it to looks and talent.' He glanced at his clipboard and added, 'Julie,' as if it was in a different, but equally contemptuous, sentence. 'You can go now.'

As Julie rose, the door burst open, and Missy appeared. 'Baby Lamb, you were wonderful,' she gushed. 'You have it. I saw it. You will be huge. I'll make you a star. Kiss me. Hug me. I want to meet your Mum. God, we'll have a great time. You like champagne? We'll drink magnums. I love you, I love you, I love you. Go home. When you come back, I'll teach you how to deal with queens like him.' Missy pointed at the cowering man. 'We will have so much fun. So much fun.'

The press were obsessed with Missy's sex life. Gossip about her adventures over the years fired the imaginations of editors, but there was little printable. It was understood that she had conducted liaisons with numerous well-known people, but most of them were before she burst on to prime-time television. The redtops scraped around for kiss-and-tells tells, but the majority of the men involved with Missy had more to lose by exposure. So she remained an enigma. 'I don't need men, I don't need love,' she repeated in almost every interview. It merely made stronger the public's appetite to see her lovestruck and in a relationship.

She did yearn for one man, though. For two decades, her father had been the only male she had not toyed with. He kept her going when she was at her weakest and most vulnerable and asked nothing in return. After the death of his wife, he invested all his emotional stock in his child and this little Irishman, somebody who seemed to operate in a different, rural dimension, took it in his stride as his little girl shaped her life in the world of entertainment. He never seemed to grasp the enormity of the household names who shuffled in and out of his daughter's life and through the terraced property they shared in the no-man's land between Essex and London.

He never lived to see Missy famous. He would not have understood his own notoriety, either. Film stars, soap-opera actors and musicians swapped tales of his hospitality and unintelligibility. After a night of outrageous antics in a nightclub or at a party, Missy would drag the privileged few across the capital, often arriving home as her father met the new day. After a traditional breakfast – soda bread and a fry up – and a top up of love, Missy would be ready for the next adventure. 'What a little monkey you are,' her father would say indulgently after the latest episode of mayhem was recounted. It was about the only thing most people could recall him saying. When addressing his daughter's friends, his accent became preposterously dense. He seemed permanently to misunderstand how or why some of the most recognisable people in the land arrived on his doorstep. The more sober and astute began to think the old man was taking the mickey out of them. After all, his daughter was doing the same.

It was the worst day of Missy's life when she lost him.

Men like this did not reach old age. Ground down by poverty, exile and loss, they work themselves into ill health and their families rarely notice until it is too late. Their children live in the same world but with parallel existences. Awareness of the older generation's plight and strength often arrives too late. It came to Missy, who had retained the frivolity of youth long into her thirties, just before fame transformed everything.

Like her father, Missy wasted little time on reflection. Life was for doing and being. So they both let the spectre of death creep up without too much sentiment. The old man was not old, but the end was coming. They both knew.

In his 20s, after arriving in London, he had worked on building sites. He was 'on the lump', a casual labourer, undocumented, untaxed, and unprotected. Like many in the building and demolition trade, he tore apart walls and ripped down ceilings packed full of asbestos. Those tiny, invisible spores had been sucked deep into his lungs, unexpellable. Over the years, the sharp little edges of the fibres tore at the spongy tissue and left him breathless.

Slowly, stealthily, the dust of a different era was killing him. A dry cough became the soundtrack to life as the energy was drained from his busy little body. He had always moved with a breathless force. Now he became merely breathless. He shuffled about the house, rejecting his daughter's attempts to make life easier, and hung on to his independence to the end. His hands became clubbed and useless, but still he rose from sleepless nights to clang pans in the dawn. Only now no one came back for breakfast.

Stairs became an insurmountable climb, so Missy had the room downstairs converted into a bedroom. One night, about nine o'clock, he headed for bed with a cup of tea, vibrating gently with the pain of everyday life. When Missy went to check on him, half an hour later, he was dead.

It did not come as a shock. It was a moment she had been rehearsing mentally for some months. He was slumped rather than lying, and she gently moved him into a prone position, as if she was tucking him in. Then she climbed beside him and held him. It was clear he was gone. There was nothing that could bring him back.

At first, she was dry-eyed. She stroked his hair and kissed him lightly. There was relief, too, because the pain had been growing, and she could see the agony in his eyes and hear the torture in his voice. But slowly the tears came.

They lay nose to nose, but he did not seem comfortable, she thought, so she turned his slight body outward and hugged him from behind. He was tiny. Missy's nose nestled in his hair and his smell, a distinct, otherworldy odour, brought back her earliest memories. And suddenly she was aware that this smell would fade into the background of the world and disappear. Yes, it would linger for months but, insidiously, it would be overwhelmed by the stink of everyday life. That special tang, that hogo of safety, would evaporate and be replaced by the smell of a future without love.

As she sucked at it, trying to gulp so much that it would leave an inexhaustible supply inside her, she began to sob. It started as a jerk of the head and built a momentum that was physical and

For Julie, it was a whirlwind summer of auditions, forms, and fear. She was heading closer to appearing on the most successful television phenomena in decades. Charisma mixed and matched genres to create something entirely new. It captured the viewing audience's imagination – and that of the tabloid press – to the extent that Duncan Stevenson, the man who created it, could claim, without contradiction, that it was 'the biggest thing that happened to Britain since Princess Diana'.

The boast was given validity by being unchallenged and appearing in The Daily Telegraph's main section. Even colonels in Kent lapped up the wisdom of Mr Charisma - as he liked to be called - with their breakfast.

'She was the People's Princess. We're creating the People's Pop Stars,' he said. 'This is instant stardom. Being part of this is like winning the lottery.'

To those few who had not seen the show in its first season of spectacular growth, its format was explained simply. The entire population of the country were invited – nay, encouraged – to have their singing abilities assessed. The good and the horribly embarrassing were filmed in front of the judges for a mini-series of pre-recorded shows that set the ground and tone for the live action that dominated the autumn.

The wacky and the wild were given their moment in the limelight, while half a million dreamers were whittled down to sixteen acts. Those who survived the process were split into four sections: boys, girls, over-twenty-fives and groups. They were then cloistered in a purpose-built house for almost three months and cut off from the world.

Filmed twenty-four hours a day, they would be given intensive training in showbiz technique by day and left to interact by night. Their adventures – or lack of them – would be edited to an hour-long show every evening which focused on egos, drama, and conflict. Each Saturday night, the contestants would sing live and be judged by the panel on their performance. Then the nation could vote by phone - £1 per call – to evict one of the bottom two.

In theory, it was all about talent. In reality, the juiciest and most entertaining titbits came during the week, inside the house, as young showoffs without the experience or intelligence to deal with the intensity of the pressure-cooker atmosphere were stripped down to base emotions.

It was vicious, brutal television, but the dreamers queued up to be part of it and the public tuned in to watch. It generated millions just in phone-call fees. The advertisers lapped it up.

'Look, people say the house is cruel, but its role is crucial,' Mr Charisma said. 'Once, people would decide to be a singer. They'd start off performing to family, graduate to local pubs and clubs, and pick up a following. If they were good, they'd attract attention and bigger audiences and finally be discovered by someone like me.

'It's a slow process doing it that way. But as you go along, you develop knowledge and experience that prepares you for stardom if it eventually comes. There's lots of little staging posts: your first rejection, your first gig, the first time you're booed off, your first autograph, your first groupie, your first limo… Each event is a stepping stone to the next and it gives you the grounding to meet the next challenge. These things happen gradually over a number of years.

'The show cuts all that out. In six months, it sends you from anonymity to adulation. It's too much. The culture shock could kill these poor kids.

'So the house is like a boot camp where we give them a crash course in stardom. It's like public school: if you come out of this in one piece, you're ready for anything. I've created the Eton of entertainment.'

In thrall to his subject and the sound bites, the interviewer neglected to mention that the producers set up scenarios that encouraged the housemates to plot against each other and ostracise individuals. Instead, the journalist countered with his own, sniggering smile, calling the show's living quarters 'a malign Malory Towers'.

This is what Julie hoped to experience. Life was about to be transformed for her and twenty-four others.

The final part of the Charisma selection process dangled the temptation of glamour in front of the potential contestants for the live show. Eight hopefuls in each category – including bands – were taken to "judges' houses' in exotic locations, allowing the four talent spotters to make dramatic decisions on their final four artists against a backdrop of wealth and luxury.

In reality, these were rented villas, but they served a purpose: the contrast between the film-star setting and the life that the discarded were likely to return to in, say, Bradford or Glasgow, was almost guaranteed to provoke the hysteria and tears that powered the show up the ratings.

With seven others, Julie was jetted off to Miami – flying economy, of course – to a meeting with Missy and destiny. It involved a hectic two days of filming.

The edited show would imply that there was time for solitude and reflection in idyllic settings, but the beach and relaxation scenes were shot in two bad-tempered hours and the contestants were crammed two to a room in a cheap hotel. On their first day they were given a song to rehearse – one neatly familiar to the audience, with lyrics and tune easily digestible to a Saturday teatime viewer – and offered one chance to perform it forty-eight hours later.

Missy arrived in a limousine about an hour before recording was due to commence after spending the night in a swanky hotel. It was hot; she was cranky, and contact with the eight performers was minimal. Within two hours, she was on the road again. The decision-making scenes would be captured back at the hotel that night, before the contestants learnt their fate the following morning. The discarded foursome would be packed off to the airport immediately. The winners kept around for another day to have lunch with their mentor and be given instructions on the next phase.

Judging had developed its own formulaic system after the first series. Missy would be videoed standing in front of a wall decorated with photographs of the hopefuls, pointing at one, making a dismissive comment here and there, asking for and rejecting the opinion of her sidekick – usually a down-on-their-luck pop star in need of an injection of publicity.

It was theatre. She knew who she would be coaching before she left London. Any battles were fought and won weeks before in discussion with the man who owned the show, her former lover. It was in low-key, probing disagreements that she would use her stock phrase: 'You're wrong, Mr Charisma. I can see something. This one has something. I can see it.' And always she would get her way.

As much as he sometimes resented her and the way she used his nickname in that teasing, mocking manner, Stevenson knew he owed much of his fame to her instincts. So Julie, waiting nervously in the heat, sweating and worrying that Missy had not even acknowledged her existence while she sang for her life, had already booked her slot on the live shows and her bunk in the house. All the rest was a facade. It just felt like real life. What happened in Florida illustrated how far Julie was moving from reality.

Missy's final four in the over-25s category were a mixed bunch. Julie was plain but presentable; no boyfriend would ever be embarrassed to introduce her to friends, but she was no captivating beauty. She was unselfconsciously funny when comfortable in company and naturally empathetic.

The other three were very different. One was a twenty-six-year-old South London diva, Nola, all false fingernails and rapping asides; a baby mother whose backstory was symbolic of the meltdown of Afro-Caribbean life in Britain. She was attractive in a hard-faced way that scared middle-class people but a potential winner of the show if she could control her abrasiveness and take a little direction. The all-white crew said she was "sassy," without ever understanding the racist bias implicit in the term.

Another was Sharon, a forty-five-year-old waitress from Yorkshire with a weight problem and a voice like Shirley Bassey. She would win sympathy and help with the illusion that anyone, whatever their age and looks, could come from nowhere and become a star. The last was Mitch, a demented forty-three-year-old mechanic, a disappointed lothario and crazed northern soul-style dancer. He was in for three reasons: lack of competition, the freak-show factor and because it allowed the show's dictator to ad-lib the phrase: 'He's living the jerrycan dream,' at the first live show. Which, after a week in the house trying to seduce every woman and girl, everyone expected would end with a one-way ticket back to Nottingham. It was Julie that the Charisma judge seemed drawn to, though. On the last night before the return to London, Missy called Julie at her hotel. 'Meet me downstairs in twenty minutes, Baby Lamb. Don't, under any circumstances, be late. We are going to have fun.'

Miami Beach was warm. Miami Beach was cool. Miami Beach was pink and pastel. It was made for champagne.

There were friends of Missy in town: two actresses from a soap opera at home. They had spent a week in the Dominican Republic and had hated the place, staying holed up in their five-star suite for the entire time, living off room service and the wares of a local drug dealer recommended by a colleague in London. "The place was filthy," the one who the nation believed was a hard-hearted bitch told Missy in the clinical, air-conditioned chill of antiseptic America. Her screen daughter told, to gales of laughter, how she had shat in a pillowcase and left it outside for third-world room service to deal with.

These women, three of them so familiar in Britain, were anonymous in Florida. The foursome headed out on the town.

'Champagne,' Missy said seriously to the maitre'd in the Bordello, a pink, pink boutique hotel at the frontiers of trendiness. The others squealed. But Missy's gravitas was misleading. Mischief beckoned.

At the bar there was a muscled, shaven-headed man with fat straining to burst out of his taut skin. His eyes were shaded with makeup, his cropped hair bleached platinum. He wore a tight white tee-shirt to emphasise his tanned flesh tones and burgundy trousers fashioned from the softest kidskin. The sun, or a facelift, had stretched his features like tanned leather.

'Look at Queenie,' Missy said, and waved brightly to the man.

'Coo-ee, love. Come and have a drink with us. Pink champagne.'

The man considered the scene and then walked across.

'Isn't he lovely,' Missy said. 'Look at his mince! Can I take you home with me, Baby Lamb? We're from England.'

'She,' the man said, correcting Missy with a sibilant lisp. Missy shrieked. 'She! She! Come on, girl, join us! You in the business? Love your pants. Don't your balls sweat in this heat, or have you had them clipped off? I think I'm going to call you Queenie.'

The man winced, but Missy rescued the situation. She touched him lightly on the shoulder and said, 'Baby Lamb, we're Brits. We love our Queen. God save her.'

He laughed at last, not recognising the Johnny Rotten allusion, and signalled for another magnum. 'So you're in the business? What business? Fashion?'

'Showbiz, darling,' Missy said. 'The only business.'

'Can your friends talk?' he asked.

'No,' Missy laughed. 'Lips sealed except for blowjobs.'

They were getting on famously.

The girl watched the performance with awe. Missy was in total command of the situation. Queenie, evidently a big-shot in Bordello, generously allowed her latitude on his territory and, as the club filled up, his acolytes surrounded the kiosk where they sat and pouted and posed as they circled around Missy.

Julie, out of her depth, said little. She watched the men and marvelled that the full gamut of male homosexual stereotypes were on display. What came first, the cliché or the culture? The same question could be asked of the world that created Missy, although her mentor's key attribute was her capacity to surprise. These thoughts clouded Julie's mind, and she retreated into a blank muteness.

Neither were the actresses disposed to speak much without the aid of a script. They drank and whispered between themselves until the older one leant over to Queenie and said: 'Coke?'

Queenie shrank away and turned to Missy. 'Jesus,' he said, petulant suddenly. 'Who are these people? They're embarrassing me. Here. In my place.'

'Baby Lamb, Baby Lamb, don't worry. They're stars in England. They don't know. They don't mean anything. They just want a little toot.'

And Missy, tactile as ever, soothed him down with a stroke and then made him jump with a slight grab of the groin and a screaming cackle.

'As it happens,' Queenie said with a haughty but amused tone, 'I can help. But not here. We can party in my suite. With the boys.'

'Oooh, nice,' Missy said. But when the group trooped up in the lift, Julie felt nervous. The soap twins were in a world of their own, and Missy was trading camp gibes with the host. The dozen or so boys who trailed along varied between flutteringly effeminate and sullenly butch. It was volatile enough with bubbly, but now drugs were on the menu.

Missy was unconcerned. She was locked in a closed circuit with Queenie. Except he was no longer Queenie. 'What's going on down there?' she asked him, returning to the earlier subject. 'You must have the sweatiest balls in Miami.'

'The air-conditioning keeps me cool.'

'Dries them crusty, more like,' she said. 'Come on, Crusty Balls, show me a good time.'

The man stopped. The new nickname was even less palatable. The whole group paused outside the suite door while he wavered on the edge of a hissy fit. But again Missy outmanoeuvred him by suddenly turning and lifting up her skirt – a demure, knee-length affair – to expose an uncovered arse. 'I've got air-conditioning, too.'

It drew a laugh, and the party began anew with the pop of corks inside the room. The fridge was packed full of Bollinger and music pumped from a place that Julie could not locate. She was drunk now and slightly tearful. Since arriving at the hotel and meeting Crusty Balls, hardly anyone had spoken to her. The actresses were off snorting somewhere, and the boys had little use for a young woman or polite conversation. She was lonely.

Then another man came into the room. He was very youthful, walking a tenuous line between camp and butch, and dressed like a High School quarterback in a letterman jacket and jeans. To Julie, he seemed the all-American dreamboat. To Missy's experienced eye, he looked like a user, swinging wherever there was a dollar to be made or an easy victim to be had.

He immediately headed for the girl, giving her the wide-beam smile that had charmed cash and favours out of people for more than a decade.

'Hi,' he said.

'Hiya,' Julie responded, her blush verbalised.

'What a great accent. I could listen to you talk forever...'

Missy stiffened. The champagne haze cleared, and she began to pay attention. No pansy was going to queer her property.

Their host stiffened, too. Missy, distracted by her concern for the girl, failed to notice. The older man was jealous.

As the heads of the young couple moved closer together, Missy and her companion watched like angry Sicilian chaperones.

'Who does that little bitch think she is?'

'I don't know, Crusty, but it looks like trouble.' They were at cross-purposes, each referring to a different person.

'I won't have this.'

Julie and her new friend quickly reached the stage of body contact and whispering. The girl said something in the all-American's ear and he laughed, looking up into his host's eyes to pique his jealousy.

It worked.

The tensed face torqued tighter with anger and he moved rapidly to grab the girl. 'You little bitch!' he shouted. 'Leave him alone.' Julie backed away, and the middle-aged homosexual slapped her across the face.

Missy was there a moment too late. 'Leave her alone, you haggard old queer!' she shouted.

And suddenly the music went silent. The man stood there, fury on his face and, in an instant, his adolescent apostles were lined up behind him. It felt like a lynch mob.

Missy said nothing. She reached down under her skirt in a movement that confused everyone in the room. There was a flash of bare quim and the hand was out again.

A collective shriek went up, and all the boys in the room shrunk away. Crusty Balls alone stood still in horror. Missy had pulled a bloodied tampon from under her skirt, and she brandished it like a gauntlet, whacking the host across the right cheek. He stood rigid, his mouth open in an unarticulated scream. So she slapped him on the left cheek. Then she stepped away as a jolt of shock animated the room again.

She grabbed Julie. 'Come on,' she said, heading for the door. The boys moved angrily after her, but she stalled the posse by hurling the tampon back at the chasing group. They squealed again and backed off as Missy and the girl ran for the lift.

'Like vampires with a cross, lovely,' Missy said as the elevator doors closed.

They reached the lobby and Julie, dazed, was ushered into a cab. As they drove away, she said to Missy: 'What about your friends? What will happen to them?' The two actresses were still upstairs, probably happily snorting cocaine in a toilet or bedroom.

'They're not going to get gang raped, darling,' Missy chortled. 'They can take care of themselves. You should learn something from tonight, Baby Lamb. You've got to know how to make a big entrance. But the big exit can be more important.'

Julie shut her eyes, and the world spun. There was, indeed, a lot to learn.

There was something that worried her about Missy. The sexual exhibitionism disturbed the girl from the north. Everyone laughed at her mentor's antics, but they were sordid. Missy scared her.

Julie made it through to the live weekend shows and did reasonably well, but in truth she won the competition not as a result of her performances on stage but because of her behaviour in the house. Amid all the hysterics and divaish antics, she was a reassuring mother hen, diffusing arguments with homely northern good sense, a calming influence on hothoused emotions. She kept the place tidy and dispensed cups of tea. There was no hint of arrogance about her, and people warmed to her personality.

Four times in the twelve week series she was in the bottom two and forced into a sing-off with a rival. Each time Missy voted to keep her in. At least one of the other judges concurred when the nation's favourite dominatrix narrowed her eyes and said: 'I can see something in her, and the British public will see it, too.' And they did. Every time her continued presence was on the line, Julie won the public vote.

In the final, a week before Christmas, she polled more than a very marketable boy band to take the Charisma title. She had the festive No 1. The boys would go on to become Britain's biggest pop stars for the next half-decade.

Mr Charisma, for all his complaining about Julie's success, was happy in the end. For the next season of the show, however, they dumped the idea of putting all the contestants in a house and got rid of the nightly show. Missy gloated, but the programme became more stage-managed than ever after Julie's victory.

The only woman on the judging panel had called it right. The viewers loved the down-to-earth northern lass who could hold a tune. She had no charisma, but she was nice.

The shortcut to fame had worked. In the 2000s only shortcuts mattered.

WHERE THE MUSIC
TAKES ME

The next time the boy saw Billy was in early 1975, nearly a decade after those captivating words on the stairs. All the hope of those days had been stripped away. Billy walked into the church looking thin, pale, and shabby. The circumstances of their reunion could hardly have been worse.

He had been out of prison for some months. Initially, he had been charged with attempted murder, but was eventually convicted of grievous bodily harm. The slow task of rebuilding his life had just begun. He no longer had a wife and was denied access to his children. He had barely known them, but it did not lessen the pain of being exiled from their lives.

Here, I have to stop talking about the boy in the third person. Billy's story is so entwined with mine that I have to accept that I am a character in this pathetic tale. It still does not feel like me. There are many years to go before I recognise myself.

Billy was released just in time to see my father die. The men were never close – the age gap was just too big – but he looked up to Duke and Duke adored his brother. In October, my father had a stubborn cough. He was buried by February. Cancer was common in men of his age, but the sudden, savage nature of his death stunned everyone in the extended family.

Except me. Joey Moran might have been a big-shot in clubland, but he was a bit-part player in his child's life. He was gone for long periods of time and those absences were never explained. It was clear he wasn't away at sea. Sometimes he was not even in jail.

For the first seven years of my life, I lived with my aunts. He would show up occasionally, carrying a crate of fruit or some other perishable goods that had come into his possession. Twice in that period, my mother disappeared and re-emerged with another child. It was unsettling. By the time we set up home as a family, I didn't want the sort of everyday male influence he provided.

We moved into a council house on one of the new estates near Stanley Road. He did not feel like a parent. To me, he seemed a rather annoying and brutish lodger who was a disruptive influence on the household. I didn't like it. I spent as much time as possible with my mother's sisters back in Burly.

You could see the grief that his death inspired, but his eldest son looked on at the anguish with a cold, juvenile insensitivity. He had barely been around during my first ten years of existence. His attempt to reconnect with family life met with distain from me, his death with indifference.

He was admitted to hospital in early December. Twelve days before Christmas, my mother went on her daily visit. About an hour before her usual time of return, friends and family members started descending upon our new-build terrace. Something was wrong, that much was clear. Duke arrived, looking ashen. When I asked what was wrong, he said. 'Your mum's had a fall. Why don't you go and stay in Burly? You don't want to hang around with all these oldies.' He gave me a pound note. I was delighted.

It is a sign of my dislocation that I did not speculate about what might be happening, even when she came in and sat quaking in an armchair. I just said my goodbyes and headed out. How could a teenager be so stupid? Like I said, the gap between that kid and me is so wide as to be incomprehensible.

I found out he was dying five days before he passed away. Since Christmas, the entire family had spent most of our time at my aunts' flat. They had a phone in the hall by the door. The bedroom was three yards away and on Sunday night I was squeezed into a single bed with my younger brother, in that half-world that precedes sleep. My mother was talking on the phone.

At first, the words drifted over me. Then they made some sort of sense: '… the drugs will shorten his time,' she was saying, 'but he won't be in pain.' There was silence while someone spoke at the other end of the line. 'Soon,' she said. 'Not long. Weeks. Probably days.'

My mother sounded very composed. The tone was matter-of-fact. The conversation continued, but the boy — sorry, me — was no longer listening.

I waited for a good while after she hung up. Then I went into the tiny living room.

My aunties were proud of their flat. When the block was renovated and the coal hearths replaced with gas fires, they paid a local handyman to put in a wall-long fireplace constructed with coloured bricks, topped by varnished wood panels that went to the ceiling. It was incongruous in a tenement block, but they thought it was the height of chic.

The trio of women were sitting across the three-piece suite when I entered. My mother was in the armchair closest to the fire, smoking an Embassy cigarette. One aunt was in the chair under the window sucking on a Woodbine. The other was on the couch, knitting. I sat on the sofa, at the end nearest to my mother. 'What are you doing up, slyboots?' the auntie with the Woodbine said.

'I heard the phone,' I said, and turned to my mother. 'Why didn't you tell me?' I said, simply. She looked at me, groping for words. There were none.

After thirty seconds of silence, I got up and went back to bed. That was that. Well, not quite.

On the Wednesday, I got home from school and grabbed my ball to go out to play. My mother stopped me at the door. 'Come the hospital tonight,' she said.

'No,' I replied.

'He's been asking for you.' She started to cry.

'No.'

73

'But he's been asking for you…'

I was already gone. Usually, I'd go into the block and fire shots at the outer wall of the old school playground – it was a community centre now ¬– and the siren call of plastic hitting brick would bring the kids flooding along the landings and down the stairs. Instead, I went into Portland Gardens and chipped the Wembley Trophy at the sign over the arch that said 'no ball games' until some of the lads came and joined me.

Two days later, he was dead. The phone call came at 7am. At least I got the day off school.

Billy had turned up at the house to pay his respects, but I was out playing during his visit. So, it was a shock to see how beaten down he looked at the church.

Duke was devastated. I felt for him. He carried the coffin. His suit was as sharp as ever, but he momentarily lost his swagger. He was crushed. Billy was a pallbearer, too, and was bereft.

Joey Moran, my father, was forty-three. I learnt a big lesson when he died. He was a hard man, admired by many and feared by more. After the funeral, we went back to the Bryom Arms, at the top of Great Crosshall Street. Everyone knew it as the Pieshop. It had been a favourite of the deceased, but it was an ugly, modern pub. It fitted its purpose on this bleak winter's day. There, as I nursed the one half-pint glass of lager I was allowed, progressively drunken men came forward to tell me what a wonderful person my parent had been. They all attested to his toughness and his steadfastness as a friend. As the drink kicked in, the stories became more extravagant. He had taken on six men and knocked them all out; he had chased a Commonwealth champion boxer down the street; he had a punch people dreaded. Late on, a man came to me and shook my hand. 'Your dad was my hero,' he said. 'First man I ever saw firing a gun in Liverpool. Popping it off down Lime Street.' He laughed. 'The Krays and their boys were on the first train back to London.'

And what was his legacy? At his death, he left a young widow, five children, and £96 in the bank. In the pocket of his trousers was a single 50p piece, the one produced for Britain's entry into the Common Market with nine hands linking on the tails side of the coin. That is all his life added up to. Some hero.

My mother kept the keepsake coin on the mantelpiece in a jug. Within a year, I spent it on a 'Docker.' This was a portion of chips stuffed into half a Vienna loaf, the favoured dinner of me and my mates at school. The rest went on sweets. She cried when she realised what I'd done, but my little bastard heart was hard.

That day of the funeral, though, I kept my hostility under wraps, projecting a blank defensiveness that the congregation took to be despondency. I was most concerned about not showing any weakness to the two rows of classmates who sat in the pews at the front of the right aisle of the church. They stared across at me, willing me to crack. I didn't. The Brothers must have issued stern warnings to them because no one interrupted the requiem with a booming fart, which was a favourite trick whenever we went to church. Every service I had attended with the school had been disrupted by the bellowing, echoing sound of breaking wind. Standing there, determined to show no fragility, I longed for the squeak of a squeezed-out fart. They were respectful, though, if a bit fidgety. I tried to remain absolutely still because any movement could be misconstrued as frailty.

I was already thinking about the positives that would come from the situation. The death of a parent meant you were eligible for free school dinners. That was a bonus. In the popular imagination, free meals made you an outcast in the playground and led to recipients being bullied. Not in our school. Other kids envied you. I'll bet there were a couple of them looking across that church at me thinking, 'jammy bastard.'

At Ford cemetery, in the bone-hard icy winter, the sound of weeping made no impact as I stood there in my school uniform. I shivered, but only with the cold. Billy came up behind me and draped his thin, cheap overcoat on my shoulders. He moved beside me, reached his arm around my shoulder, and gently pulled me towards him. I was touched. If someone had taken a picture of this episode, it would have been less heart-breaking than the one of us at his wedding. 'It feels as if it will never get better,' he whispered in my ear, 'but it will. Keep strong and things will improve. I promise.' Despite myself, something in me believed him.

A return to sea was out of the question. Not because of Billy's criminal record, but due to the opportunism of his brother, Jimmy. The first thing Billy did on returning home from his final trip was to register with the pool for another ship. While he was on remand, a letter came to his mother's house offering another berth. Jimmy calculated, rightly, that no one on the next voyage would have met his brother. He accepted the job and turned up as if he was his incarcerated sibling. No one noticed. For the next few years Jimmy sailed across the world, explaining to those who asked that he'd rather be known by his middle name than the title on his paybook. The family seafaring tradition was kept alive.

Lilly had gone to Marie's house and collected Billy's meagre belongings after his arrest. From that point on, she never saw her grandchildren again in the flesh. They moved out of the area with no forwarding address. Every birthday and Christmas Billy's mother sent money and presents care of some relatives. The children were given the gifts but never told their source. Despite the lack of interaction, no birthday or festive season went forgotten by the estranged grandmother.

Lilly retrieved her son's guitar. It had been maltreated and needed refurbishment, but it gave Billy consolation. He began to play. By day he worked on building sites, hod-carrying where he could. By night, he strummed away, desperate to reach the level of expertise of his pre-marriage days.

The mood in Liverpool had turned. The conveyer belt to pop

fame had seized up. Fewer young men were forming bands in the mid-1970s, but there were enough relics of the previous decade casting around for playing partners to give Billy a chance to perform live again. He began to duet with a local country and western singer in the little club next to the church on Eldon Street for £2.50 a night. Within weeks, he was the senior member of the duo. His partner, peeved, engineered a split by connecting Billy with a showband he knew from Kirkby. Their act was part cabaret, part comedy, part rock'n'roll. They needed a rhythm guitarist, and the newcomer doubled the money he had been earning for playing country music.

Soon Billy was the front man for his new group. There were pre-existing tensions in the showband. The lead singer departed with a broken nose after a fractious night in New Brighton, where the drummer took umbrage at his bandmate's sarcastic commentary on his stickwork. Billy took over the vocals. He had to tell jokes between songs and perform ribald cover versions of popular hits. The novelty wore off quickly. It left him unsatisfied, but he was able to scrape a living from performing as long as his income was supplemented by the dole. At least he could leave the building sites behind.

The band was never going to last, but Billy was at least learning his trade. His voice could occasionally quieten a crowd, but he was now developing a comedian's craft: how to still a heckler and the value of wrongfooting an audience by switching between pathos and humour. He learnt how and when to deal with female admirers – not when their boyfriends or husbands were around – and how to handle the mayhem when he misjudged the situation.

For a year he hauled around the northwest in transit vans, loading and unloading amps before attempting to charm or bulldoze audiences in working-men's clubs that had arrived predisposed to barracking the entertainers. He learnt that charisma is a gift, but technique is the key to survival.

The band dressed in dinner suits, frilly shirts and dicky bows, and their cabaret act brought them plenty of bookings. The attention from women made Billy feel like he was sixteen again. He began to enjoy the sort of sexual liberation associated with the Sixties. It had been delayed by almost a decade. Things could hardly be better in that area of his life, but he knew this situation could not continue indefinitely.

The group even had a brief glimpse of the power of television. Before Billy joined, they had been in line for a performance on the TV talent show New Faces. It was a Saturday-night staple, and the acts were judged by a four-person panel of industry insiders. Their chance came along about three months after he joined. It was not an episode Billy would remember with affection. The harshest of the panellists, Mickey Most, slaughtered the act. Showbands were dead, he said, and this one smelt like it had been dug up. He was right.

It confirmed what Billy knew. He was bored. Every day, he was experimenting with his own tunes and trying to write lyrics. He dreaded wearing the velvet suit and hated the gags and magic tricks that were part of the show. It felt like he was back in the flat in Burly, playing the 'old songs' for the family. Belatedly, he decided to become an artist. It was time to trust his own voice and own words.

Things were going well for Duke. He acquired a share in a club after a particularly vicious clubland spat. The owner thought it prudent to give his most prominent bouncer – and bodyguard – a financial interest in staying loyal. He married, too, which was a surprise, but the wedding was one of the few episodes in Duke's mid-seventies life in which a shotgun did not play a role. The marital union had no impact on his romantic life.

If he had been sharp and modish in the 1960s, Duke became fashionable and flamboyant in his thirties. His three-piece suits with big lapels and wide flares made him stand out. An ill-conceived Zapata moustache completed the look.

There seemed to be a little more money in his pocket, at least to the outsider. He bought a Bentley and loved its varnished wooden dashboard and luxury interior. Duke took a special glee when parking it in front of the social security office on Newington Street when he went to sign on.

The police were watching him, but he had friends on the force. If they came to the club, they were given VIP treatment, and some were rewarded with an envelope of cash. There was an understanding that he would not practice his daytime job of theft within the city limits. The sub post offices of the Wirral and the Lancashire hinterland were fair game.

Joey's death hit him hard. Growing up, Duke had piggy-backed his brother's reputation. There were some whispers that the younger man would not be able to maintain his jurisdiction without the threat of family backup. The young bucks in the club tried it on and the up-and-coming hard cases toned down their respect a notch. It was a mistake. For a month or so after the funeral, there were frequent challenges to Duke's authority. They were dispatched with a brutality that few had associated with him. When everything settled down, his reputation was stronger than ever.

Things were beginning to change. A new wave of criminality was starting to sweep the port. In Liverpool 8, where the black community of the city were grouped, there had long been a tradition of smoking weed. Soft drugs were nothing new in the south end.

It was different on the other side of town. Even when The Beatles and Bob Dylan popularised cannabis, it had made little impact on the streets of the north end, where alcohol was the mood-changer of choice. Now weed began to spread. Importing and selling it would soon become more lucrative – and less dangerous – than armed robbery. Before long, Merseyside's underworld would be able to make a career choice. The new generation could see this development looming. Duke didn't. His quick wits had carried him a long way, but he did not recognise the changes occurring under his nose.

Billy blew out a plume of blue smoke and laughed a high-pitched giggle. 'Not sure I like that stuff,' Duke said, nursing a squat tin of Long-life beer. They were in a flat on the fourteenth floor of Canterbury Heights, one of the towers in a three-block complex on the slopes of Everton. The high-rises were less than a decade old but had already acquired a nickname that reflected their squalor: the Piggeries. The lifts were broken that day and it was a long haul to the top.

'It relaxes you,' Billy said. 'And helps the creative process. You can write songs on weed. You can't do that drunk. It's harmless. Have a go.'

'Just don't smoke it in the club,' Duke said. 'Even my mates at Rose Hill,' – the police station – 'wouldn't turn a blind eye to that. And if your mate sells it in my place, I'll break his legs.'

It was a rare spat. Duke was delighted with his cousin's career progress. The era of velvet and jokes was over. Billy had teamed up with a former member of a Merseybeat group and created a band called Scouse Pie.

After leaving the showband, the aspiring singer-songwriter had begun to hang around the local gig scene. He got wind of a weekly Wednesday afternoon football game that musicians played on the all-weather pitch – it was really just hard-packed sand and gravel - at the bottom of Everton Valley.

The kickabout was the entrée he needed to the incestuous world of Liverpool's pop clique. No one was interested in Billy in the bars and venues of the city, but that changed when he took his kit and stood on the sidelines at the Valley. When one team had a no-show, he asked to fill in. As soon as he got on the pitch, the other putative music legends saw his star quality. The boy from Burly could dribble, shoot, and had a fearsome tackle. Football means something on Merseyside. The performances on the stony pitch at Everton Valley catapulted Billy to prominence.

It was division two stuff, though. The more successful pop figures in the area had their game in Skelmersdale, where chart stars like Liverpool Express enjoyed their exercise. The players in L6 dreamt of promotion to matches in the new town on the outskirts of Wigan, where the men seen on Top of the Pops had their weekly runout.

The Valley was good enough for Billy. One of the regulars had a couple of hits under his belt, but could not be bothered to drag himself out to Skem. He soon demanded that the newcomer play on his team. They became friendly and, before long, were jamming together. It seemed natural to take the next step and perform as partners.

They formed Scouse Pie and soon developed a local following. They headlined at the Montrose and the Wooky Hollow traditional cabaret venues, but there were no gags or repartee. This was a serious band. They were reviewed in the New Musical Express and Melody Maker. The interest of the press brought A&R men to Liverpool. The prospect of a record deal felt very real in the first weeks of 1976.

Duke looked around the shabby flat and pulled a face. 'From the Piggeries to the Palladium,' he said. 'Don't let the junk you're smoking get in the way.'

Billy laughed. He extinguished his joint and popped a Long Life. 'This,' he said with certainty, waving the tin, 'ruins more careers.'

His cousin took a deep breath. 'The fella who lives next door to Joan sells that shit,' Duke said, returning to the subject of cannabis and pointing at the ashtray. Joan was his brother's widow, my mother. 'Smokes too much of it himself. Nothing creative about that destructive gobshite. I'm hearing bad things about him. I might need to have a word.'

Billy sat up. 'She's said nothing to me.' He had visited the family the previous week. 'You sure?'

'Yeah. Nothing to me, either. Well, we'll see. So, when you playing London?'

'Next week,' Billy said. 'And I sent some of my songs to a publisher down there. I'll meet him, too. The money's in writing songs. I love singing, but I wouldn't mind a few quid.' He laughed.

'It's been a bad few years,' Duke said, looking from the window down the slope and over the Mersey. 'But things are getting better for you.' He reached into his pocket and pulled out a wad of notes. 'Judging by the way you're living,' he said, 'you're skint. Here.' He placed a pile of five-pound notes on the windowsill. It was a lot of money. 'This will see you through the next couple of weeks. You can't go to London looking like a tramp. Go down there like you own the place. And don't spend it on that shit you're smoking.'

Shaking his head, Billy smiled. He wanted to say no. But no sane person said no to Duke when his mind was made up. 'A big job?' The younger man imagined a horrified sub post office manager cowering in fear as Duke emptied the till.

Duke shrugged. 'Let's just say a little win on the horses. Go down there. I want to see you on Top of the Pops. You might even be able to pull as many birds as me then. Come on, let's go for a pint. Do you know the lift's broken? No? At least it's all downhill from here.'

There were big things happening in 1976. Billy was heading towards a London where the cultural goalposts were shifting in a way he could not yet comprehend. Scouse Pie were on the soft wing of pub rock, but at the other extreme of the genre there was a youth movement growing that would destabilise the pop world that the Liverpudlian duo knew. Punk was about to smash its way into the national consciousness, and the music industry was not ready for it.

Under Billy's nose, a different sort of teenage culture was developing, and it was a style that would outlast punk and influence the way young people dressed for decades.

Some half-a-mile to the northwest of Canterbury Heights was Arden House, a huge, gothic, Salvation Army hostel. It sat on Scotland Road with the Kingsway tunnel one hundred yards or so away to its north. To its south there was a vast swathe of wasteland up to Leeds Street, which was being converted into a new ring road. This empty space at the top of Blackstock Street, where the slums had been cleared would become the crucible for a new fashion.

Why? Because lorry drivers who converged on the docks would park up here and spend the night in Arden House, a cheap resting place close enough to town's pubs to make it convenient. Local youths, myself included, nicknamed it 'the loadies'. We tried to break into the wagons and generally failed, but we were just kids. The older boys who were following in Duke's footsteps were more expert in their lock breaking skills and made off with as much of the cargo as possible.

How did this have an impact on fashion? In the streets around Scotland Road, the young lads were already wearing Adidas Samba training shoes under their flared jeans. Other pieces soon began to fall into place.

That summer, ITV's answer to BBC's coverage of the Montreal Olympics was the mini-series Rich Man, Poor Man. It was set in the immediate post-war era and the protagonists had short-back-and-sides haircuts with floppy fringes. Teenagers like me loved the Tom Jordache character, a tough-guy boxer who counldn't compete with his intellectual brother but who could beat any antagonist half to death. We all wanted to be the hard man, not the rich man. Suddenly, feather cuts and mullets disappeared among my age group on the streets of L3 and L5 and shorter, clean-cut hairstyles replaced them.

Then, at some point in that scorching summer, someone illicitly opened a vehicle at the loadies and discovered a shipment of Adidas tee-shirts. They were the round-necked, short-sleeved type with the trefoil on the chest and three stripes down the arms. They were similar to the Bruges shirts the Belgium team had worn in the UEFA Cup final against Liverpool earlier in the spring, and all the young lads loved the look. By the next day, the Adidas tops were available for sale in Tate & Lyle's factory. My auntie came home with three, one for each of her nephews. Within forty-eight hours, most of the young boys in the area were wearing them.

The entire consignment seemed orange, a colour usually anathema on this side of Great Homer Street, but everyone wanted one. Sectarianism didn't matter in this style uprising.

Fashion used to be brought back on ships. Now it was delivered in lorries. Horizons had shrunk, and we'd soon expand them again.

No one worried about buying stolen goods in the district. The same youths who pillaged the loadies were also talented shoplifters. While big consignments sold in the factories, items purloined from town's department stores were offered door to door. The robbers quickly worked out what clothes and goods were favoured by individual households and would knock on their neighbours' doors with products they thought would appeal to the residents. The money they earned was spent on beer, the horses and, crucially, football. We all went the match. It was the great leveller.

When kids from Huyton, Kirkby, and Bootle saw the germinating Scotland Road look, they copied it. The older generation looked on askance, tutted, and called us "scallywags," a term of distain common among my father's generation. We embraced it. We liked being Scallies. We were happy to describe our style as Scal, but that would come later. In 1976, we didn't realise we were part of a menswear revolution.

The new fashion might've withered over the long, hot summer without football, but the trip to Bruges in May was an eye-opener. The youths who went to Belgium loved the beer and food, but most of all they appreciated the naivety of the shopkeepers. Back home, the stores were sharpening up their security, and the thieves were recognised the moment they set foot in town. In Europe, they pillaged places they would never visit again.

The new season was around the corner. The warm-up tour was to the Netherlands, and groups of lads went to Rotterdam, Roda, and Enschede. One fella from Burroughs Gardens brought back a pair of blue Kickers in my size.

They cost me £8 half the retail price in town, and were a ridiculous extravagance, but the fashion was beginning to take shape. Like the rest of my mates, I was eager to be at the forefront of it. A buzz went round the district. The Continent was like a big loadies with easier access. The blaggers could hardly wait for the European Cup campaign in the autumn, and I was desperate to be part of it. I was just a little too young and a little too cowardly.

I started going to regular away games. Until then, I'd alternated between Liverpool and Everton home games, sometimes going to Goodison with Billy. Now it was just the team I supported, and I was a Kopite. We began to be conscious of how we dressed at matches. Punk's biggest impact for us was the rejection of flared trousers; but we wore straight-legged Lee Riders, Farah, and Levi 501s instead of bondage pants.

But I run ahead.

In the late spring of '76 I was hanging around, lurking on the same crook in the stairs where Billy had played cards and thrilled his audience all those years ago. He came up the street after visiting his mother and spotted me. He was wearing a denim shirt, Birmingham bags, hair on his shoulders, and a drooping moustache with the same unfortunate consequences as Duke.

'Look at you, you little square,' he said, noting the short hair. 'How old are you now? Fifteen?' I nodded. 'Come and see the band play in town. I'll get you in; even let you have a beer.' There was no chance of me taking up the offer. To me, he reeked of the past.

Neither of us recognised, or could articulate, what was happening. So, he gave me a pound note. That was enough. I still loved him. He had learnt how to win over an antagonistic audience.

The London gig was not quite the triumph Billy had expected. There were quite a few A&R men at the Windsor Castle on the Harrow Road, but they had an offhand insolence that did not bode well. Although the Abbey Road studios were only a fifteen-minute walk away, they might have been on a different planet. The crowd, in the throes of the punk uprising, were hostile and alien-looking. Someone shouted "hippies!" from the floor. Billy had that grim feeling that he knew from the tail end of his showband days, although he was buoyed that one of his own compositions was the least badly received of the set. Scouse Pie were dead. He knew it before the closing song. The recriminations in the poky dressing-room confirmed it. There was no encore.

He had an appointment the next day with Richman and Richman, a tin-pan alley music publisher that Billy had sent a tape. There were four songs on it, written for a solo performer. They were quite distinct from the band's sound. He had always intended to go it alone.

Billy went down to Denmark Street for a 2pm appointment and was told to take a seat by a dismissive secretary. At 3.30, he was still there, unseen and unheard. He rose and towered over the girl, who could hardly have left school, such was her youth.

'Your boss know I'm here?' he said.

The girl looked at him as if noticing his presence for the first time. 'He does,' she said, holding his gaze just too long for him to be comfortable. She picked up the phone and pressed the intercom button. 'Mr Richman, the pop star's beginning to get angry. I'm scared,' she emphasised. 'He's going to trash the office.' She put down the phone and smiled at him. 'He knows you're here.'

Forty frustrating minutes later, Raoul Richman opened the door of the office and angrily waved Billy in. He chomped a huge cigar, wore a pinstriped suit, and acted, as he looked, like a caricature. He pointed to a stool, sat down on a leather sofa, and snapped: 'Play the song.'

Billy fumbled with his instrument and began to tune up, but Richman shouted 'play!' Barely ten seconds into the first song, the publisher threw up his arms and said: 'Not that one! Stop wasting my time.'

He was completely unnerved, but was allowed to get through the remaining three tunes. Richman harrumphed and went back behind his desk.

'Is that how you dress on stage?' Billy's senseless gape suggested the answer was affirmative. 'You look like a tramp. Tramps don't sell. Someone else will have to sing them. How many more songs have you got?'

That was the moment when Billy realised that he was underprepared, an amateur in a professional world. 'Er...'

'Don't er me. Go back to your hovel and write some more songs. Come and see me in a month. You've got one more chance. Go, go. And arrive on time next time.'

His head spinning, Billy went back to the waiting room. The secretary smiled sweetly. 'Went well?' He fought off the urge to swear at her. It wasn't easy to be mocked by a girl.

'I have to come back in a month.' She took a business card and wrote a date and time on it.

'I'll cry every night until I see you again. Give my love to The Beatles.' He snatched the card and went down the stairs. Behind him, he heard the girl's voice, projected, so she was sure he could hear. 'I think it's sweet the way they all think they're going to be stars, boss. Yes, he's gone. I don't think he'll be back.'

In the off licence at Euston, Billy bought six cans of Younger's Tartan and drank them on the rattler back to Lime Street. It was cheaper than the buffet. He was not despondent. Three days in London had induced an epiphany. Over the previous few months, Billy had come to believe he was talented enough to write and sell records. He thought he had the awareness and acumen to negotiate the music business. Because he was from the roughest of areas, had been away to sea, and had spent time in prison, Billy had mistakenly assumed that he was streetwise enough to cope in any situation. Now he understood he was out of his depth.

He went home, hauled his guitar up fourteen flights of stairs, and decided on a new course of action. He would sleep tonight. Tomorrow he would work on the dozens of fragments of songs and lyrics that he had discarded for lack of inspiration. This was not about being inspired. It was time for hard graft; harder than humping a hod full of bricks up a ladder. He smoked the last of his weed and resolved not to buy any more. At least for a month. The next time Billy went to Denmark Street, he would be prepared.

After my father's death, it was not so easy for me to spend time away from home. At weekends we all – my mother, me, and the kids – stayed in her sisters' flat in Burly, but during the week I was obliged to go to the house close to Stanley Road. It was a mere twenty minutes' walk or a ten-minute bus journey from where my mates lived and where I was comfortable. It felt like a different world.

There were problems brewing with the next-door neighbour. They had started as soon as we moved in. The twenty-two-year-old man was dealing dope. He liked to play his music loud and slept at odd hours. This did not go down well with my father. In the brief interlude between us arriving and Joey Moran's death, there was trouble. He immediately labelled the dealer next door "the Divvy" and his contempt for the young man was palpable.

I can only imagine the neighbour knew about my dad's reputation but was too stoned or drunk – or a combination of both – to care. It came to a head less than three months before my father died. Ironically, the confrontation was sparked by someone else.

It was mid-November. The couple next door, but one had just had a baby. Around midnight, the new father knocked on the Divvy's door to politely request he turn down the music. This perfectly reasonable action provoked a frenzy of violence. The Divvy threw himself out of the door, butted the new dad and screams resonated down the walkway between the two rows of houses. In pain from a series of lung biopsies, Joey went outside.

People used to say he walked into a melee like Clint Eastwood and even I, who felt the opposite of hero worship for him, was impressed by his composure and clinical actions. He strode up to the Divvy without a word and when the young man turned; it became clear that he was armed with a cosh. He showed it to my father, and said: 'Come on, old man. Let's see if you're as good as they say.'

He was. He blocked the thrust of the blackjack and lifted the Divvy off his feet with a straight left. The power of the punch knocked the recipient out, but it caused as much pain as the man who threw it. Joey could barely move.

For a moment, my father stood over him and seemed poised to hit the prone body again. But he was not shaping up to land another blow. He was frozen in agony. Striding back to the house, he betrayed no evidence of his weakness until he collapsed on the couch, gasping desperately for breath.

He was still in the same position half an hour later when the sound of shattering glass made him sit up. The Divvy had kicked in the front door and was back for the second round, armed with a four-foot fencepole. Joey used all his strength to stand up and went outside into the tiny front garden, where the aggressor had retreated to give himself room to swing his staff.

The street was full of neighbours watching the confrontation. No one moved to help. Even I wondered if this was a fight too far for my father. There was no cagey moving about from him, however. He walked straight towards the Divvy and took the impact of the stick on his forearm without breaking stride. This time he butted the man on the bridge of his nose, knocking him over the fence. Then he picked up the remains of the fencepole and beat the injured drug dealer for a good minute; slowly, deliberately, without any indication of rage. Every blow brought a whelp of discomfort from my father, but he carried on, determined that this would teach the Divvy a lesson that would stay with him for ever.

Two policemen came into the close and faltered. The sergeant, with his long nightstick, seemed as if they would leave, but my father beckoned them over.

'He's drunk and disorderly,' he said. 'He fell over and might need patching up before a night in the cells.'

The senior officer nodded. 'He's a little gobshite, this one. You haven't hit him hard enough, Joe.'

I've never liked Busies. That's one of the things my father taught me. But this one spoke the truth. I never met many others who did.

Life was difficult for the neighbours. They banged on the wall and shouted to Billy to stop playing the same songs over and over again. They screamed in frustration as the noise continued after midnight and turned up their own music centres to blot out and discourage Billy. That was impossible. He felt he was getting somewhere.

The last song he worked on had been written in a prison cell, but he had been too embarrassed to send it to the Richman brothers. It needed something extra, but every time he played it, the memories flooded back. He put it aside. The humiliation in London changed that. High up in the Piggeries, he began to hone something of beauty. He called it 'Slamming Doors' and played it over and over again. It had been inspired by anger after the collapse of his marriage, but even after his fury dissipated, the shame remained. Screw it, he thought. He wrote down the lyrics and perfected the melody.

'The lights on, there's a car on the drive,
Never thought that she'd have lied,
My mind's gone, so tired of life,
Result of all those sleepless nights,
And I would shift the world to see her,
One more chance, and I'd believe her,
I know I can't take no more,
To stop the sound of slamming doors.'

He could hear the timbre of his voice buzz like a trumpet. Billy could feel his own conviction. It had been missing for more than half a decade, and he could sense it growing again inside him.

'Spare a thought,
Look at me now,
We have to stay together,
But show me how,
All along, it's been suspected,
To her friends, it's just what they expected,
And I would shift the world to see her,
One more chance, and I'd believe her,
I know I can't take no more,
To stop the sound of slamming doors.'

Here, he stopped. This was his problem. At this point, he could not work out how to move the song forward. For two days, he played it and tried idea after idea. It did not help. Finally, he slapped the fretboard four times in frustration and attacked the strings in anger. Remarkably, it sparked something inside him, and suddenly the song coalesced without Billy's conscious effort. He followed his inadvertent key change, and the words poured out.

'Living with me would never be the same,
I know he's got letters after his name,
But he'll get bored with her,
His type always do,
Always do.'

Then he was out of the break, and it was easy to complete.

'Lights on, shadows move round the room,

Feeling sick, but I'll be talking to her soon,
If I close my eyes, it won't happen,
Count to ten, it might go away,
And I would shift the world to see her,
One more chance, and I'd believe her,
I know I can't take no more,
To stop the sound of slamming doors....'

It was almost an out-of-body moment for Billy and one that he had never felt while smoking cannabis. For the first time, he understood the process of turning experience into fiction, into art. After spending so many hours trying to wring lyrics and chord progressions from an uncompliant mind, he realised he had been overthinking everything and inspiration was inside him. Hard work would drive him in its direction and help him unlock it.

He stood up and watched the Mersey turn from black to silver as the sun rose behind him. It was a turning point. The creative process had begun.

The next afternoon, he passed a neighbour on the long trek up and down the stairs. 'I liked that one you sang last night,' the man said. 'If you're going to keep me awake, at least do it with songs like that.'

At last Billy was onto something.

The next time Billy went to London, it was different. He had bought a pair of straight-legged jeans for a start. He noticed many of the younger men on Denmark Street had shed their flares. His leather jacket and hair were still assiduously stuck in the early 1970s, but his look, if not quite contemporary, appeared less like an anachronism in Soho. His attitude had changed, too.

He walked into the office, went straight to the secretary and said: 'Alright luv, tell Richman I'm here and I've only got half an hour. I need to be somewhere else this afternoon.' The girl looked at him with keener interest. Billy reciprocated.

She was young, definitely not much past eighteen, if that, but was confident in a way he had only experienced in bold older women. There was a difference. She did not radiate the world-weariness of his quick conquests on the working-men's club circuit.

It was impossible to tell whether she was beautiful or not. The girl's hair was cropped short in what appeared to be an amateurish manner and she wore pale pancake makeup with black, exaggerated eyes sweeping up towards the temples. Her garb was equally confusing. The top half looked like she was a disturbed public schoolboy: a white shirt, baggy at the neck but with the top button secured over a loosely dangling school tie. The effect was confirmed by a stripped blazer with the pockets ripped off. When she stood up, the jacket came down to the top of her thighs, falling lower than the leather miniskirt she wore. The ensemble was completed by black tights and flat monkey boots. She was an intriguing mess. He watched her while he checked the tuning on the guitar.

He asked: 'What do you call your style?'

'Gorgeous,' she replied.

The door opened and Richman was there, along with his hitherto unseen brother. Billy went through and sat with them. 'Let's hear your songs,' the man he'd seen before said.

'This is a new one. It's on this tape,' Billy said, placing the cassette on the desk. 'I'll do just this one. Then I've got to go. You can listen to the tape later.' The brothers looked at each other, eyebrows raised slightly, and then the man who had not been introduced said: 'You've got five minutes.'

Billy didn't need it. He backstrummed E minor twice and began singing Slamming Doors. He could see a scintilla of interest in their eyes. Then he stopped caring about them. His voice buzzed off the walls of the small room, filling the empty space with thrilling, vibrating waves. Billy lost consciousness and became a vehicle for the song, staring into the void and funnelling every emotion through his vocal cords. When he came to the change, he stopped. As the words "slamming doors" faded, he let silence engulf the vacuum. He held the moment: not so long that the publishers would think the song was complete, but just enough for the tension to build. In the quiet moment, he refocused, looked both men in the eyes, and then slapped the body of the guitar four times with a swift, rhythmic movement.

The key change caught them by surprise. He growled the words out low and then let his voice spiral up the scale. Across the room, the brothers looked on, rapt, and Billy experienced the same feeling he had felt back on the stairs more than a decade earlier. He had them. He controlled the audience. They were in thrall to his charisma. But how long could it hold?

The end of the song was close. It would last until then. It did. At the finish, he looked up. 'How's that?' he said.

'I've heard worse,' said the man he had originally met. 'I'll tell you what. Maybe we'll put up a couple of hundred quid to get you in the studio and do a professional demo. You might be able to sing your own songs. We'll see. How about we draw up a contract? How long are you in London?'

Billy thought. He could stay with a friend in Walthamstow that he knew from going away to sea. The offer was there. 'A couple of days.'

'OK, maybe come back tomorrow. Give us a chance to have a chat about you. Maybe I can get some studio time for you over the next few weeks.'

'Great, thanks. I really appreciate it.' The confidence, the aura he had conjured up during the song, had dispelled. He was back to being a needy, desperate, hopeful. 'Go on, get out of here,' the second brother said gruffly. 'We're busy. Leave your tape.'

He went to the waiting room and put away his guitar. 'You fancy a drink tonight, Gorgeous?' he said. The girl stared at him, aghast. 'Who said you could call me gorgeous?'

'You said that's your look. What's your name, then?'

'I never said anything of the sort.' There was silence.

'Eileen.'

'No, no, you can't be an Eileen,' he said, shaking his head in disgust. 'Every third girl round ours is an Eileen. Where's the glamour in it? You look like someone else.'

She raised her eyebrows. He thought. 'OK, I'll try this. You look like an Eileen from another planet.'

Did she like that? He couldn't tell. Probably, he thought.

'You're too old for me,' she said dismissively and put a digit in the rotary dial of the phone and started to turn the disc around. Billy put his finger on one of the stubby connectors to kill the call. 'I didn't ask your age. I asked if you'd like a drink. I assume you like lager and lime?'

'Rum and black,' she said insolently. 'I could hear you in there. It wasn't bad. I finish at six. Maybe one drink. We'll have that and when that's finished, I'll know whether I like you. There's a lot of boys,' - she accentuated the word - 'who come through here. I don't like many of them. Let's see if you're different.'

Billy was unusually nervous as he waited in the darkness on the pavement in Denmark Street. The girl finally exited the office door nearer 7pm and did a theatrical jump at the sight of the man waiting for her. 'What are you doing here?' she asked in a manner that suggested it was a surprise meeting. 'The drink,' he said nervously. 'Oh that,' she exclaimed, as if being told she was required to do unpaid overtime. She sighed. 'Is this your first time away from home?' she asked. 'Are you easily impressed? Is this Billy-Boy's big adventure?'

'I've been across the world. I've been away to sea,' Billy said, miffed. 'I've seen things you can't imagine.'

Eileen sniggered. 'I can imagine. There's plenty of places in Soho where you, er, sailor boys can enjoy a bit of male companionship. Three to a hammock, eh?' She tweaked his backside. 'Let's go over the road. You'll be impressed.'

They went to the Fitzroy Tavern, and he was impressed. Dylan Thomas, Brendan Behan, and George Orwell had drunk there, and all had been on Billy's rather perfunctory reading list. She was amused that he was star-struck.

'Behan was drinking in the Honky Tonk on Scotland Road the night he was arrested,' he said with pride. 'Round ours.'

'One of my favourites used to come here, too,' Eileen said. 'You ever heard of Aleister Crowley? He liked a good time. Or maybe a bad time would be a better description.'

The name meant nothing to Billy. The conversation stalled. 'I asked you about your clothes,' Billy said. 'Tell me about the way you dress. I've never seen anything like it.'

'It's called Punk,' she said. 'It's about the young idea. Why would you know about it? It's a long way from your music. You wouldn't like it.'

He was irritated. 'How do you know? I haven't heard it.'

'You wouldn't like it. I have to go soon. I'm going to see a band tonight. I have to meet some people.'

'Can I come?'

She reached over and squeezed his crotch. 'I'm sure you'd love to, big boy. And so would I. But I'm off to see The Jam. They're only a bit punky. Too much for you, though. See you around.' With one gulp of the rum and black, she was gone.

Perturbed, Billy sat alone for some minutes. He swilled away the dregs of weak sulphury IPA and went out into the gloom. After finding a phone box, he called his mate in Walthamstow and told him he was on the way. Then he walked down Rathbone Place to Oxford Street, intending to take the Victoria Line north from Oxford Circus. On his way, he saw some strangely dressed young people gathered on the street. It was the 100 Club. That night The Jam were playing. For a moment, he thought about going in. Instead, he headed for the tube.

Just before he was about to step into the Underground, he had second thoughts. He took his indecision to the Argyll Arms and drank another four pints in one of its small, cloistered lounges. After a final swig from his pint glass, he crossed the road back to the venue.

The bouncers gave Billy strange looks when he entered, but allowed him in. He went downstairs, straight to the bar, and bought a drink. He felt very out of place, but not intimidated. The room buzzed with aggression, but it was forced, manufactured. The Hotsy on a Saturday night was significantly more dangerous and some of the working mens' clubs fizzed with way more unfocused anger. Too many people here were trying too hard to act tough.

The girl was thrashing around in front of the stage with her friends. It was not dancing, as Billy knew it. He lurked in the shadows, waiting for the band to come on. He did not want Eileen to see him.

With six pints down him, Billy was in that dangerous state where elation, mental fuzziness, and anger vie for control of the psyche. Young men bumped into him at the bar and met his gaze with brittle tough-guy stares. The mood could have turned ugly, and he clenched and unclenched his fists a few times. Then the band came on and everything changed.

They were a three-piece combo in badly fitting suits and looked young enough to be playing a school fete, Billy thought, even though he had never been near any such event. Even before they started, feedback wailed from their amps. Automatically, he sniggered at their lack of professionalism. He had spent the past couple of years learning how to avoid making such an unpleasant noise.

Eventually, with a gruff 'One-two-three-four,' they began to play. Billy was not prepared for what he saw and heard: the visceral fury, the energy, the rawness of the voices, and the string-ripping strumming. They made no attempt to be cool, to project the aura of stardom. For this band, sweat was a prop to be embraced and celebrated, not something to be wiped away. The level of commitment astounded him. This was music-making as a physical act, providing the adrenaline-squirting euphoria of a brawl. Against all his preconceptions, he loved it.

He recognised Slow Down, the Larry Williams standard he had played and sung a thousand times, but it was like hearing it for the first time. The performance was intensely brutal, pop music as a contact sport.

It was reflected by the audience. The crowd fought on the dancefloor, threw glasses, and spat randomly into the air.

The man who had that afternoon been trying to become a

1970s pop star was destabilised, undermined and thrilled. Life would never be the same. It was a forty-minute assault on every musical belief Billy had held. He almost forgot the girl as his mind spun wildly. Although he remained perched at the bar, he was exhausted at the end of the set. He gulped down what was left of his drink and headed for the exit.

As he was leaving, he saw the girl involved in a pushing match with a skinhead on the dance floor. She stormed off towards the toilets and the skin chased her, shouting abuse. Billy followed them. At the toilet door, the youth grabbed Eileen's wrist and pulled her back. She hurled a foul mouthful of invective, and Billy began to move out of the darkness. His fists were bunched, and he was calm; it was not the raw aggression that had sent him to jail but a settled, composed intent that was even more dangerous.

To Billy's surprise, the girl pulled the man towards her and kissed him, thrusting her tongue into his mouth as if she were the predator. She stepped back to the door and pulled the skinhead into the toilets. As she pushed him inside, she turned back and looked into the blackness. Billy thought she had not seen him until she winked and cackled. He was stunned. He wanted to hate her. Instead, he just wanted her.

When Eileen emerged from the club alone, she found Billy loitering. This time, she expressed no surprise. 'Waiting for me, Scouse?' It was mocking. 'Yeah,' he said. 'Can I see you home?'

She snorted out a laugh. 'Think you're getting sloppy seconds? But I'll take you with me. We're going to a party.'

They went back to Denmark Street, to another building, and went through an open door to what was clearly a squat. A number of angry young men were drinking and talking. Three or four girls– all with frightening makeup– were hanging about, but the atmosphere was not sexual. 'Meet,' the girl said loudly, 'the worst band in history. The Sex Pistols. People will talk about them when your Beatles are forgotten. And this,' she spread one arm to make a theatrical introduction, 'is my pet Liverpudlian. Don't provoke him. He may be dangerous. I don't think he has been house trained.' If anyone heard, they did not acknowledge his presence. There were cans of warm Harp sitting on a wooden crate. She took two. 'Welcome to the new age.' Billy looked around. The wall was full of graffiti, and one snippet caught his eye. 'Depressed, miserable, tired, ill, sick, booed & bored.' A buffoon in a studded leather jacket squared up to him and said, 'Fuck off, hippy,' waving a bicycle chain. Billy slapped him with the back of the hand, and that appeared to earn the approval of the room.

There were no seats, so he leaned against the wall. A red-headed teenager that appeared to be the ringleader looked at him with bug eyes. 'We played Eric's last month,' he said.

'They'd never seen nothing like it in Mathew Street. We disgusted them.' The boy let loose a music-hall chuckle.

Billy had never heard of Eric's, but he resolved to go there as soon as he got home. 'I'll be there next time you play. We need more disgust.'

'You're growing on me,' the girl said. 'Maybe we'll snog. I'm beginning to think you have something about you. Come on, I think it's time for some Hole.' And she was off, with Billy trailing in her wake, wondering whether he could cope with sloppy seconds.

Duke thought it was hilarious. They were in The Grapes. There was a famous photograph of The Beatles sitting in this exact spot on the wall above them, but Billy could not stop talking about the new sound. 'I'm too old. I can't do it, but it's brilliant.'

'You've changed since you went to London,' Duke said. 'I like it. After you came out of jail, you seemed beaten. You've got a bit of bounce about you. You writing more songs?'

'Yeah, they're putting me in the studio before Christmas. Can't wait. Jail changes you, Duke. It changed Joey. You be careful. They've never got you, but they want you. Don't take the piss.'

Somehow, by a mixture of good luck, reasonable planning and easy-going charm, Duke had never been locked up for longer than a night or two. Even he sometimes didn't understand how he'd got away with it. 'I've got five years coming,' he laughed. 'It's a matter of time.'

Billy did not find it funny. 'Seriously,' Duke said, 'I'm getting too old for all the madness. The day of the shotgun is coming to an end. Can't be doing with drugs, though. But people will always want clubs and a bit of protection.'

Billy was wearing Wrangler jeans, sixteen-inch at the ankle, Converse basketball boots, a white shirt, and one of his dad's old suit jackets with the lapels turned up. When Duke left to go to the club, Billy put on his old Archbishop Whiteside school tie and went to Eric's. Every day he was injecting more energy into his compositions and trying to utilise punk sensibility. He knew that his best song was a ballad, but understood that there was a change in the air. At the kickabouts at Everton Valley, he spoke with the obsessive certainty of a seer. Yes, he was a prophet late to the cause, but he could see the pop world realigning.

He was also obsessed with Eileen. He had long gotten over the notions of fidelity and monogamy, but the girl fascinated him. She had shown interest, too. He phoned her at the office from a box on Soho Street near the Piggeries and she had taken the number and rung him back. Twice a day, at 1pm and 5.30pm, she would call him. They would talk until her bosses noticed and demanded she do some work.

The couple found plenty in common once the barriers came down. Both had a parent who had worked in Tate & Lyle's, and each had relatives in Ireland. The phone conversations started to become intimate.

In a week or so, he would be back in London for four days of recording. His seaman friend was away. He had access to the flat at the end of the Victoria Line. In his imagination, he would spend the nights with the girl and his days recording. It did not quite work out like that.

The Richman brothers had plenty of contacts and knew how to get cheap studio time. Essentially, they were on standby for when there were no bookings. Billy found he had to be ready to record whenever there was a free slot.

The girl liked him. She approved of his change of image, even if she mocked him as a pensioner. He was recording in a studio in Pimlico, and, after work, she came and watched Billy play, hanging around all night in one case. He was cutting four tracks and while Slamming Doors was the most marketable – he did it straight, without any punk influence – the other three songs were infused with energy.

Once recording finished, they went to The Hole, the place she had taken him on the night of his epiphany. That first time was an eyeopener.

After leaving the squat, the girl stopped outside a shop that sold hot-dog trolleys and began shrieking at an upper-floor window. Eventually, someone hurled a key into the road and Eileen let herself in. On the first floor was an ad hoc bar and dancefloor where salsa music was blasting out. 'Rodo's,' the girl said, waving hello to the customers. 'They're all Colombian. They like to dance.' She continued upstairs.

On the next floor, she stopped. 'The Hole,' she said. 'It's really the Spanish Rooms, but all these lovely spics call it El Hueco. We can drink until dawn. Or when I go into work.'

It was a classic drinking den. 'All of life is here,' the girl declaimed. 'Illegals, Irish, layabouts, gangsters, blacks, lesbians and homos. And you and me. Isn't it lovely?'

Billy had been nowhere lovelier. It became their favourite place and sometimes they joined the dancers in Rodo. He loved it.

When the drinking and dancing finished early, they went to Billy's mate's place in a tower block in E17. The couple lay in bed and held each other tight. Eileen was serious for once. 'I have something,' she said, 'an ability I can't explain. I know what people like. I know what people want, even if it's crap. People love crap, you know. You've got a bit of it.' Billy laughed, but in a slightly peeved tone.

She did not find it funny. 'I don't mean you're crap,' she said. 'It means you've got something people will warm to. You're not great, but I can see something. I can see what people want. You've got enough of it. But it will never come out if you try on your own. You need to listen to me. I can make you a star. Not a big one. But any sort of stardom is better than none.'

'You'll manage me?' He sniggered. Unexpectedly she said: 'Yes, but you will have to do exactly as I say.'

He sat up and looked at her. 'Wow. You're something else. You're a bossy little madam.' He guffawed with real joy. 'You're like a teacher. Yes miss, no miss.' He looked at her intently, seriously. 'So, if I listen to you, miss, I'll be OK?'

'Yes,' she said. 'Yes. You will be.'

'Well, little missy, I'm in your hands.' She groped him and they both laughed. He never called her Eileen again. He was looking for any excuse to give her a nickname. Her baptism name suggested barefoot, pregnant, and worn out by forty.

Unexpectedly, in the unlikely surroundings of Walthamstow, Missy was born. She entered a world of love. Holding Billy closely, she resolved that there would be no more casual sex, no more eccentric wildness, no more provocative sensuality. Love was the loveliest of surprises.

The tape was disappointing. Everyone at the mixing desk had been hugely positive during the session, and the studio had pulsed with excitement, but the playback left listeners puzzled.

The sound that thrilled human ears alchemised into something ordinary and tinny when it met tape. All Billy's charisma – what little there was of it – was crammed into the moment. It could not be captured. The tape was serviceable enough to tout around to record companies, but it gave no hint of how the singer could lift and thrill a room.

It was painful to hear back. The sound was nasally and thin. The small sonic boom he could employ in person failed to penetrate the microphones in the cloistered setting of the studio. He had only ever played live to relatively small audiences where the throbbing intensity of his voice overrode the amplification, and its resonance transcended any electronic projection. Recording, his voice drained the charisma from it. Now he feared that he had no future as a performer. The chart success he dreamt about would not be possible. He remembered reading about Australian aborigines, believing that photographs stole their souls. Billy felt the same way about the demo tape.

Was the engineer to blame? The studio? He thrashed around for answers, for scapegoats. For long hours he played and sang for his girlfriend and then listened once again to the cassette for clues as to why there was so little personality projecting itself from the machine. How could the voice that sounded so big and vibrant to human ears become scrawny and pallid when filtered through technology?

Missy was still optimistic. 'It just might be that you won't sell a million records,' she said. 'But there's worse recording artists out there. People will love you. They'll see you live; buy the singles and LPs, and you'll be successful.' She pulled a face. 'Yes, they'll be disappointed when they get home, but you'll get enough radio play to sell enough records to be a star. I can see it.'

Looking into her sincere blue eyes, he would have believed anything. He wanted to believe in her. She was very convincing.

The relationship was becoming more intense, and Billy stayed in London for most of December. He was taken to a terraced house and introduced to the girl's incomprehensible Irish parents. The couple lurked on the fringes of the punk scene, and he was introduced to those on the margins of change. It was the most thrilling time in his life, and he went back home for Christmas with a heavy heart.

At Euston, the lovers parted. 'I don't know how I'll survive without my wicked little Missy,' he said. 'You'll be back in ten days,' she said. 'Sentimentality is for hippies and OAPs.' They kissed.

'I think I should move down in the new year,' he said. 'Liverpool's a dead end.' She nodded. 'You need to get out of there,' she said. 'It will happen. I'm going to make sure you're a success. Now go, or you'll miss the train.'

As the guard blew his whistle, Billy jumped on the carriage. The door slammed behind him. The train pulled slowly out in the direction of the future. He went to the buffet and bought a can of McEwans. He could not have been happier.

I was happy, too. A flat had become available back in Burly, and we would be moving in January. We would be back close to family and friends in that tight tenement community and away from the Divvy next door.

The further we got from my father's death, the bolder the neighbour became. The music was turned up a notch, went on longer into the night and when he was high and drunk, the Divvy would bang on the walls and shout: 'He's dead. You and your kids are next.'

My mother said nothing. We would be out of that house and away from him by February. Despite being married to such a violent man – or perhaps because of it –she would go to almost any lengths to avoid conflict.

It's the one lesson I learnt from her. Sometimes you need to force the issue and control the direction of fate. If it takes hold of you, then anything can happen.

We spent New Year's Eve in Burlington Street, going out onto the landing at midnight to hear the foghorns blast on the Mersey. Neighbours were in the block, hugging, singing. Auld Lang Syne croaked out across the squares. I had been to town and went into the Yankee Clipper in Cumberland Street. The bouncers were friends of my father. They would not let me, or my two mates, buy a drink, and glass after glass appeared on our table. By 11.30, we were struggling to cope with the weight of beer, and one of the lads ordered a rum and black. That was the path to hell. I decided to go home. They stayed. I'd already seen too much of clubland to make such a mistake. They were supposed to meet me at the match the next day. Neither showed. They still looked queasy on Tuesday when we were back at school.

Relatively fresh, I went to Anfield for the first game of the year. Outside the Kop, there was something I had never seen before. There were men in Harrington and flying jackets trying to hand out National Front leaflets. It was an ugly portent of things to come but, for the moment, no one seemed to care. They were largely ignored.

It was a routine win over Sunderland. Alan Kennedy scored early, and Phil Thompson added a second after half-time. Generally, the Kop were subdued on New Year's Day, and the straightforward nature of the victory made it an unremarkable afternoon. From where I stood behind the goal, I could see Duke in the front row of the Main Stand where he had his season ticket. He looked relaxed, although his shirt wrenched free of his trousers when the second goal went in. He was standing up to tuck it back in when Sunderland kicked off again. I would, I thought, tease him about his scruffiness when I next saw him. Duke Moran rarely looked so untidy.

After the game, I went down to the Anfield Road with a couple of other mates to see if there was any trouble. Well, not quite. The burgeoning Anny Road Army, a mob of young scallies, were as keen on fashion as they were on violence. I wanted to check what everyone else was wearing and whether the look had moved on in the three days since we drew with Man City at Maine Road.

There was very little action, so we walked down to the Jester at the bottom of Everton Valley. It was a new pub on another of the modern estates. It was a good base to ambush the escort of away fans as they snaked down the Valley towards Scotland Road and town.

There wasn't much appetite for trouble. It was fairly calm. We had three pints there and went our separate ways. It was Saturday night, but everyone was a bit jaded. It was about 8.30 when I crossed Smith Street and walked into the close. No one was around. It was calm.

That was, until I opened the door of the house. I could hear kids crying. I assumed one of them had misbehaved and had been given a smack. That was not unusual. As I shut the door, I heard my mother say: 'Stop it now!'

The television was off in the living room, which was strange. My mother looked strained, sitting upright and upset. It reminded me of the night she had returned from Whiston Hospital after being told her husband would die within three months.

'What's going on?' I said.

'Nothing,' she replied. But my younger brother spoke up. 'The Divvy hit her.'

They had arrived home unmolested but, the day before, she

had left some washing on the line in the back garden. When she went out to bring it in, about an hour before my return, the man next door jumped the fence, punched her and, according to my eleven-year-old sibling, told her he was going to get a bottle and come back and slash everyone's throats.

We did not have a phone. I knew there was only one reasonable option: call Duke. She tried to stop me. 'We'll be away from here soon. Let's just get ready and go to Burly until we can move. Don't call him. Bad things will happen.'

I was too old to stop. I took a bread knife from the kitchen as protection and headed towards the phone box on Stanley Road to ring Duke. He would be at the club soon. As I walked up the narrow walkway between houses, the Divvy came into his garden. I stopped. He did not advance, but drew his finger across his neck in a cutthroat gesture. I reciprocated, showing him the knife, and backed slowly out of the close. Then I ran as fast as I could to the phone box. It was outside Stanley Road police station, but it never crossed my mind to go in and try to get help there. That was not the way I had been brought up.

Billy planned to go to Eric's. Yes, he was a bit older than many of the young punks trying to develop an identity on Mathew Street, but his brief experience of mixing in London music circles (and his ability to intimidate anyone who mocked him) had won him credibility. At the last moment, he decided to go to see Duke at the club while things were still quiet.

The club was a converted warehouse with three floors. The main one, on the entrance level, was where the DJ and dancers congregated. Downstairs was a danker and seedier space, where deals were done and seductions attempted. Upstairs was an attempt to create a dining room. Only the very drunk or strong of stomach ate the chicken in a basket there.

The walls were dark, with 60s-style murals painted on them. Behind the DJ, in the thick rear wall, were a number of bullet holes where Duke and his friends had practiced their shooting with illegal revolvers. The weapons were status symbols rather than tools of the trade, but firing them enhanced the shooters' sense of prestige.

Billy had just arrived when the phone rang. Duke was not yet there, I was told. The bouncer who answered the call was gruff and did not seem to understand the gravity of the situation. I gave him the number of the phone box and told him to get Duke to ring as soon as he arrived.

Idly, the doorman chatted to Billy. 'A kid's just phoned looking for Duke. Said he's Joey's boy. There's been some trouble with his mam. Kids and their mams, eh…'

All Billy's alarm bells went off. 'Give me the number,' he said. When I picked up the handset, it was not the voice I expected. It gave me a series of instructions.

Ten minutes later, a black taxi pulled up in front of the phone box and Billy gestured me in. We went around the corner and parked at the end of the close. The driver waited and Billy strode towards the Divvy's house with evil intent and then stopped. He beckoned me to open the front door to our place. He went in and looked at my mother, saying in a soft voice:

'Come on, girl, let's get you out of here.' Then he supervised the scooping up of clothes and children. He took us back to the taxi, said to the driver, 'Take them to Burly,' and gave the man a £10 note. 'I've left a message to meet Duke here,' he said and took the front-door key from me.

'I'll stay with you,' I said. He was having none of it. 'You go with the family. Your job is to make sure they're alright.' I grimaced. 'Now!' he shouted. There was authority in his tone. Yet again, you could see why men would follow him and obey his wishes. There were times when Billy's intangible qualities exploded out of him and his voice boomed around the silent estate. It was not threatening, but it was in control.

So I got in the cab. I did not see what happened that night. I can only piece together the events of the next few hours from the snippets told later by those involved and second-hand stories that spread like wildfire.

Billy took the key and went to the house. He lingered for a long look at next door, then let himself in. There was no music pounding through the wall, just silence. After turning the television on, he went into the kitchen and found a bottle of whisky. He poured himself a nip and sat down to wait.

Nearly an hour later, he heard banging on the door. It was Duke and one of his armed-robber mates known as the Gasman. A sinking feeling washed over Billy when he looked at his cousin.

They came inside. 'What happened?' Duke was outwardly calm, but it was a façade. 'That's your killing face,' Billy said. The comment was ignored.

'What happened?'

The Gasman caught Billy's eye and shrugged. He noticed the whisky, picked up the glass and went in search of the bottle, leaving family matters to the other two. The spirit was on the sink's draining board. The Gasman found another two tumblers and put a healthy slug into all three glasses and then took a long swig from the bottle. By the time he returned with the drinks, Billy had given a condensed version of the story.

'Did you knock on his door?'

Billy shrugged. 'Waiting for you.'

'Drink up. We'll give him a knock.' Duke slipped a cosh out of his pocket and slid it up his sleeve. His friend put on brass knuckles.

'They're moving soon,' Billy said. 'Do it when they're gone.

Pick him up one Friday night when he's stoned and coming out the pub. Or run him over on Stanley Road in the early hours. He won't be in now. He'll have shit and run because he knows you're coming.'

Duke nodded sagely. 'Let's give him a knock anyway,' he said casually, as if calling on a man to propose a visit to the pub. 'We're here now. We might as well.'

They went down the narrow path, walked ten yards to next door's gate, and approached the front door. All lights were off. Duke rapped on the knocker.

There was no movement or sound inside. Gazza stepped back into the unkempt garden and looked at the upper storey. Nothing moved there, either.

'I'll take a look around the back,' he said, strutting off to the top of the close to check the rear windows and garden.

The other two men went back into the street. They waited for a few minutes, wordlessly conscious of the twitching curtains of the other residents. The Gasman came back. 'All quiet there. Nothing we can do tonight,' he said. 'And everyone's blimping us out their windows. Billy's right. Let's get a drink and work out when and where.'

Duke sighed. He nodded towards the walkway that led to a small car park on the estate. A taxi was waiting, driven by a mate of Duke's. They strolled cautiously in its direction and turned into the entry.

Coming the other way was the Divvy. All four men stopped and stared at each other, mere yards apart. The lone man swayed. He was drunk, and because of the intoxication, showed no fear. More than that, he smirked and nodded his head.

And then Billy saw why. The Divvy was holding an empty Schofields' lemonade bottle, gripped around the neck with the glass vessel half hidden behind his buttock.

Coming back with a bottle to kill them, Billy thought, but his body was already moving, even as the idea flashed across his consciousness. All three of them leapt on the Divvy as their quarry swung his arms wildly.

Duke hit him three times with back-and-forth swings of the cosh. The blows tore a hole under the man's right eye and echoed with a clunk in the narrow walkway. Gazza was on him next, ramming his metalled fist into the Divvy's nose, pulping the ethmoid bone, and tearing the septum. Features were no longer distinct on the man's face. He did not scream or even howl, but gave out huge, liquidy gasps. Billy landed a punch and then wrestled the bottle from his prey's possession.

Then Billy lost his grip on the glass. The blood on his hands made them slippy. The vessel dropped to the floor and smashed. Its base shattered. The neck held together with the screw top still on, its bottom splintery and razor sharp.

Duke and his mate leaned over the body, pummelling the mangled head in fury. People had come out of the houses to watch, peeking around the corner of the entry. The Gasman stood up and looked around.

'Someone will have called the busies,' he said. 'Let's get out of here.' Duke stood up and nodded. Even though his suit was flecked with blood, he straightened his jacket and shot his cuffs, determined to display both his dominance and style.

Then the Divvy made his big mistake. He smiled, showing derelict teeth, and said: 'I'll kill them. You can't be here all the time. Even if they move, I'll find them.'

Billy snapped. He snatched up the bottle and drove it down towards the middle of the man's face, grinding it in and twisting. He pulled it out to repeat the act. Duke went to grab his cousin, but slipped on a piece of detached flesh. The broken bottle pumped downwards again, and the Divvy squirmed to turn his face away. It exposed his neck. The glass sliced through the skin and severed the artery. It sounded like a water-balloon ripping, a squelchy plop, and a fountain of blood sprayed fifteen yards down the entry and into the parking area where the taxi waited.

It was less than ninety seconds since they first saw the man. In another minute, he would be dead.

Duke grabbed the bottle. 'Fuck,' he said, and whipped off his jacket and wrapped the lethal weapon in it. Billy was standing over the body, a squirt of blood flashed across his face as if it was Ziggy Stardust makeup. Calmly, but with authority, Duke pushed him into movement. 'Come on,' he said, and led them to the cab. The driver, who had been out of sight but within earshot of the brawl, had heard the screams of onlookers. He was already white with shock.

'Go north. Towards Crosby,' Duke said.

'What the fuck have you done?' the Gasman said, but Duke shut down the recriminations. 'We need to think, not shout. We need to work out the best way to get out of this with the minimum damage.'

He turned to the driver. 'When we get to Bankhall, get out, get the next train into town, and once you get there, and report the cab stolen. After that, go to Ma Moores, the Pieshop and the Mitre and find John the Dog. He'll be in one of them.' That was another of Duke's criminal cohort. 'Tell him we're going to that place we've talked about. We'll have an hour or so before they start rounding people up.'

After dropping the driver off, Duke drove north for a mile and stopped at a phone box. He made a call and within five minutes; they were at a pub near Bootle Town Hall. They slipped in the side door that led to the upstairs living quarters. A man carrying a can of flammable liquid and firelighters took the keys to the vehicle. Ten minutes later, the cab was burning on waste ground near Marsh Lane; the bottle smashed to smithereens in Duke's jacket, which was doused in the petrol and used to help set the fire. Burnt-out stolen cars were not unusual round here, and the police trod warily in this area at night. For the moment, the killers were safe.

We were packed tightly in my auntie's flat. In the room where I was born, there was a double bed and one of my mother's sisters slept there with the two youngest children. The other aunt was in a single bed in the small bedroom, the one where I had heard about my father's looming death. The largest sleeping quarters in the house had twin beds. My mother was in one with the baby, me and my brother in the other. We were all in bed before midnight.

So, this is the way a police raid goes. There is pounding on the door, followed by shouting and chaos. Men charge into every room and in the bedrooms tear away the covers from the beds, all the time roaring abuse and obscenities.

A detective dragged me to my feet and weighed me up. 'Not him,' he said. 'Too young.' They ushered my mother into the narrow hallway in her nightie and then hustled her out into the night, barely stopping to drape an overcoat around her. She knew nothing, but they understood she would be part of the bait to bring Duke in.

I had seen one policeman outside Anfield with my uncle. They were going the match together. They were mates. He noticed I recognised him and put his face close to mine. 'He'll be in jail by the morning,' the detective said nastily. 'No more match for Bob the Beaut.' I looked at him with hate. 'You'll join him in chokey one day,' he said, enjoying the moment. 'It's in the Moran blood. Destined for jail from the moment you're born.'

In such a small flat, there were no hiding places, and the

detectives knew it, but they opened the wardrobes and hurled clothes and hangers onto the floor out of malice. This was the last place Duke would come, but the policemen wanted their presence to be unsettling. No doubt they hoped word of their casual vandalism would get back to him. Pressure on the family would be the key to catching their man.

'What do you think happened?' my little brother said when they were gone, and we were ushered back to bed. 'Duke must have beat the Div up,' was my best guess. We had no idea how bad it was.

Neither did Billy. Everyone ignored him. Duke was in the kitchen area of the pub's living quarters, talking quietly but urgently to the landlord. The Gasman was clearly angry, but kept his counsel. They had been there about two hours when another of Duke's mates arrived in a car with clean clothes for the trio. The bloodstained garments were collected. Duke addressed the group.

'Well, we're fucked,' he said with certainty. 'They're looking everywhere for me. They've nicked a couple of the lads. We've got to get out of here. They don't want youse, they want me. But we need to get you away for a while. Both of you.'

'I need to call a few people,' Billy said gormlessly. 'I'm supposed to be back in the studio in London next week.'

'You should have thought about that before you killed the cunt, you daft twat,' Gazza said with exasperation.

'And there's a girl…'

'You can't talk to anyone,' Duke said with crisp authority. 'If you do, you'll end up doing life. I need time to think. There're a couple of places we can go. But you do exactly what I say. If you don't, it'll be more than jail you need to worry about. You first,' he pointed at Billy. He motioned to the man who had arrived with the car. Billy knew him as 'the Panther.' 'Take him, come back for us.'

Billy was helped up from his seat rather roughly. Duke came to the bottom of the stairs with him. 'You can't call anyone. He's taking you to a place that doesn't have a phone. I'm going to have to carry the can for this. Don't make it worse by fucking up again. Do you understand?' There was no reply, so Duke slapped his cousin's face. 'Do. You. Under. Stand.'

Billy shook his head. 'No, Bob. You can't take the blame. It was me. I'll turn myself in.'

Duke laughed. 'I've told you. I've got five…' he thought again, 'ten years coming. If they don't get me for this, they'll get me for something else. Gazza's already on bail for armed robbery. He'll go away for ages. You'll get life. You couldn't handle it. Think how bad it was last time. If we do it right, you two can stay on the outside.' He laughed sadly. 'Nothing can save me now, you silly bastard.

'Now a lot will happen in the next few days. We'll get word to your mam. Write down the number of the girl and I'll get a message to her as soon as things calm down.'

Duke went back upstairs and came down with a pen and paper. 'Her name and number.' Billy scribbled it, noting the time and date the girl would be back at work. 'I don't want you in the next cell to me,' Duke said. 'The only chance you have of being a pop star is if you do exactly as you're told.'

'Any chance of getting my guitar?'

'Get in the fucking car before I kill you.'

The Panther stood beside the vehicle, checked up and down the street, and nodded, beckoning the fugitive to his transport. Duke shut the door behind them. He went back upstairs and looked at the paper. 'Fucking hell,' he said. 'He's fucked up everyone's life tonight, and all he can think about is a fucking tart called Missy. I should leave him to the fucking murder squad.'

He took the paper to the ashtray and set it alight. 'Fucking Missy,' he said again.

The next five days left Billy disoriented. That night he was taken to a block of flats in Formby and told to stay there. The apartment belonged to a woman and was very feminine. There was no food in the fridge, which suggested the occupant had gone away for the holidays. The bathroom was full of beauty products. Billy assumed she was one of Duke's girlfriends. Then he thought again. The police would check anyone who'd had an affair with his cousin.

It was a very bourgeois place. There were cheap copies of oil paintings on the wall and inexpensive, chintzy ornaments positioned on every flat space. The absent owner collected thimbles. Billy groaned and sat on the couch. He could smell the sea was not far away and wanted to go out to the beach and look at the waves.

'You'll be here for a few days,' the Panther said. 'Don't go out. Don't use the record player. If you watch telly, keep the sound down low. Do nothing to attract attention. I'll be back with food, booze, and news tomorrow. You got that?'

He had it. There was no phone in the flat. One had recently been removed, he suspected. There was no one to call, anyway. His mother would get told he'd gone away. Duke would call Missy. She would not be back in the office for some thirty-six hours, anyway. There was no other way of contacting her other than the work number.

There was nothing to do but wait. On Tuesday he considered looking for a phone box but, as lovelorn as he was, Billy was not stupid. That would mean leaving the flat during daylight hours, and that would be dangerous. He imagined the Echo printing his picture or Look North news running a small TV segment on the killing. He started to grow a beard.

On Wednesday afternoon, the Panther came around and brought a Chinese meal. 'You'll be moving tonight,' he said. 'I've got a van. You'll be in the back.'

The news was not good. Duke was still on the run. Gazza was being taken out of the country. Because he was on bail, he was the priority. The police had been all over their friends and families.

'We were seen by too many people,' Billy said with resignation.

'And your fingerprints were all over the whisky glasses in the house,' his companion said. 'They're scouring Scottie looking for you.'

At 8pm they went to the van. All was quiet in the street, and Billy jumped into the windowless cargo compartment and lay flat on the floor. He had no way of knowing where they were going. The driver put on the radio and moved off.

At length the Panther said: 'We're heading towards Manchester and then we'll swing round and catch the M56. We don't dare go through the tunnel. We'll go to Wales. You might be there for a week or two.'

It was after midnight when they stopped. There was a moment of panic for the fugitive when he saw they had pulled up on a pitch-black country lane. Billy had seen too many gangster films and his imagination, fed by his escort's nickname, briefly spun out of control, but the Panther merely wanted him in the passenger seat when they arrived at their destination.

It was a caravan park. Billy recognised where they were, even in the dark. It was Talacre, where he had spent his childhood holidays in a bus converted into a holiday home. A man with a torch obviously expected them. He unlocked a gate to a private roadway, chatted easily with the driver, who he clearly knew well, relocked the gate, and disappeared into the night.

There were two hundred or more caravans on the site, and Billy was taken to one right in the centre of the park, as far from public roads as possible. It was equipped with a small oven, powered by bottled gas, a portable TV with dreadful reception and a tiny cooler box. Someone had stocked it with food and a couple of four packs of Long Life before his arrival.

There was no one around in the depths of midwinter except the caretaker, whose name was not disclosed to Billy. What tale the Welshman had been told to explain his presence was never discussed. The Panther said he'd spend the night with him. He went back to the cab of the van and reappeared with a half-bottle of Paddy, twelve more cans of beer, and a pack of cards.

'Rummy?' he said, pouring the whiskey and opening up two cans of Long Life. 'I'll leave the cards when I go. You'll play a lot of patience, I reckon.'

They played hand after hand. 'What's your real name?' Billy asked. 'I feel a bit soft calling you the Panther.'

The man laughed. 'Jim,' he said. 'Call me Jim.'

'How did you get your nickname?' Billy continued, imagining the man stalking his prey in the dingy back streets of Liverpool's clubland and pouncing with sudden and decisive violence.

'Me?' Jim said. 'I wore a pink shirt one night. Duke took one look at me and then I was the Pink Panther for years. Then everyone stopped using pink. It became just the Panther.'

They both laughed. Jim was hard. Only someone like Duke could have got away with giving him such a pisstaking moniker. 'It's worked quite well over the years. I don't mind if people think I'm a hunter. Yeah, at first, I was annoyed, but it's done well for me. I haven't had to throw many punches as the Panther. Jim would have had much more knuckle.' He looked into Billy's eyes, laughing but sincere. 'Just don't spread the pink stuff around. The colour didn't suit me, anyway.'

The next day, Jim left around mid-morning and returned with more food and beer about an hour later. 'I'll be back in two, three days,' he said. 'Remember, don't go out. There are no strangers around here in winter. The Welsh will notice you. Enjoy some peace and quiet. And any time you think of going walkabout, remember that this is better than Strangeways. Oh, and I'll hunt you down pretty quickly. They don't call me the Panther for nothing.' He winked.

'I've been in Walton,' Billy said. 'And away to sea. I won't go anywhere. Tell Duke thanks for everything.'

'Duke will turn himself in soon,' Jim said. 'Maybe he has already. He could have turned you over and settled for five years, you know.' Billy knew. 'He'll get life.' He stopped at the door, shook his head, and looked intently back at Billy, who braced himself for admonishment. 'Mind you,' the Panther said, 'he had ten years coming. I'll see you in three days or so.'

Jim returned on Saturday. Only a week had passed since the incident, but Billy felt like it had been years. The visitor entered without knocking and dumped groceries on the floor. 'Put them away,' he said by way of greeting. 'I've got something for you.'

He came back with a guitar. It was a cheap instrument, the sort that you might buy a child just beginning to learn. 'Duke said you needed one. He wanted you to have one.'

'How is he?'

'Pretty shit, I should think. He went in yesterday.'

Billy sat down with a thud and groaned. 'It's done now,' Jim said. 'We've got to make the best of it. He doesn't want you to be in the same position. Gazza should be safe within a week or so. Then we can get you out of here.'

'What then?'

'You stay away. Out of sight. At least until he's convicted. Longer. Me? I'd give it at least a year. They'll have moved on to other people then. I'll be off.'

'Jim,' Billy said as the man unlocked the door to his van. 'Did Bob call that girl for me?'

The Panther looked back at him and shook his head. 'He's going down for murder, and all you're arsed about is a bird?' Billy went red. 'Oh, by the way, his missus is pregnant. She thought she was before Christmas, but didn't want to tell Duke until she'd been the doctors. I don't know if he called your tart, but if it slipped his mind in the circumstances, you'll understand. He's had a lot going on.'

Billy went back into the caravan and put his head in his hands. Not for Duke and his unborn baby, but for a love he now knew he had destroyed, along with a man's life. He cried for hours, grateful that there were no neighbours to hear his weeping.

In Talacre, Billy felt lost. He paced the caravan, cursed his existence, and pounded his head against the table. Then he picked up the tinny, discordant guitar and strummed it. After tuning it, he began to play. It did not release any frustration, but it numbed his mind. The strings slipped sharp and flat at frequent intervals, but he persisted and played.

If anyone had been near enough to hear, they would have been concerned. The first day or two he played every song he knew, reaching back to the old songs of Burly and mixing them up with his own material. As time passed, he began to narrow down his range. After a week, he was only playing four songs. After ten days, just one.

It became almost trance-like. He stared ahead and saw nothing. He played Slamming Doors for hours, changing the lyrics from one break-up that barely registered any more to the recent enforced separation that tore up his soul.

There, alone, with no other human being within five hundred yards, he gave the show of his life. The air sizzled with energy; his voice buzzed like a trumpet. All his personality and melancholy condensed into a black hole of loss and anger before exploding into a performance of hair-raising beauty. Even his nemesis, the magnetic tape that recorded his voice with such contempt, might have succumbed to such passion and commitment. And there was no one to hear him.

He rose in the morning and played until his fingerpads were sore and his voice hoarse. When he could only croak, he adapted the song so that the gruff verbalisation was still compelling. Billy's instincts became attuned to the range and variety of his own intonations. In the harsh training grounds of heartbreak and loss, he found another quality in his talent. And now there was nowhere to express it except a caravan on an empty site.

Then it distilled further. He telescoped his repertoire down to four bars. For hours on end, he would play the same chords and repeat the same refrain: 'And I would shift the world to see her,' over and over again with manic intensity.

The repetition was hypnotic, agonising and somehow reassuring. It was the only thing that seemed certain in Billy's life.

PURSUIT

Missy expected to hear from Billy on Monday. She had breathless tales of a drunken Irish Christmas. The visiting family from Cork had become involved in an absurd series of events during the festive period. The girl was also excited to tell him some news: she had been offered a job.

At a gig between Christmas and New Year, she bumped into a young A&R man she had met the previous summer and then seen at various concerts. They had fumbling sex before she became involved with Billy, but did not ignore each other afterward. They often talked about bands when they crossed paths. The talent spotter was very interested in Missy's opinions. During the holidays, he told her he was leaving a major record company to start an independent operation. He was allowed to recruit two staff, and the money on offer would double her wages as a secretary. It was less secure, sure, but she could do whatever she wanted with her days. There were no second thoughts. Even before Christmas, she was getting to the point where the sound of a ringing phone made her feel nauseous.

Except at lunchtime and the half hour before closing. In the new year, her stomach leapt every time the ringer buzzed. She hoped it might be Billy.

On the first day back, she was amused by his silence. She imagined him hungover and hung up; trying to work out whether he should relocate to London and mulling over the level of commitment he should show to his new girlfriend. 'Men,' she sniggered to herself.

By the third day, she was angry. He was selfish and probably shacked up with a blonde somewhere. She'd rip his balls off when she saw him. By Friday, she was concerned.

In the late afternoon, she finally snapped. She rang a number Billy had given her to leave messages with his mother. The call was answered quickly. 'Mrs Green?'

A man's voice, suspicious, said: 'Who wants her?'

'My name's…' she hesitated. 'I'm a friend of Billy's.' There was silence. 'His girlfriend in London.' It went quiet, but she heard the clunk of a receiver being set down on a table. There were family-life noises in the background. A child cried.

Missy could not know that this was not the Green household. It was a neighbour's flat three doors along the landing. It was the only phone on the block and therefore a community asset. The man who answered had to leave his residence and fetch Lilly.

In London, the girl could not imagine what was happening. She listened intently to the clunks and voices at the other end of the line, desperately trying to get an insight into Billy's life. Eventually, after a scraping noise, a wary woman's voice said: 'Who is this?'

'I'm a friend of Billy's, Mrs Green. He's called me every day at work for a couple of months. I haven't heard from him this week, not since he went home for Christmas. He's supposed to be recording down here in London soon, and I'm worried about him.'

Lilly had been warned that the authorities would try anything to get to her son. There was no chance of her giving any information to a stranger. It was probably a policewoman.

'Don't know,' Lilly said. 'He goes away to sea. He's been on a ship for about six weeks now. I haven't seen or heard from him. He's on a tanker. Don't expect him home anytime soon. Don't ring here again.'

Missy put the phone down in shock. So that was that. She gathered her stuff, went to the office, and opened the door without knocking.

'Mr Richman,' she said sweetly. 'You need a new secretary, you old fruit. Goodbye.'

With no more explanation, she walked out into Denmark Street and the next phase of her life. She had learnt a crucial, bruising lesson: never fall in love with any man who wanted to be involved in showbusiness. Part of her was angry at herself. She had seen the way band members and musicians behaved, their selfishness and contempt for women. How had Billy conned her? He had appeared vulnerable, sensitive, and trustworthy. She had seen something in him. It turned out not to be there.

'That,' she said aloud, 'is the last time. I will not let anyone do that to me again.'

Not a single tear was shed in east London. Yet the brief relationship had two lasting effects on the girl. It hardened her heart in the most brutal manner and she now completely uncoupled sex and love. Every relationship she would enter into would be on her terms and to her benefit.

The other lasting legacy was the nickname. Eileen had always been too workaday for her anyway, and in the glorious weeks of infatuation, her friends on the punk scene had responded well when they heard her called Missy. The dominatrix overtones chimed perfectly with the era of bondage trousers. So, she not only answered to it but built part of her developing persona around it.

The new job suited her as perfectly as the new name. She met the A&R man in the Pillars of Hercules in Greek Street. His name was Duncan Stevenson, and he had learnt his trade at EMI. Now it was time to strike out alone.

He explained the brief she would work to. Punk was about to go mainstream, but Stevenson believed it would burn out quickly. There was money to be made, though.

'I want you to find bands that are not as threatening as the punks,' he said. 'You like The Jam?' She nodded. 'Groups like them but less angry. I want to sign bands that will make the middle-class kids feel wild, but not so wild. They and their parents get scared off. Understand? Pop bands rather than punk. With a bit of punk power.'

'Power pop?' she said.

'You've got it. I don't mind one-hit wonders. If they've got one song, get them in the studio, crank the record out and count the cash.' She thought briefly of Billy and his one potential big seller. 'Then give them another chance to see if they can repeat the trick. If they can't, drop them. We'll pay peanuts for the advance. They're all so desperate to get a deal and get in the studio they'd sign away their balls.'

'I can do this, Duncy. Why me?'

'Because when I've talked to you, it's clear you've an eye for potential. You've got experience with a publishing company. And I want to fuck you again.'

'That can be arranged,' she said, running her hand up his thigh and squeezing his groin slowly in full view of the rest of the pub.

'Come back to my flat in Victoria,' he said. 'An American friend brought me some cocaine. You ever tried it?'

'Only speed and weed.'

'You'll love this. It's a different experience.'

Missy was more interested in the drug than the sex. 'How do you take it?' she giggled. 'I don't mind your little needle entering me,' she slapped his groin now, feeling his penis erect under his jeans, 'but I don't want to inject drugs.'

'No, no,' he said. 'You roll up a pound note and snort it up your nose. But you can sniff it off anywhere. I want to snort it off your nipples.'

'As long as I can sniff it off your cock, Duncy,' she whispered down his ear, drawing her bottom lip over his neck and under the lobe. 'If it's big enough.' She pulled away quickly, projecting her voice so the clientele could hear the comment while she cackled like a scornful crone. The tone was set for their professional relationship.

It was hard for a woman in the pop world. The men with power assumed the girls without it were fair game. Predators used their fame, wealth, and status to take what they wanted. Missy was in the line of fire from her first foray into the A&R world.

Bands were reluctant to take her seriously. In pokey dressing-rooms, egocentric lead singers would stroke her hair as she tried to talk business. Leering drummers touched her up while breathing heavily down her ear. In tiny rooms full of sweat and masculinity, she doubled down on the sexuality. Over-excitable vocalists suddenly found their genitals grabbed and manhandled with a rough urgency that surprised them. 'I want to talk contracts, big boy,' she would say with a heavy dose of mockery. 'Are you man enough to put your balls on the table?' Then she would laugh. It was the sort of guffaw that caused droopiness in everyone except the most spaced-out sex fiends. It quickly became clear to the wannabee pop stars who was in charge. She would slap bassists' backsides hard and express a desire to tie them up with their E strings and make their body vibrate. She marked her territory as the hunter.

Most of the callow youths trying to crack the music scene had their bluster punctured easily. Missy learnt to turn the tables on boyish bravado and take control of the situation. She doled out sexual favours on her terms and record contracts to those in whom she saw potential. Her instincts were unerring.

The hits came rolling in. Post-punk power pop fizzled for a moment and then died, but before it expired, Missy managed to get three rather tepid combos into the Top 30. She rode the mini-Mod revival at the end of the 1970s until it crashed. While The Jam imitators were still selling records, she had already latched on to the New Romantic movement. Her portfolio was full of footnotes to pop history, but they raked in the money for her company and made her wealthier than any of the bands.

The turning point in her career came when she championed a group that was part of the 'new wave of British heavy metal.' Jeans, flairs, and long hair were a standing joke when Sounds magazine and a few DJs began to get behind a slew of mainly dreadful bands. Missy checked a few out and dismissed even their single-hit potential. Then she watched a five-piece from Newcastle called Audio Seizure. She saw something. It was impossible to explain, but she knew that their raw, infantile sound and lyrics would generate cash.

Duncan Stevenson was not convinced. His tiny record company – and his reputation – had grown hugely. He took credit for the succession of successful records. His first nickname – the Hitman – began to appear in the music papers, largely on the back of Missy's instincts. This, though, was a gamble too far.

She badgered him constantly, teased him with the offer of sex and, finally, threatened to leave for a bigger label if he failed to sign the band. He relented and allowed her to offer Audio Seizure a small contract. It was a mere £20,000, barely enough to put out and promote a single, an album, and finance a transit-van tour.

There were flops on her resume, but that was always going to happen given the label's policy. She had never staked her instinct – and status – in such a big way. Remarkably, vindication came with the first single.

The whole concept was laughable. It was six minutes long, called 'Bang Your Head' and was played at punk pace except for a slowed-down guitar solo coda that comprised the final one-hundred-and-twenty seconds. Everyone in the industry who heard the finished version turned the tape off before ninety seconds had elapsed. Stevenson only sanctioned the release to restore the power balance with Missy. He wanted her chastened by failure.

Certain record stores across the country had their sales recorded and averaged out as representative of the entire nation to generate that week's charts. It was a simple and flawed system because the labels were aware of the supposedly secret locations and sent people out to buy large amounts of individual records from these shops to create a false illusion of national demand. Done cleverly, this could catapult a single on to Top of the Pops, the BBC showcase. An appearance on TOTP, which had an audience of millions, could change the fate of a band. Stevenson kept his regiment of secretive buyers away from Audio Seizure's debut. His pluggers – more senior operatives who schmoozed radio and television DJs and producers – were instructed to ignore the single.

Against all expectations, Bang Your Head began to sell. Radio stations in the northeast supported their local band, and word of mouth began to create a buzz. From nowhere, it made the Top 50 in its second week of release. It was hovering around the 30 mark a week later. Missy had done it again. She was delighted.

Yet even she did not expect what happened next. The single crashed the Top 20 despite receiving no national airplay. The entire music press ran features on the band and a TOTP appearance beckoned.

Missy liked the lads. They glugged crates of Newcastle Brown Ale and swigged whisky from the bottle. They were in their late twenties and womanised rabidly, engaging whenever they could with their female followers. On occasion they would smash up equipment, a room, a car, or a bar. But they were always respectful to Missy. She was at least five years younger than "the boys" but they treated her like a serious record exccutive. Within weeks, she started mothering them and cleaning up the chaos they left behind. None of the band made a clumsy pass at her, although it was clear they all fancied her. They acted like she was out of their league. There was never any need for her to project her ferocious, dangerous sexuality towards them.

The band asked her to come to Television Centre in White City for their debut on national television. They were nervous. She was only too happy to go along and reassure them.

Missy had been to TOTPs before. This was the big stage. From the perspective of living-room sofas across the nation, it appeared to be harmless family entertainment. Inside the studios, it was a hothouse of lust.

Underage girls roamed around while predatory men looked for victims. Missy was used to the culture of groupies, so it made little impact on her. During this filming, she felt relaxed and in charge. It was the first time she had been at a show presented by Jimmy Savile.

Like almost everyone in the industry, she had heard about Savile. Rumours of his dark carnal appetite abounded. There were even tales that he used his volunteer work in hospitals to molest helpless patients and had parlayed his massive celebrity status to gain access to morgues where he engaged in necrophilia. All this while establishing friendships with the Royal Family and Prime Minister and hosting an extremely popular children's show called Jim'll Fix It.

Part of Missy could not believe the stories. It was a business where exaggeration and bluster were common. But she was fascinated to see what the man was like in the flesh.

Brazenly, she caught his eye during rehearsals. He was nearing sixty and looked every day of it. He was dressed in a tracksuit top and running shorts that were damp and stained at the crotch. An ominous bulge hung between wiry thighs. When the crowd surrounded him to rehearse the shots of him announcing the artists, a young girl at his side flinched as an unseen finger probed her private regions. Missy watched with amusement. He clearly had impunity to act as he desired here.

In the gap between run-throughs and filming, he took a young woman – certainly; she appeared to have nudged just past girlhood – into his dressing room. When she emerged five minutes later, it was clear Missy had overestimated the girl's age. She was crying and distressed. Embarrassed, too. She tried to compose herself as she walked past. At that point, Savile popped his head out into the corridor, a fat Havana between his teeth, and looked straight at Missy. 'Come in,' he said. 'I've heard you know a hit record when you hear it.'

A small thrill of excitement shivered through her. If the rumour mill had any substance, this was the next best thing to meeting Aleister Crowley. She walked into the room and Savile locked the door. The wet stain on the satin running shorts was bigger, sopping, and sticky.

He leaned over her, a threatening presence, and pushed her towards the dressing-table ledge in front of the mirror. He smelt of rancid sweat and criminal sex. The assault was near.

He still had the cigar in his mouth. Missy was more concerned about being burnt than raped. He pushed against her and fumbled with her leather trousers. It crossed her mind that a man of his age must be loading up on drugs to maintain such an erection – she could feel it pressing. As he groped – rather inexpertly, she mused – she squirmed sideways, but not enough for him to think it was any more than token resistance. While he was distracted, she reached around, slid her hand under the skimpy running shorts, and rammed a sharp finger up his rectum. He leapt away, shocked at the role reversal, and the cigar tumbled out of his mouth.

'Fix it for me to watch you have sex with a dead body, Jim,' she said, referencing the title of his show. 'We could be partners. I'll give you pleasure like you've never had.'

Savile froze, shaped to slap her, and then backed away. Missy straightened her clothes, unlocked the door, and minced out into the corridor. She was happy. Not many people stare the devil in the eye and walk away a winner. She saw the look. Satan was scared of her. In the toilets, she took another big hit of cocaine and felt like no one could stop her.

They couldn't. Audio Seizure played New York and college radio stations went crazy for this bunch of Geordie headbangers. Their fame spread despite scant promotion. Missy oversaw their route to stardom like a proud, filthy mother.

Things were changing in the music business. The mid-to-late 1980s became the age of the producer. As if to counter Missy's success breaking America, Duncan Stevenson, still pursuing one-hit wonders, found himself a studio engineer who had a magic touch. In Britain, the second half of the decade was defined by a certain sound. It didn't matter whether the artists were a talented bunch of musicians and singers or squeaky-voiced soap stars; The Hitman had a song for them and the producers to create something the public wanted. The tiny, independent record company that Missy joined in the waning days of punk was bought by a huge conglomerate. It made her and her on-off sexual partner rich. Both were still dissatisfied.

Corporate life did not suit either. They began planning an alternative route. In the early 1990s, they were regarded as anachronisms by the people who worked with them. It was only a matter of time before they were offered a pay-off to leave. They took the money.

It was corporate tunnel vision. Stevenson and Missy were not tied to the past. They were visionaries. Instead of setting up a new record company, they created a management business. Forget looking for new bands: they were going to manufacture their own pop sensations.

The plan was to develop two acts: a boy band and a girl band. Instead of searching for groups of mates where one talented kid would have to bear the weight of three drudges just because they went to school together, the new business auditioned scores of accomplished singers and combined those with the most ability and charisma. The idea was to recruit a combo that would appeal to a wide range of teenagers and adolescent girls. They wanted stars who could cross genres.

It was cynical, brilliant, and lucrative. The first success was five young women. The Modern Girls were not particularly glamorous. Their voices were satisfactory rather than scintillating. Each of the quintet needed a distinct look that appealed to a section of their teenage fanbase. The blueprint was to find a middle-class princess, an athletic tomboy, a soft, fuzzy, compliant blonde, and an abrasive, mouthy redhead. After months of auditions, they had a foursome. At the last minute, Missy saw a flaw in the plan: the band was too white. After a short search, they added a bookish black girl. Everything was ready. Songs and producers were already in place. The creative process had more in common with an actors' casting than pop music. Their impact was sensational.

The boy band needed a more subtle approach. The aim was to develop a group whose sexuality was ambivalent. In post-AIDS society, both Missy and her mentor believed the world was becoming a gayer place. Ecstasy and experimentation were the order of the day. The lads' night out that comprised a bellyful of ale and a brawl was becoming something in Britain's past.

There were dangers in the process. Bandmates with shared histories continue to stay together like bad marriages even when money and fame begin to sour relationships. People who had only been acquaintances since the audition have no loyalty. Missy and Stevenson chose wisely, though. They picked pliable young people with a psychotic ambition that they were unlikely to fulfil on their own. Boys Alone, the male composite, were almost as successful as their female counterparts. And, of course, both sexes were tied to contracts that no artist in the right mind would sign. They were not artists. They were empty vessels.

The Hitman and Missy had their credentials underlined. They now looked to expand their empire.

Missy was an expert at manipulating publicity. Early on in her career, before the money really started rolling in, she had made a little cash on the side from a variety of extracurricular activities.

She knew the secrets of the bands under her wing and other figures in the industry. One rock star built his image around ferocious womanising. In reality, he was gay. Missy had a drink with a contact from the News of the World, and within weeks, the nation would learn the true nature of the rocker's sexuality. A wholesome crooner was cheating on his wife. Missy steered the reporter in the direction of the mistress. All for a fee, of course.

By the mid-1980s, when the red tops were running wild and almost every celebrity's private life was fair game, she had high-level contacts behind the fences at Wapping. Inside 'the Fortress' – as Rupert Murdoch's News International, union-free plant was known – Missy was regarded as someone who could provide reliable, salacious material.

Many of the youngsters she placed on the fast-track to stardom saw her as a shoulder to cry on and turned to Missy for advice and solace. She exuded an empathy that they were too young or too ambitious to see through. It was easy to cover her tracks. Once the showbusiness desk at the Fortress had all the information, journalists could squeeze the various parties involved in the scandals. No one, except Missy's favourite reporter, knew the source of the sensational exclusives. This was a jealously guarded contact. Missy made sure she worked with just one journalist and one newspaper for the biggest stories.

She was extremely careful to protect her own credibility. At the same time, she placed lesser stories around various other newspapers to give the illusion that rival reporters across the media were also in her confidence.

When Charisma became successful, she ran her own black publicity campaign that complemented Stevenson's PR machine. Her boss was frequently sent into a fury by the sort of tales Missy placed at the Screws. He had no idea she was behind some of the exposes, and she enjoyed the power that this gave her. 'Remember,' she would say when he raged at the way his latest protégé's sex life had been laid bare in print, 'all publicity is good publicity. And you should be happy. You're creating stars who are so big that the tabloids target them. They sell records and they sell papers.'

These days she didn't need the money. She just liked doing it. Manipulating people, taking people from obscurity to fame and back again, was a game she enjoyed.

In the middle part of her career, back when she was an employee and did not have a slice of the company, Missy was resentful. Her bosses – even Stevenson – were stupid, sexist pricks, and they used her instinct to build their empires. Those houses in Weybridge with their Lennonesque white carpets and massive lawns? They would not have been able to buy them without her knack for knowing the British public's baser tastes.

There was another easy way to make extra cash. She would give desk engineers a tenner and a tape – and sometimes a blowjob – to record the live performances of her bands. At first, it was just selling copied cassettes to fans.

In the early-1980s she accompanied a group to Amsterdam. They were in a coffee shop, getting high before a visit to a brothel, when she thought she heard a voice she recognised. It was Scouse, with a particular inflection. It pulsed through her brain, provoking instant anger. It was no one she knew, though. But she stared through the darkness long enough for the man to notice.

'Alright, luv,' he said. 'You OK?'

'I thought you were someone I used to know.'

He laughed, looked her leather-clad body up and down and said with affable jollity, 'I'd remember such an impressive rock chick. You in a band?'

'No, I'm not a performer,' she said.

'That's a shame. You've got the look of a star,' he replied. 'I'm in the record business.'

That intrigued her. They talked for a while. The one-hit wonders she was guiding around the red-light district disappeared for what they thought were rock'n'roll adventures, but Missy stayed. She wanted to know more.

'Really?' She arched her eyebrows. He took it as encouragement.

'Yeah. I'm a producer. Of sorts.'

'That turns me on,' she said. 'I was going to go window shopping and pick a girl to fuck, but you're more interesting.' He was hooked.

By the time the bar shut, she had established that he was a bootlegger. Gently, she rebuffed his advances. Instead, she took his number, went back to the hotel, and thought about her strategy for a day or two. Then she rang him. 'I'm back in Amsterdam in a couple of weeks,' she said. 'You can buy me dinner, Mr Big-shot record mogul. I have a proposition for you.'

The man at the other end of the line thought he was going to get laid. He even fantasised that he might get a wild, bisexual girlfriend who lived far enough away to rarely interfere with his lifestyle. It was obvious that the girl was in thrall to the pop-music business, and she gave no suggestion that she was anything more than a putative groupie. She'll do for a while, he thought.

Well, he got himself a partner. Just not the sort he expected. And from the second she heard his accent, there was never a chance that the Gasman would get into her knickers.

A TOWN CALLED MALICE

'There have been seven murders in the family. One was at sea, where the fella was lobbed overboard. One was a scrap in Cape Town that went wrong. The rest were here. One of the early ones was a bare-fisted fight around the turn of the century. Is that a murder?'

Billy was sitting in the Green Man opposite me. It was a Sunday night early in July, well past last orders. The door and windows were open because of the heat and humidity. Normally, this would invite a patrol car to stop and investigate. After-hours drinking would be stopped, and the pub closed down.

There were no police visits that night. Liverpool 8 was burning. Radio City was on behind the bar and most of the customers were listening intently. Billy wanted to talk.

'We've got High Rippers in the family. The High Rip caused a national sensation, you know. Jack the Ripper nicked their name. One of ours was involved in the Blackstone Street killing of a Spanish sailor. They hanged one of his mates for it. Can't claim that one because they say he only hit the Spic with a belt.'

I wondered whether he was counting his own incident in the murderous tally. It was that time of night when awkward questions get asked. 'What's it like to kill someone?'

'It's difficult,' he said. 'Go get another round.' He nodded to his mate behind the bar. 'You destroy things. There's no going back. You lose so much. At least I did.'

It was hard to comprehend. Billy lost so much? What about the guilt?

'The guilt is hard to live with. I let a lot of people down. A lot of people suffered. I'd do it all differently if I could.'

Did he think about his victim? Did he have nightmares about the gargling last moments of the man, when the severed artery and skin made raspberry noises and the blood plumed into the cold night? It seemed we were talking about a very different conscience.

He laughed loud and unselfconsciously. 'The Divvy? I'd cut his throat again now. He was a cancer in the neighbourhood. He should have been taken in hand long before. My dad would have killed him. Your dad would have killed him. Duke was planning to run him over, but it came to a head too fast. I have never missed a minute's sleep over him. I couldn't have lived with myself if he had done anything to your mum and you kids. That's the way people like him were always dealt with round here. It used to be that they were scared off – or killed off – before they became too much of a problem.

'Does anyone care? People know I did the right thing. It's not like I'm a pariah, is it?'

That was true. Everyone in the area secmed glad to see him back after four long years. A steady flow of well-wishers came over to our table, and quite a few drinks were sent across. It was not quite the returning hero treatment, but the affection for Billy was clear. It was also obvious that it was not inspired by fear.

He told me his story in a shortened version. After more than two months in Talacre, he was driven south to Dover and inserted on to a coach of Liverpool fans heading towards Saint-Etienne for the quarter-final of the European Cup. There were no checks at border control on either side of the channel, and he entered France unnoticed and unrecognised. It was galling for him. Billy was an Everton fan. He did not go to the match.

After leaving the coach, he took a train to Amsterdam, where the Gasman had been living for a couple of months. There was a small Liverpool contingent in the Dutch city, and, for a while, he hung around smoking weed and doing the sort of odd jobs that can't be advertised in a newspaper. He assiduously avoided Gazza. In late spring, he took a plane from Schiphol to New York. His brother had jumped ship in Manhattan and had set up home in Greenwich Village. Billy joined him and, within days, had a job bartending in a folk club that was soon to turn gay. There were substantial Scouse and Irish communities to slot into, and they could always find a paid position for a newcomer. Bar work was easy, and he was comfortable in the changing environment of the Village – he was an ex-seaman, after all.

There were still enough music outlets along Bleeker for Billy to start performing again as soon as he had saved enough money to buy a guitar. He was miserable, though.

Once he was out of Britain and on his own, he called the office on Denmark Street and asked for Missy. She was long gone.

There was no other way of contacting her. He could not even remember where her family's house was located. He had been led there drunk in the early hours of the morning and invariably left hungover and giddy with love the next afternoon. His thoughts were focused on the girl, not the surroundings.

In his dreams he trawled the London clubs: the Marquee, the Vortex, the 100, ending up in The Hole, looking for the person that had metastasised into his ideal woman. It was all fantasy. All he could do was sit tight and wait to be told it was safe to come home. He would linger miserably in Sonny Newcome's bar on 56th Street and yearn for a return. Sonny had sympathy. He was a friend of Duke's who had done something so unspeakable that there would never be an opportunity to go back. They would talk of the Honky Tonk and the Foot Hospital, of Anfield and Goodison, and mourn for the places they'd rather be. Billy could never let slip that he longed for Fitzrovia.

'Sounds like the Southenders are giving it to the busies,' the barman said after a particularly frantic broadcast from a reporter on Upper Parliament Street. That brought us back to the present. A small cheer went up. Someone said: 'We should go to town and help ourselves. There'll be no one protecting the shops.' There was a laugh. 'While they're still serving here?' another voice asked.

Billy became serious again. 'I think she's dead.'

'Who?'

'Missy. The girl I met.' I didn't have much to say, so I let him talk. 'She just vanished. There has to be a reason. I was in London and went round all the places we used to drink. We used to go to a place called the Spanish Rooms. We called it The Hole.' For a moment, he was misty-eyed.

'It was great. Salsa music, Colombian's dancing, Jamaicans on the weed, London wide boys, working girls and rent boys…'

'Sounds wonderful,' I said with a laugh.

'It was. But there was a fire. Some fella got thrown out and put petrol though the letterbox and set the place alight.'

'Jesus, When?'

'Last year. Nearly forty dead. I think she's one of them. It would explain why she disappeared without a trace.' He looked away and settled into a long, mournful silence, oblivious to the frantic updates from the south end. There was little to say. We sat, mute, while the radio cackled away in the background with a running commentary of urban insurrection.

Then Billy turned back to me. 'How's Duke? Could I go to see him?'

I'd seen Duke twice in the four years since his conviction. He had waited a week after the killing until he was sure his companions were safe. Eventually, he walked into Rose Hill and surrendered. He stuck to his principles and never said a single word to the police while they interrogated him. 'Don't say anything,' he always stated. 'Get into a discussion, and they've got you. Don't take a ciggy off them, don't tell them you need a piss. Do it in your kex. They'll get the hang of your hand gestures after they see the puddle on the floor.'

God, Duke could have been anything in life. You wanted to listen to him. He was funny, self-depreciating and optimistic even in the visiting room of Wakefield Prison. He was sincere, too. Leaning across he said: 'Never feel sorry for me. I had ten years coming. It was my job to protect your mum and you kids.' There was a moment of silence. 'And the people who were helping me. You tell anyone who asks that I have no regrets. I would do it all again.'

I looked across at his infant son squirming on his mother's knee and wondered how that kid would eventually compute his father's words; whether he would feel cheated of a relationship and how he would react to his dad's return. By then, the toddler would be a fully formed person. Duke's sense of responsibility was admirable, but his child might see it differently.

Try as I might, I can't remember the high security jail as the fearful gothic monstrosity I want it to be. I recall it as part school gymnasium, part refectory. Duke's wife wore a huge coat with a number of inside pockets full of contraband and passed food and drink to him throughout the visit. When we arrived, the couple kissed passionately: she was passing £20 notes from her mouth to his. They repeated the clinch before we left. I suspect more money changed tongues.

He pointed out some of the other inmates with pride. This was the all-star game, and Duke was proud to be in such exalted company. 'There's my mate,' he said. 'One of the Birmingham Six. Didn't do it. Fitted up and beaten up by the bastards. He's not got a bad bone in his body. It's criminal what they've done to him.' He scanned the room. 'There's another of my buddies. He's one of the Bank of America crew. He did do it. He's got millions hidden away. Not doing him much good in here, like. But you'd like him. Stand-up fella.'

It was obvious he had a good relationship with the robbers and hard-cases, and he seemed very friendly with the screws. He introduced me to a passing prison officer. 'Our Joey's lad.' We shook hands. 'Don't you end up in here, young fella,' the prison officer said with a smile. 'Even if it's in uniform like me.'

Duke laughed. 'He's going to university, right?' It was not really a question. There was an element of threat implicit. 'Maybe,' I said.

'You'd better. I've started an Open University degree. It's great. I can't wait for the summer camp.' He let me digest that. It took a while for the penny to drop.

There was a moment when he seemed to realise that his charisma had almost made jail fascinating. 'I look at you and I think about the fun you can have going to college. All the girls you'll meet, all the books you'll read, all the beers you'll drink. I'm doing my learning here. You do it while you're free and make sure you never come to a college like this.

'I want to be the last of the Morans who end up in places like this. Go to university for me, eh? Get a degree before me. If you ever think you owe me anything, you don't. But that's what I want.'

Did I see a tear in his eye? He changed tack quickly. 'Did I tell you about Christmas? There's a fella in here called the Beast of Barnsley. He did horrible things to two young girls and killed them. Well, on Chrimbo day, the screws had a little drink and some of my mates bumped into the Beast, even though he was supposed to be in isolation. They poured a kettle of boiling water on his balls and broke his legs.' He laughed loudly. 'That's the way fellas like that need to be dealt with.'

For all he tried not to, Duke had a way of making prison seem glamorous. He could not help himself, and I was too young and too stupid to know any different.

No one had ever mentioned university to me before that moment in late 1977. I was still sixteen and not highly regarded at the Brothers' school I attended. There were no jobs available that summer. No apprenticeships. So, with a paltry five O levels, I went into sixth form. 'You might,' a teacher said, 'get lucky and get two A levels. A Poly will have you.'

The mood was changing. Punk was a symptom of something bigger and more powerful happening in the country. A shift in the psyche of the British people was taking place. We didn't see it because we were part of it.

Like Billy, I was swept away by The Jam. I joined Eric's and became a regular at gigs. There was a substantial group of young men frequently seen at concerts who were also matchgoers. Football and music became twin obsessions.

Actually, there were three. Politics was beginning to feel important. As Liverpool slipped into decline, the young men around me embraced socialist beliefs in an unfocused, vague form. The National Front targeted football fans as recruits. They figured angry, dispossessed youngsters with a predilection for violence were perfect fodder for right-wing thuggery. They picked the wrong city when they turned up outside Anfield and Goodison selling their filthy fascist newspaper. They were punched and kicked senseless. I had no qualms about putting the boot in.

By then I'd realised something. 173-174. The English have a fore-man class, a corporal class, a sergeant class. They take and obey orders and need someone to command them. It is a legacy of Empire. No matter how poor, stupid, disadvantaged and hopeless Albion's lower orders are there is always someone below them to look down upon: an Irishman, an Indian, a West Indian.

The NF was trying to exploit the anger and fear built into England's NCO culture as it be-came increasingly clear that the immigrants and underlings were no longer prepared to be bossed around. At Chelsea, West Ham and Leeds it worked. It didn't succeed in Liverpool. On the Celtic fringe, there was a real working class and we knew that the English despised us, too. After all, the term Scouse was originally an insult aimed at the most impoverished Irish immigrants around Scotland Road. Some might forget that but I never will.

By the time I was in my teens I understood that I was lined up alongside the ranks of the minorities who were supposed to be inferior to their Little Englander imperial masters. Now they were beginning to ask for respect, there was a backlash from large elements of white society who had an inflated sense of their own status.

No Irish, no blacks, no dogs, the signs used to say. Well, I was aligned to the outsiders. And the muzzle was off. It was time to bite back.

The NF's papers and faces got torn. They wanted disorder on the streets, and they got it from us. The fascists just didn't expect that we would direct the violence at them. They wanted hate and easy targets. We gave them the hate, and they provided easy targets for us.

I never enjoyed violence for its own sake. It is exhilarating, win or lose, but it's not fun unless it's got a purpose. It was entertaining when you caught the Paki-Bashers and Nazi boot boys at their own game and left them in an agonised heap.

The foreman class looked down on Scousers. We were thieves, half-Irish aboriginals, fodder for heavy labour, bred for battle. Well, us young lads wanted combat, but it would be on our own terms, not those of generals or governments. We wanted to be outside the pale of British society.

It always amuses me that people disapprove so much of violence. It is nothing more than a form of communication. It's the simplest, most effective way of getting a message across. It is the greatest leveller. The poorest in society can use it. Those with no negotiating power have one last fallback. The fist.

That worries the wealthy and powerful. They bully people with status and money. The upper and middle classes use their articulacy and education to make the disadvantaged feel small. Their social mores are designed to humiliate those further down the economic scale. It is institutionalised bullying. Of course, they don't see it that way. Politely, with calculated passive aggression, the middle classes will assert their superiority wherever they can. That was the only thing I learnt at university.

But many of the uppity Scouse teenagers I knew were ready to fight back whatever way we could. Instinctively, we knew we were outsiders.

When football took us to other cities, we could see the contempt the locals had for us. Even before the phrase was used, we knew we were the enemy within. It made us swagger more, steal more, and express our pride more volubly.

It was a glorious time to be young and Scouse. Liverpool Football Club were dominant at home, abroad, and the focus for civic pride. The iconography of the club suited our political beliefs. The shirts were blood red, with a Liver Bird symbol over the heart. Billy Shankly, the man who transformed Anfield's fortunes in the 60s, talked about socialism and the importance of everyone working for a common purpose. We believed it.

Everything in life was political. From the Rock Against Racism concerts to Saturday afternoons on the terraces, the bloody skirmishes had a clear social component.

Football hooliganism? It's the most misunderstood concept in modern British history. Mostly, it was young, lower-class men placed in confrontational situations, often after consuming an unhealthy amount of alcohol. Certainly, in the late 1970s and 1980s, I never saw any evidence of organisation. It was an organic expression of Scouse power for us.

Me and my mates tried to avoid knuckle if we could. But we were not inclined to back down if confronted. We were class warriors, not hooligans. At least that was our story.

How do I look back on that young man that I no longer recognise? Like many kids from a poor background, he craved status. How do you get it? Duke earned it with his toughness. No, that is not true. Yes, the power in his forehead and fists brought a certain glamour, but there was much more to his persona. The money he spent freely garnered him friends and admirers, but that was the least of it. He had a winning personality. He listened to people. He seemed to care about them. I believe he did. Why did people love him? In the end, you could only say he had charisma.

Young, dumb scallywags like the one I had once been didn't see the wider view. We got respect from going the match, especially away games.

Most of those who followed Liverpool across the country took the Football Special trains from Lime Street. Those transports went direct to the city where the game was taking place, were comprised of the oldest, most decrepit rolling stock and were shoehorned in around the regular timetable. Journeys took longer, and the trains were met at their destination by a huge police presence. Fans were disembarked, formed into columns, and marched to the ground under heavy escort. Generally, the police kept the local thugs at bay. Specials were a relatively safe way of attending away games.

Those who craved danger and adventure took the regular, timetabled trains that were part of the normal service. The opposite of special is ordinary. So, we took the ordinary trains.

Ideally, we would plan to arrive before the police had set up their reception operation at the railway station.

This was not just a Merseyside phenomenon. Across the country, groups of youths banded together and spent Saturdays travelling up and down the rail network to watch football and, sometimes, cause havoc in someone else's town. Hooliganism became a national scandal and some of the bands of wannabe street warriors created names for themselves to exploit the publicity. West Ham's Inter City Firm generated huge headlines. Leeds called their mob the Service Crew. We had no truck with these vainglorious titles and PR-hungry mythologizing. We referred to ourselves as Ordinary Boys, but it was a generic, non-specific term, not the moniker of a mob.

We enjoyed the subversion of language. We were the elite. When you walked into the Yankee three hours after the special had returned, drinkers would murmur 'the Ordinary's in' and the inevitable question would be posed: 'Any trouble?'

The best answer was a smirk, a shrug, and a rolling-shouldered strut. 'Nah, it was a doddle.'

That's how I see the boy sitting opposite Billy in the Green Man while L8 burned. He is wearing a modish, black, three-buttoned leather jacket, a burgundy John Smedley crew neck jumper over a pale blue buttoned-down shirt. On the sweater, over the heart, there is a tiny, quarter-inch, circular enamel badge with a Liver Bird on it.

He is clad in 501s, bought in New York and shrunk to fit in the bath in Burlington Street and then bleached pale in the same tub. On his feet are a pair of grey Hush Puppy suede boots.

I like the way he looks. The hair is short on the sides and back, but the fringe is still long enough to hint at foppishness. He is thin in a way that no longer seems to exist. It is a 1980s leanness; vaguely undernourished but wirily strong from manual work. There was no need to go to the gym. It is a body shape that belongs in the past; men his age today have either a comfortable chubbiness or display weights-room sculptured torsos.

Earlier in the Scally era, the fashion was for labels - Lacoste, Fila, and Kappa - in bold primary colours. By 1981 that look was discarded by those at the cutting edge, the bright clothes handed down to younger brothers. Now he wore muted shades. It was symbolic. I imagine him at the cusp of a darker, less flamboyant era when political vindictiveness would blight an entire city.

The clothes he wears are not designed to attract women but to signal to other, like-minded youths (for or against) that he is not to be taken lightly. He has enough prestige to feel content.

Of course, he would not have been dressed like this in July. I see him in his winter, match going gear. I visualise him as the essence of Scal.

To the outsider, he looks nihilistic. He is not. He worries about the future. Even now he can foresee a time when the confrontations will move beyond concerts and terraces and his enemies will be the authorities. The bloodletting in the south end confirms his concerns. He is certain a clampdown is coming and ready for the challenge. Idealism and anger course through his being. I shall now drive him from my mind, the little prick.

In the autumn of 1981, my grandmother died. She was a large woman, with whom I'd never established a connection. This was a shame. It would be a decade more before I heard about the night of Duke's birth and her widowhood. No one spoke of the past when I was growing up, except to tell bizarre, generally inconsequential stories. Important emotional events only slipped out by accident, it seemed. History was a luxury the poor could not afford.

Duke arrived for the funeral accompanied by two prison officers and was handcuffed to the most physically imposing of the duo. The requiem was at Holy Cross. St. Bridget's, my grandmother's preferred church, was long gone. Our Lady's, further north along Vauxhall Road, was closer to her old stamping ground, but she had a ghetto snobbery. The nearer to the city centre, the better. Eldon Street, and Our Lady's, was perilously close to the border with Liverpool 5 and people beyond Burlington Street were out-of-towners in her mind.

We went to Ford cemetery again. I did not see Billy in the church, but I noticed him lurking at the back of the crowd around the grave. We had not met since the Green Man, but I heard there was a buzz around the new band he had formed. They were drawing crowds to pubs from Cantril Farm to Crosby.

He looked ashen. It was the first time he had seen Duke in person since that fateful incident six years earlier. Sensibly, he kept his distance, but when the two men whose lives had changed completely that night made eye contact, Duke's sadness lifted for a moment and was replaced by a dazzling smile. Billy put his head in his hands.

We went back to the dining room in Gulliver's club on London Road. Duke and his guards sat down at the back of the seated area and my uncle beckoned me over.

'Get a drink for my mates,' he said with no hint of sarcasm. They wanted halves of lager and were grateful for the beer when I returned. Duke held up a wrist. 'I need the toilet. Any chance?' The men looked at each other and exchanged an imperceptible nod. Unlocked, Duke stood up. 'You keep them occupied while I jump out the toilet window,' he whispered to me. He laughed at my horrified look.

'Go get these gentlemen some food,' he said loudly. 'They've been very good to me, so treat them well.' He walked off. 'And where's Billy?' I pointed to the bar.

To be completely honest, I was nervous while he was in the toilet. His escort was not. When he emerged a few minutes later, he gestured across to the guards and indicated that he was going to the bar. They nodded assent. He went straight to Billy and hugged him. They spoke briefly, and then Duke returned to the table. He held up his wrist and said: 'We've got a long journey back. Whenever you two are ready.' Billy was sobbing at the bar.

'Go and do your goodbyes,' one of the screws said. 'We've got a few minutes.' So Duke went and hugged his wife and little boy again, but not before detailing me to refresh his mates' drinks. Billy was nowhere to be seen.

The Manchester Street Wine Lodge was a truly awful place, but we felt comfortable there. It was a long, thin bar with wooden floors and furniture that showed the rips and burns of two decades. The back entrance opened onto Preston Street, next door to the Ministry rehearsal rooms where Billy was working on his own material. This was not with the band. He was trying to revive the songs of the previous decade.

'I had to leave,' he said about the aftermath of the funeral. 'I couldn't bear to see him handcuffed again. And watch him say goodbye to the little fella. I know what it's like not to be around your kids. It breaks my heart. That poor little boy. It was my fault.'

It seemed safer to get on to a different subject. 'I'll have to come and see the band,' I said. 'All the boys love you.'

'It's cover versions,' he said. 'It's good. The money's rolling in. I'm a bit disappointed you haven't been to see us yet.'

In truth, I did not like what I'd heard about Billy's most recent career turn. The group played an eclectic mix of crowd pleasers that ranged from Genesis songs to Country Music classics. Gushing Scallies had told me that when they played Duelling Banjos or the theme from the Beverly Hillbillies, the venues went wild. There was bedlam. It was like punk gigs; they said. To me, it felt like punk had never happened.

'I've been too busy,' I said. 'All the Young Socialist meetings, trying to get people behind the council. That and the match.'

Billy saw through it. He laughed. 'I'm old, I know. But come and see us if you get a chance. You'll be on the guest list.'

I changed the subject. 'You seeing anyone?'

'A few,' he said without boastfulness. 'They come and go.'

'You never really got over Marie,' I said, the fixed image of the photograph having lodged itself in my memory. He looked at me, aghast. 'You on the Bismarcks before I came in?' He laughed.

'I never got into Marie. It was a mistake. A blunder. If it happened today, we would never have married. It was just that mad world we lived in where people were more concerned with appearances than what made us happy. I was forced into that marriage; she was forced into it. From what I hear, she's made a go of it with Larty. My only regret is I don't see my kids. They're his now.' He went the bar. Two Guinness, two Bismarcks. Shit, I thought, I've blundered into deep waters.

'It's the one in London I think about,' he said, downing the fortified port in one bilious gulp. 'She took me to places I'd never been before.'

He saw my eyes widen. 'Punk clubs, dirty ticket. She opened me up to a different way of approaching music. She may have been the love of my life. I killed that when I killed the Divvy.'

'Did you look for her again?'

'Yeah,' he said sadly. 'Had another go a couple of months ago. I went to the area she was from, but I never got the name of her street and couldn't recognise the house. No one knew where Eileen went. She disappeared off the face of the earth. Even tried to find out exactly who died in that fire in the club we went to.' There was silence for a moment.

'I vanished, too,' he continued. 'I wonder whether she looked for me? No one knew where I was, I suppose. She probably just thought I was one of those fellas who…'

There was little more to say. And I did not want to get into it again. Big issues - the politics of millions of people and the great philosophical battles of the age - were the things I cared about. The emotions of the human heart, the feelings that crush and curse an individual, I dismissed as self-indulgence.

They embarrassed me. I liked it when we laughed, sang loud and channelled our intensity into anything except personal, emotional pain. I was willing to die for a cause. But not for love.

Billy's return was just about the only good thing about 1981. It started badly. In January Tate & Lyle shut. The long swathe of factories that stretched along Vauxhall Road stopped belching out sugary smoke and nearly two thousand people were thrown out of work.

Turbaned women with their blue and white chequered headscarves poured out of the buildings after the final six-till-two shift with the excitement of college graduates on commencement day. They flocked into the Glass House, the Castle and the Green Man and drank with abandon. They burnt their turbans over ashtrays and all along Vauxy the festivities ran late into the night. When everyone woke up the next morning, unemployment in the area had leapt from manageable levels to more than seventy per cent. You wouldn't have noticed.

Holidays to Benidorm were booked, three-piece suites purchased. It was as if the final redundancy paycheque was a bonus, and another job would be along any moment. Those days were long gone.

The older generation had worked all their lives. They had been insulated against the decline in the city's economy in the sugar refinery. Where the school leavers of my vintage had emerged from their education with the awareness, the job market was shrinking terminally. Many of the Tate's workers had imagined that the desire for sugar would keep them employed until retirement.

It was heart-breaking watching them. Men in their fifties who had come of age during the war and toiled relentlessly in rebuilding the nation now had nothing to do. They had lived through the boom years of the 1960s and their sense of self was tied into work. Now it had been removed. Some went the pub and betting shop. They were the minority. Most had families to worry about.

Their pride was linked to employment. One man came out every day and brushed the landings and stairs on his block. He wanted to be busy. You could feel the bewilderment and sadness with every sweep of the brush. I watched with narrow, unsympathetic eyes. His efforts would never impress the wealthy, the powerful, those with a vested interest in writing him, and us, off as lazy and feckless. His outlet was the hopeless task of maintaining a decaying tenement that was rotting into a slum.

Perhaps us young men did our elders a disservice. They could not comprehend what was happening, and we sneered at their confusion. We implicitly understood the direction the nation was taking. It was in revolt against traditional Toryism and the class system was mutating in front of our eyes. The 'you've never had it so good' ethos of the ruling class was about to be destroyed. One-nation Conservativism had ceased to exist. The age of patronage was over.

It was a two-pronged uprising. On one side there was Thatcherism. On the other, the Militant Tendency. They were two faces of the same coin.

There was a rejection of cap-doffing Toryism across the political spectrum. On the left, we wanted opportunity and the chance to advance as far as our talents allowed. There was an awareness, though, that a safety net was necessary for the most vulnerable people in the community.

To the right, they were looking for a similar route of advancement. The grammar school generation wanted to get to the top and not be held back by barriers erected around notions of class. The problem was that the right-wingers believed their responsibilities were only to themselves. There is no society, said the cocktail-party philosophy of people who drove the thinking of Margaret Thatcher. James Goldsmith, a huge influence on the greengrocer's daughter in No 10, said: 'When you see signs of vulgarity, it means that new people are breaking through. Vulgarity is a sign of vigour.'

The Vulgarists were in power. They cared nothing about anyone else. No society. History is over. All that mattered was they were able to sit at the top table. The rest of us were left to fend for ourselves. Their Tory predecessors spoke of their 'duty' to the poor. It was mere lip service, but at least they recognised a connection with the lower orders. With vulgarism, it was every man for himself.

It got worse. This political ideology was vindictive. We did not know in that tense summer after the riots that in Downing Street they were discussing the 'managed decline' of our city; that they were considering deliberately depriving an entire metropolis of resources despite the misery it would cause hundreds of thousands of people. We suspected it. But even people who were supposed to be on our side thought we were mad.

Terrorism. Everyone falls back lazily on Mao's quote about the purpose of terrorism being to cause terror. It's stupidly simple. Actually, most of what we call terrorism is intended to apply political pressure. It's a gruesome form of public relations; politics by fear and negotiation by violence.

Few consider how Governments inflict terror. I saw it first-hand. They don't mix with people who are terrified wondering whether their meagre income will stretch to the end of the week. Or understood the fear of a parent whose child has no prospect of work when they leave school and can't gather the resources to 'get on their bike' and look for employment at the other end of the country. The terrorists who cut budgets through political maliciousness and force people into long, slow, miserable existences so that they can make a profit are as morally obscene – maybe more – as anyone who has ever set an explosive device to go off in a crowd. The complacent, comfortable, smug proponents of vulgarism brought so much fear and despondency to Britain that it created a philosophical civil war.

You might imagine that we were wallowing in misery and digging mental trenches as 1982 loomed, but that would be the wrong impression. Liverpool was abuzz. The pubs were full, bands were springing up everywhere, and vibrant debates were commonplace. The Daily Mirror, talking about the city, said 'they should build a fence around it and charge admission. For sadly it has become a showcase of everything that has gone wrong in Britain's major cities.' It did not feel like that. At least in town.

The musical doldrums of the late 1970s were over. A new class of bands were beginning to make an impact. Once again, Billy was in the wrong place at the wrong time. Echo and the Bunnymen, Wah, Dead or Alive and Frankie Goes to Hollywood were storming the charts. Billy was playing other people's songs. He was becoming a Scouse icon, but that's something very different to the pop star he dreamt of being. London had no interest in what he was doing. He could have been a metaphor for the city.

I disappointed Duke. University was a disaster. The teachers at school downplayed my chances of getting the qualifications needed to earn a place in higher education. They were fond of telling us that only the top two per cent made the grades. When the A level results came out, I'd got the passes I needed with ease.

For the first time, being poor became an advantage. I received a full grant. Suddenly I was richer than everyone around me, or so it seemed. My student contemporaries complained that their suburbanite parents could not afford to top up their meagre public allowances and whinged about their penury. I provided the drinks until I exhausted the grant. At that point, the people for whom I'd bought round after round discovered a cache of money they had never admitted to before. Few of them expressed any interest in filling my empty glass. Again, a lesson: the poor rarely cry poverty, the affluent often do.

That was not my biggest problem. I had been led to believe I would be mixing with the best and brightest (within reason, for even someone as naïve as I was knew this was way down the rung of universities). It turned out that the middle classes were not very intelligent at all. They were more polished, more superficially articulate – they could pronounce words I had only read and never heard spoken – but as thinkers they were a disappointment.

It was disillusioning. And being a cocky young fool, I believed I could breeze through with little effort. That might have been true. If I had kept my head down and gone through the motions, that is.

Instead, I used the grant to travel to every Liverpool match I could get to. Tutorials? They could wait. I just about got away with disappearing to Paris in May '81 for the European Cup final. A trip to Bulgaria for the quarter final against CSKA Sofia ten months later was probably the tipping point. It was a double whammy: we got beat, and I got sent down that summer.

I avoided visits to Wakefield. I would hear stories, though. The Monday work party was met outside the prison with two bottles of whisky for Duke. He had passed his exams for the Open University and was beginning to write a memoir.

The possibility of parole was not too far away. He was coming up to his seventh year inside, and that was the standard for a crime of this nature.

Unexpectedly, staggering news arrived. He had cancer. Like his brother, illness hit hard and quick. It was in his brain, spine, and liver. There were plans to send him to a half-way house, then home. Then, out of nowhere, he was placed in a hospice. Before any arrangement could be made to get him back to Liverpool, he was dead. He was forty-three. The same age as my father. After months of grief, it occurred to me that now, at the age of twenty-two, I was the oldest living Moran male.

It was back to Holy Cross for another funeral. Duke arrived in a firestorm – literally – but he was sent off on a lovely, mild spring day. There should have been a triumphant celebration when he returned from jail. Instead, there was only a wake.

Before he came home, I went with my auntie to his house on the fringe of Knotty Ash. In the living room she put up The Sheets. "The sheets" was an old tradition that was dying out. As far as I knew, there were only three exponents of the art in the city. The other two charged for their services. My auntie did it free for friends and family; if anyone outside that circle wanted it done, she merely asked for a donation for the church.

The custom had come from Ireland and was once commonplace. It was the process of converting an everyday room into a place where the corpse could repose and visitors could come, pray, and pay their respects.

We got to the house and unpacked what we needed. We brought a stack of stiffly starched white cotton sheets. My auntie tacked one corner up on the wall and began to deftly pleat the material, doubling the cloth down the long drop before pinning a neat crease at the bottom. She worked quickly and created a pleated white grotto around the spot where the coffin would be placed. The folded white sheets covered the window and half the room, and the gathering of the stiff fabric made the walls appear padded. The carpet was covered, too. It created a separate chamber for Duke's return.

From another bag she produced a sheaf of green fronds,

which were placed strategically around the walls. The effect was completed with an anguished Jesus on the cross. While we worked, she told me of the significance of the greenery and how it had to be a particular plant. I wasn't really listening. When she died less than a decade later, her knowledge and expertise went to the grave with her. No one did The Sheets for her. It took me years to realise that in that room, awaiting Duke's return, I was witnessing the last stirrings of a culture. I was so wrapped up in the individual death that the wider picture was obscured.

The coffin arrived and was put at the centre of this white recess. A suburban living room had been transformed into a chamber where the body could lie in state. The funeral director opened the lid of the ornate wooden box and fussed a little with the body. He stepped back, took a look and judged all to be well. He turned to my aunt and offered congratulations for her work. 'Maureen,' he said, 'this is beautiful. No one does this like you. You've done Duke proud.' He was on familiar terms with the dead man. Cynically, I wondered whether Duke had generated plenty of business for him over the years.

My auntie went out and brought the widow to the coffin. She, too, was moved by the transformation of the room. The little lost boy was with her, sullen, overwhelmed, and confused. 'Kev,' I said. 'Fancy having a shootie in the back garden?' The child nodded. He needed to be away from the misery. So did I. The women would be round soon to say the rosary and the men would dribble in near the end to sip whiskey and beer and make maudlin small talk until alcohol loosened inhibitions and made them laugh. Late on, it would get raucous. Duke would not mind. Legend had it that he was the driving force in removing one of his friends from a coffin and sitting the corpse on an upright chair with a glass in his hand so the dead man could be part of the conversation. That was the sort of thing that used to happen around Scottie. It was hard to imagine it occurring in Knotty Ash. That time, and place, had passed long before Duke. Even so, it would be a long night.

There were a dozen bottles of spirits on a table opposite the coffin and a pile of twenty-four-can trays of beer in the hall. After the prayers, the women retreated to the kitchen to smoke, make tea, and prepare snacks. The men congregated around the body, pausing for a moment of contemplation when they arrived before entering the conversation. Billy showed up about 8pm. He could hardly look the widow in the eye, but she generously hugged him. 'Duke thought the world of you,' she said. It seemed to make things worse.

It was hard to get any sense out of Billy. He stood looking into the coffin for too long. A man I didn't know came in and stood by his side. For a moment Billy did not seem to notice and then he turned and you could see the realisation hit him. 'The Gasman,' he gasped.

'I didn't think you'd remember me,' the man said. 'It was a long time ago.'

'Not a night you'd forget,' Billy said. 'I never said sorry.'

The Gasman laughed. 'Come on, let's have a drink. It all turned out alright for me.' He looked at Duke. 'We've a lot to thank him for. He wouldn't want us to be miserable tonight. Tell me what's happened to you.'

A few minutes later, Billy called me over. 'This is the Gasman… Gazza. He was with me and Duke that night. You remember the kid with the knife and the big-shot ideas about staying?' They both laughed. 'This is him.'

'You back at home now?' I was unsure of the niceties of a

conversation like this. Was that a compromising question?

'No,' he said. 'I live in Holland. It's a great place.'

'What do you do?' It was a really stupid question, the sort of idle, unthinking and uninterested query one of my former university colleagues might have asked at a student party. Billy spat out a mouthful of Double Diamond. 'Christ!'

Gazza took it coolly. 'Import-export,' he said. 'Shipping goods in and out. And what do you do?'

'He's just got himself kicked out of university,' Billy said. It was a reprimand.

Again, Gazza was relaxed. He shrugged. 'Don't let it worry you. Sometimes it seems like things could not get any worse, but the situation turns into the best opportunity of your life.' What was it about funerals that made people want to tell me that things would get better?

'I'm living proof,' Gazza said, looking at Billy. 'If you're ever down on your luck and need work, give me a call. A spell abroad would do you good…'

'No!' Billy interjected, a touch too forcibly. Gazza did a double take and then chuckled. 'He's probably right.' He did not take offence.

'I just meant he should knuckle down and get that bloody degree,' Billy said, flustered. 'I mean, that's what Duke wanted.'

'He did,' Gazza said, still amused. 'Come into town with me for a drink, boys. Too much misery here.' He turned to Billy. 'We'll get a cab. It'll be better than the last time we were in a taxi.'

The day of the funeral was memorable for a few reasons. Me and Billy were bearers, the first time I had done the job. People said it was an honour.

After we placed Duke in front of the altar, a down-and-out appeared at the church door and shuffled down the aisle on his walking stick. No one was sure what was happening, and the surprise froze the congregation.

The tramp, in his sixties, reached the coffin, put both hands on it to support himself, and knelt down. For an appalling moment, the casket shifted its weight and tilted towards the man. It looked as if it would slide off its trestle but, after a short wobble, it held. Now men were moving out of the pews towards the tramp.

Before they got there, he stood up, suddenly remarkably lithe, and pointed his stick into the air. Miming a rifle, he produced a fat-cheeked boom as he issued an imaginary gun salute. He got two shots off before he was gently ushered towards the back. Duke had given him a few quid to keep going over the years, and this was his tribute.

There was one more to come. Duke had written to Billy and asked him to sing at the service. He requested 'He Aint Heavy.' It seemed that the weight of the world was on Billy as he went on to the altar to perform it. He was behind me as we carried the coffin. I could feel him shaking. 'I can't do it,' he said. 'I can't sing today. I won't be able to get the words out.'

When the moment came, he rose to it. The acoustics suited him. The song was plaintive, painful, and beautiful. All that unquantifiable, thrilling vibrancy was there in his voice that day. All the emotion, love and, curiously, joy that Billy could project were illustrated in that church. At the epicentre of despair, the sound was unbelievably uplifting.

Duke, of course, knew what would happen. That's why he wanted Billy to sing. His charisma lingered with his dead body. Soon it would be just a memory, and its resonance would fade. It has. Now, even I wonder if I'm making all this up. And I was there.

It was not all grim. It should have been, but it wasn't. In May 1983, the Conservative Government were re-elected in a landslide. A different sort of electoral avalanche happened in Liverpool. The Labour council took more than two-thirds of the seats they contested, and they did it behind a manifesto that put them on a collision course with Whitehall.

The gloves were off. We voted for jobs and services. Most of the country took a different view. That was OK. We wanted confrontation.

There was a sense of purpose, a pre-revolutionary mood, which is impossible to describe. We felt that Liverpool could take on vulgarism and beat it; that decency and social values would resonate with the British public and they would have the good sense to throw out the notion that it was every man for himself. We were wrong, of course.

When you're in a bubble where everyone agrees with you, it is easy to become delusional. At the demonstrations in support of the council, there were thousands of people. It felt like a mass movement. It was only a local phenomenon. Most of the country despised us. Even the people who should have been our allies.

That became clear during the miners' strike. We travelled to Yorkshire to bolster the picket lines. The local strikers were grateful for our support, the funds we raised, and the food we brought. But they didn't understand us. We embraced the idea of being the enemy within – hadn't we always been? But Yorkshiremen hated being thought of that way. They regarded themselves as the backbone of the nation, England's spine. You could see that they despised the way we loved the notion of being traitors. Our thought processes were alien. We wanted to destroy the essence of Englishness, sweep away the monarchy, cripple the class system, and all the faiths and fancies of Albion. Those miners wanted nothing of the sort. They suffered dreadful working conditions and backbreaking labour and all they craved was appreciation, recognition and not to be treated like dangerous outsiders. You could see how bewildered they were by our attitude. Had they not been forced into this life-or-death economic struggle with the government, they would have enjoyed running us out of their county.

The physical impact of the strike was the least of it. The miners were tough people. They could go hungry and cold, but the tangible destruction wrought by Thatcherism was not the worst affront. The metaphysical cruelty was far more insidious and barbaric.

The rhetoric from Westminster demeaned their past, made their present uncomfortable, and denied them hope for the future. I remember being outside the Grimethorpe pit on a chilly spring day, looking around and thinking, "this is terrorism." There was fear in men's eyes. They could see the long, slow torture coming their way. They knew their history and had pride in the struggles of their forefathers, but they understood, deep down, that this was a battle they could not win. You can only succeed when the opponent is rational. This was not an ordinary industrial dispute about money. This was a brutal imposition of political ideology, underpinned by a vindictiveness that made little economic sense. Thatcher and her vulgarists would impose their will, whatever it cost individuals, the nation, and those on the receiving end. The entire weight of the state was set against these people who regarded themselves as pillars of society. No backing down, no arbitration. History was over. Britain would never be the same again.

Back in bloody Manchester Street, Billy finished his pint. 'Come next door,' he said. 'You've not come to see the band play. I know you think what I'm doing is selling out. That's fine, it puts a few quid in my pocket. I'm doing quite well these days.' He was. The group had a residency at the Bierkeller at the bottom of Mount Pleasant every Saturday night, and the place was packed out. Nearly a thousand people crowded in there each week. Bands that would go on to have huge No 1 hits would never get audiences like this without record company promotion and television exposure. They were a local sensation.

As proof of his financial health, Billy pushed a £10 note across the table. 'Have a drink. Your dole doesn't go far. Anyway, I want your opinion.'

If it was a bribe, it worked. I followed next door to the Ministry and went into a room with padded walls, low lighting and a stack of amps. I thought of The Sheets and the metaphor for Billy's dead career. He approached the microphone and ran through a set of new songs. They were overtly political, and I could tell he was proud of them. I stood in front of him at first but, conscious that the amplification was draining the charisma from his voice, went and lurked beside him where I could listen to the human tones. When I heard that the thrilling timbre was still there, hairs stood up on my neck. The songs were OK. Not great, but OK. They were three years too late. After forty minutes, he stopped. 'Well?'

'Brilliant, mate.' He had given me a tenner. 'Let's go have

another pint and talk about them.' He nodded.

'I'm doing a miners' benefit,' he said. 'In Derbyshire. We all have to do what we can.' It turned out we couldn't do much.

In peacetime, there cannot be many years that were as violent as the twelve months from spring 1984 to 1985. A civil war was taking place, and we did not recognise it.

I spent a lot of time travelling. Politics, picket lines and, most of all, going to the match. Every victory for Liverpool on the pitch felt like a boost for our civic pride. We sang a song that said:

'They all laugh at us, they all mock us, they all say our days are numbered. But I was born to be Scouse, victorious are we…' The lyrics and melody were taken from the slow march of the King's Regiment, the local infantry. It was adapted for foot soldiers in a very different fight. If you think that these words were about football, you are insane.

The greatest day was just after the miners' strike began. Liverpool played Everton at Wembley in the League Cup final. It was the first time these neighbouring clubs had met in a final. It felt like the whole of the city invaded London.

The match was on Sunday. We went on the train early Saturday afternoon. Reds and Blues were mixed in the carriages and some of my Young Socialist mates were going up and down the aisles raising money for the miners and distributing 'I support Liverpool City Council' stickers in red and blue. All the young scallies, in their half-and-half ski hats – Liverpool or Everton on one side, Celtic or Rangers on the other – snapped up the badges. When we got off at Euston, the roar of 'Merseyside' resounded across the station. The chants hailed Derek Hatton and Arthur Scargill. They may have been the most hated men in Britain, but we'd support them evermore. We were colonising enemy territory. It was Scouse power in action. Thousands of us filled Soho and the West End. The locals looked at us with disgust. It was exactly how we liked it.

Mobs of young urchins performed mass smash and grab assaults on jewellery shops on Edgware Road. Others raided Bond Street for clothes. Mostly we gathered, drank, and sang loudly. The game? What did it matter?

Two months later, Liverpool went to Notts County, needing a point to win the league. We stood in the huge, open away end at Meadow Lane and chanted not about the glory of the team but about the big industrial battle that was unfolding. The Nottinghamshire miners had resisted the call to strike. Throughout the match we taunted them with the worst insult we could conjure: 'Scab, scab, scab!' Politics was entwined in our lives and existence.

Going to away matches taught you about how outsiders perceived the citizens of Liverpool. Trying to spend a £20 note in London was difficult. People did not want our money. The moment they heard the accent, cashiers began to scrutinise the currency. They would hold the note up to the light, check the aluminium strip, and analyse the watermark. Often, they would then refuse to accept it. There were forgeries around, but pubs frequently used this little charade as an excuse not to serve us. You could see friendly faces turn suspicious the moment the accent hit their eardrums. We weren't wanted outside the city and enjoyed being away all the more for making the locals uncomfortable.

My bloody year started in Italy. Liverpool faced Roma in the European Cup final. Although we were wary about playing such a big game on another team's home territory, we were not used to trouble in Europe.

Trips to the Continent were about drinking and, for the Scallier element, robbing. We laughed at the idea of the 'English disease' and the hooliganism that often accompanied

England's representatives abroad. There was little to smile about in Rome.

Even before the match, local youths were stabbing and slashing away fans. All Scousers were fair game.

I always despised the Romans. They thought their city was still the capital of the world. Their arrogance made London's self-regard look like insecurity. They expected to win and be anointed the best team in Europe. We beat them, of course.

Then they beat us, physically, outside on the streets. Just 8,000 Liverpool supporters were in the Stadio Olimpico and a fair proportion of us were on the receiving end of Italian rage. They had elevated stabbing people into a cultural symbol in the Eternal City. If you want to know what puncicate means you won't find it in an Italian-English dictionary. I'll show you my arse and you'll get the picture.

Puncicate is the act of knifing a rival in the buttock. It's meant to humiliate the victim but not cause permanent harm. Shithousery as a tradition.

When we came out of the ground, there were thousands of Romans on the road that traversed the ridge above us. They hurled down bricks, set fire to deep, metal bins and rolled them down the slope at us. When the chaos was at its worst, the police fired tear gas. Not at the troublemakers, but into those who were under attack. While I was choking and gasping for air, a cowardly Roman crept up behind and pushed a stiletto into the fleshy area a couple of inches from my right hip. In the madness, I thought I'd been kicked in the buttock. We backed off down the road and would have been in even bigger trouble without the arrival of a mob of Lazio ultras who turned up to taunt their local rivals. They were ready. They wore scarves wrapped around their faces and seemed used to the gas. The Lazio fans slashed at Roma with their own knives and, while the internecine feud continued, we retreated to the relative safety of our coaches. I was appalled to see my jeans were soaked in blood. An older man had been stabbed in the kidney – presumably the knifeman missed his target – and was in a critical condition. He was loaded into an ambulance, and I managed to hitch a ride. I was lucky by comparison.

It was carnage at the hospital. Blood everywhere. So much of it was surreal. At one point, the emergency room doors flew open and a huge blond man in a red shirt appeared. He stood and surveyed the thirty or so stab victims waiting to be treated, many of whom were wearing Liverpool jerseys.

He spoke in a braying Californian accent. 'I came all the way from LA to see the Holy City, so why the hell have I been stabbed in the ass?' I understood his confusion and dislocation. I was in a world that I couldn't comprehend, too. It was about to get worse. There were numerous stabs in the back waiting round the corner.

The stiches came out after a couple of weeks but sitting was still uncomfortable when we boarded a minibus to Yorkshire nineteen days after that night in Rome. We were going to a coking plant in South Yorkshire called Orgreave. There had been a call for a mass picket. By the time we got to our destination, the temperature was in the 80s. I don't recall much of the day. I have vague memories of standing around – everyone else was sitting in the sun – and then the next thing I can clearly remember is five days later.

The narrative of the day is readily available to anyone who cares to look for it, but the forces of the state instigated bloodshed and attacked peaceful demonstrators as they sunbathed. It seems I dodged the repeated police cavalry charges and advances by snatch squads on foot until the final mounted rout in the village. I managed to get my elbow up to deflect a blow from a baton-wielding rider, and the truncheon broke the joint. A second horsebound policeman then had a free shot at my head. I was knocked cold, but my mates got me back to the bus and revived me somewhere on the way to Liverpool. They took me to the Royal where doctors set the arm and kept me under observation for two nights. If anyone ever tells me I don't know my arse from my elbow, I inform them the arse has the scar, the elbow's misshapen. I learnt a lot that summer. I'd been a victim twice. Duke would have been ashamed of me.

Knowing that the miners' strike was a lost cause, I should have realised that Liverpool would lose its battle, too. Yet the euphoria in town made us delusional. Every night we would see news reports from Northern Ireland showing anarchy in Belfast and Derry. Street fighting with the authorities was beamed into living rooms at teatime and normalised. It was thrilling to see unarmed youths taking on the army and the police. Most of the nation was disgusted to see the soldiers, their brave boys, coming under attack from those who wanted to destroy the British way of life. My sympathy was with the rioters. The ease with which the majority accepted that troops should be deployed on the streets of cities that were, at least nominally, part of the United Kingdom was appalling. Older patrons of the Green Man reminded us that, within living memory, the army were killing civilians outside the Rat just five hundred yards down Vauxhall Road. I felt guilty not drinking in the Rat, but it was a crap pub.

It looked like history might repeat itself. There were suggestions that the government would suspend the city council and install a commissioner backed up by troops to maintain security. We looked forward to the inevitable confrontation. One of my mates stockpiled petrol bombs, siphoning inflammable fluid from cars, adding, of course, a splash of washing-up liquid after decanting it into bottles. He wanted to make sure the burning gasoline stuck to anyone hit by the improvised explosive.

They were happy days, too. In October, there was news that made us believe that there was a chance to win. The IRA planted a bomb in the Grand Hotel at Brighton months before the Conservative Party Conference. When the device finally detonated, it killed five people and narrowly missed Margaret Thatcher, the Prime Minister.

I was in the Honky Tonk on Scotland Road that night. There was a party atmosphere. Even though by then we knew that Thatcher and her vulgarist backers were alive, well, and more vindictive than ever, people were giddy with excitement. 'Close,' a man at the bar said to no one in particular. 'Next time, they'll get the bitch. Next time.'

The bitterness was entrenched. Heroin had hit the region and the bonds that held communities together were beginning to erode, which was exactly what the government wanted. Drugs were causing havoc on the edges of the city: in Croxteth to the north and on the Ford Estate across the river on the Wirral. In L8, the scene of the Toxteth riots, a place held up as a symbol of British decline, the black community resisted hard drugs. The graffiti around Granby Street read: 'This is Toxteth not Croxteth, strictly ganga.' Heroin was not welcome there. There were still relatively few smackheads. Narcotics were coming, though.

Unexpectedly, Billy walked into the Honky. He was with a couple of mates, but he immediately came over and hugged me. 'They nearly got her,' I said in his ear, elated with ale and whiskey. He shook his head.

'This is bad,' he said. 'Bad for the Six Counties, bad for us. They will come for all their enemies. The worst years are coming.'

It made me shiver. After all, he had been through; he was expecting worse. He was right, of course.

I could pick out a thousand moments and incidents that are symbolic of the seismic shift in British society that was taking place. This one is as good as any. On New Year's Day 1985, the first mobile phone calls were made in the UK. It was technology that should have brought people together by making communication and contact easier. How could this advance in science lead to people becoming more isolated and undermine personal, one-to-one interaction? It would take another twenty-five years to find out.

The immediate effects were bad enough. Before the end of that month, the newly privatised telecommunications monopoly announced that it was phasing out public phone boxes. They were a lifeline and a safety net when emergencies occurred in impoverished communities. Elsewhere, it was different.

The south of England was booming, and the foremen and their wives had their own phones, shares in British Telecom, cars on the drive, and were looking forward to buying their council houses. They didn't care about those who needed neighbourhood phones. The only message they wanted to communicate to us was that we were screwed.

Liverpool understood that. Its reaction was to dance harder, celebrate wildly, and ignore tomorrow. Billy and his covers band became even more in demand.

There was a rage that drove Billy's audiences that was more authentic and furious than punk. It did not manifest itself in violence but in crazed excess – all on a very limited budget. The group's live performances gained legendary status because of the crowd reaction. More and more people flocked to the gigs to experience the madness.

There were no jobs. I was twenty-four. Almost half of the young men below my age were unemployed. People with next to no money appeared to blow their entire bankroll as quickly as possible.

Because of this, Billy was doing well financially. The band played six nights a week, culminating in the festival of scalliness at the Bierkeller every Saturday night. He was maudlin, though. On his night off, in the Glass House, he articulated his misery.

'This can't last,' he said. 'The city's shrinking. Every year of school-leavers have less chance of making a success of their lives. When I was their age, the possibilities seemed endless. They weren't, but at least I went into adulthood with optimism. What chance do these kids have?' He was upset. 'My kids are teenagers now. God knows what they'll do. I don't.'

I shared Billy's fears. It wasn't that young people were ignored; it was worse. There seemed to be a deliberate effort to misunderstand and alienate them. Mary Whitehouse and her ilk based a whole philosophy around the cry 'Won't somebody think about the children?' but there was no real consideration for youth. If there had been, then more effort would have been put into creating jobs for school leavers.

In fact, the economy was stretching childhood way beyond where it should have ended. Without employment, young people had to remain living at home and rely on their parents. Instead of going into the world and fending for themselves, their only responsibility was to get up and sign on the dole on time once every two weeks. The economics of the 1980s were extending adolescence into people's third and fourth decades.

You can't live on the dole. You can survive, but it's no life. The giro cheque is enough for you to purchase the requisite calories to get you through two weeks, but being barely able to nourish the body while the soul withers is pointless. It's even worse than starving someone. It's torture. The fruits of a consumerist society are dangled in front of you every day from every angle, and you know you will never have the pleasure of tasting them. So, what do you do?

It is not money, cars, expensive clothes, or holidays that people crave. They want expectation and opportunity. Billy had expectation. So did I, though it dwindled on my route to adulthood. It was a brief window. Opportunity and expectation were being slowly withdrawn by the vulgarists so that most of us didn't notice. By the time it became clear what was happening, it was too late. There was no going back. The generation behind me would bear the brunt.

The idiocy and lack of self-awareness of those in power was illustrated by their advice to relocate to a city where there was more potential employment. As if it was that easy. The message to us was 'get on your bike.' Billy turned it into a lyric:

'They're telling us to move around for work, but I just got nicked for stealing a bike.'

The line got to the nub of what was going on. The women and men in control had no empathy; they made the inane assumption that if they could make a success of their lives, then anyone could. They wanted to believe life was a straight race, with everyone starting from the same point. It isn't. It's a handicap. Get the right start and you're ahead and uncatchable. And as the vulgarists disappeared into the distance, they left barriers behind them to make sure the trailing pack never got any closer.

So how do you survive? The robbers took the high-risk route. There were other ways of bringing in extra cash. Working on the side was Merseyside's staple industry.

It was cheaper for some companies to employ the unemployed at paltry rates as casual workers under false names. I started to earn an extra few quid working in a warehouse in Canning Place, across the road from where the Albert Dock was being turned from a derelict swamp into a showpiece attraction.

This was a legitimate firm that was contracted to do mailshots for the big catalogue companies. These brochures were effectively department stores operating through the Royal Mail. Their advantage for the buyers was that the payments were staggered up to thirty-six months. These were the days before credit cards were widespread, so it made a wide variety of products available to those with little cash.

The bulky catalogues were backed up with promotional mailouts; anything from a single printed note in an envelope to an extra magazine-style supplement packed into a polybag to emphasise the latest bargains.

The post room of this business was crammed with two hundred or more shabby women stuffing envelopes and polybags for as little as £5 per thousand items. The dextrous and speedy could perhaps earn a fiver in two hours. For most, it took much longer. The room was bare, dirty, cold, and clogged with cigarette smoke. It buzzed with the murmur of downbeat womanhood. Me and the other warehouse boys delivered pallets of printed materials and envelopes to the working floor and removed the completed correspondence after it was packed into sacks. The heavy bags were hurled into cages, dragged to huge lifts and taken to the loading bay to be flung on to the back of forty-foot articulated lorries.

Of the four hundred or so people that worked for this company every day, ninety-five per cent were illegal. Periodically, social security investigators would raid the building. The women worked on the sixth floor so there was invariably a short warning given, but those who were not quick enough to scamper down the fire escape or disappear on to another floor were prosecuted for working while claiming benefits. The inspectors never sanctioned the company, who were profiting from the women. Government unemployment cheques effectively subsidised this commercial operation.

I was brighter and more articulate than the average warehouse lad, and the managing director took a shine to me. He was a sharp, ruthless sort from the Wirral and saw exploitation as part of his birth right. He was not a bad man. He tried to give me a leg up and it would have been madness to turn down his offer of a job. Part of it was simple. He was a huge Liverpool fan and took vicarious pleasure in my away-game exploits. There was one problem. The removal of my bi-monthly giro cheque cut my income by a quarter.

One of the facts of British life was the 'fiddle.' Everyone had one, it seemed, at least in Liverpool. This was a way of making extra money from your employment. It usually involved some form of robbery. But 'fiddle' was a nice, fuzzy, inoffensive term, and it was considered a perk of the position.

The company was responsible for maintaining two warehouses. One was a secure area that housed returned consumer goods that mail-order customers sent back. Some were damaged, some had been delivered to the wrong addresses. It was tempting to raid this security warehouse and sell on the stock. Most of it was eventually destroyed, anyway. This would be more than a fiddle. It was clearly straightforward theft.

There was a less dangerous route. In the back warehouse sat pallet upon pallet of catalogues linked with promotions that had expired. Even the cheapest, most basic waste paper would earn £15 a ton. There were more than a hundred tons' worth. There was one problem.

This was the warehouse manager's fiddle, passed down with the position and almost part of the job description. He was a fat Evertonian who marched in the Orange Lodge. His name was Brian, a cowardly, thirtysomething bully. I watched him closely when I was working illegally. Vans would arrive with the words 'we buy all grades of used wastepaper' on the side and he would order the lads to load them up, disappearing into the office while the deed was completed. It struck me that the other boys – especially the legal workers – had no idea they were complicit in this fiddle. As soon as the managing director gave me a proper job, I was ready to take Brian on.

There was an ideological element to it. One of the mailshots sent out by the company was for the privatisation of British Telecom. While I humped sacks of letters offering the shares to the public on to a lorry, I listened to Brian talk to the Lancastrian driver of the truck. They probably did not realise I was paying attention; and anyway, why would either have cared about the sweat-drenched scally lugging sacks?

They talked about buying their council houses. They were excited about the new opportunities to buy shares. Both wanted to be part of the Thatcherite revolution. The idea struck me that Fatboy Brian was using his fiddles to finance his foray into property and share ownership.

When he went on holiday, I convened a meeting of the lads in the pub. The four boys – they were all younger than me – expressed shock that getting rid of the unused pallets could be anything other than company policy. Fatboy's demeanour told me different. I took a chance.

I had made a note of the telephone number on the side of the truck. On the second day of the warehouse manager's break, I rang it. 'Can you send a van round today? We've got stuff building up in the warehouse,' I said. The voice at the other end was sceptical. 'Your boss didn't mention it.'

'He told me on Friday before he shot off on holiday,' I said. The man was not convinced, but a wagon arrived to take a load that afternoon.

For the rest of the week, I had them come in twice a day, sometimes three times. On Fridays, I'd noticed Brian disappeared for an hour just after lunchtime. It was about the length of time it would take to get to the wastepaper yard and back.

So I went. The owner was suspicious. 'The boss said come and get the cash,' I said.

'We only deal with Brian,' the man said. 'He gets the money.'

I was calm and smiled. 'He gives the boys a few quid on Friday for a night out. He asked me to make sure they got it when he was away. You wouldn't want to see the lads go without a pint?'

He counted out the cash. It was £130, more than my weekly wage. As I went to take it, he held onto it for a moment. He looked like a hard fella. 'You be sure it gets to Brian,' he said. 'And I'll get you to sign a receipt.' Now I knew for certain I was right.

'Are you taking the piss because I'm on the dole?' I asked, staring him down. He let the money go.

'There better not be any funny business. I'll be talking to your boss as soon as he gets back.'

With that, I was off. I went back to the loading bay and gave each of the lads £20. I kept £50 for myself. We were sharing the risk, but I was the one who would have to face down Fatboy. That's how the fiddle worked. Everyone in the building seemed to be on the take from top to bottom. Only the underclass of women envelope stuffers weren't getting their fair share.

Billy's song about life on the dole, Is That The Way It Is?, was recorded at Strawberry Studios in Stockport some time in October 1984. Billy had saved enough money to buy three days of recording time and he did a version of Slamming Doors, which he renamed Pursuit. It was an astute change. It made the song more enigmatic.

He brought me a tape when we met in Streets, a wine bar on Baltimore Street opposite Kirklands. It was quite trendy there, but the bouncers were friendly and tolerated me and my mates when we arrived for a late drink on Saturday nights after away games. They always wanted to know whether there'd been any action. On a Tuesday, it was dead.

'I need to do more creative stuff,' Billy said. 'Covers are fine and pay the rent.' He underlined that by sliding a tenner across to me. 'Go and get the ale in.'

When I came back, he returned to the theme. 'But I'm thirty-four now. I still look young enough to get away with it, but the clock's ticking.'

I thought of those wasted years. He was still in his twenties when he had to disappear and, while he was never a convincing punk, he might have fitted perfectly into the new wave aftermath. Although he still looked youthful, he was a man out of time. Since his return, he had been playing catch up. That was clear when I listened to the Strawberry sessions. If I had heard this tape four years earlier, I might have got excited. It wasn't bad, but things had moved on.

He sent the tape to Wild Momentum records, which was run by a talent spotter called Duncan Stevenson, a man who had developed a reputation for taking a chance on unknown bands and turning their best songs into quick hits. The cassette was returned, and it had either been stopped after about twenty seconds or Stevenson had not rewound it properly. Only one out of those two options was plausible.

When Billy told me, I consoled him by saying he needed to play these songs live. A&R men were crawling all over The Farm and The La's because of the buzz their performances were causing. The irony was that Billy was playing in front of the biggest following in the city every Saturday, but only those in the audience cared.

I also suggested he restructure the tape and place Pursuit first rather than one of the more political songs. He had left the best to last. That never works.

The disappointment was too much, though. He had the air of a man who had given up. The instinctive charisma was being beaten out of him. He was stuck in a blind alley and did not know how to escape. Weren't we all?

Surprisingly, Brian was conciliatory. He rang me on the sixth floor while the senior management team were having their morning meeting and asked for a word. 'I know what you did,' he said when I got down to his office. 'And how much you got? I don't mind. You had a bright idea. In future, I'll cut you in.' Then he pulled a mean face. 'But I want half that money. This is my fiddle. That won't change. Give me my money by end of play today.'

I told him I would have to see the lads and used that as the excuse to take a long lunch in the Dolphin Pub above the warehouse. The boys were scared. Quite deliberately I let them take the lead and make suggestions. They were all for giving him half the money.

When they finished, I spoke. 'What can he do? Snitch on us? He can't go upstairs and say to the boss, "the lads are on the fiddle."' He's got more to lose than us if it all comes out.

'I say we give him a fiver each. He took no risk. He'll get £25 and he'll be happy with that.' Two of them grimaced. 'I'll tell you what. Put your fivers in an envelope and give them to me by three. I'll give him the money. I'll give him the five envelopes, so he knows everyone's paid up. OK?'

They nodded. That afternoon, after I collected their offerings, I went to the toilet, locked myself in a cubicle, and ripped open the seals. All four of them had put a £10 note inside. Shithouses, I thought.

Taking a fresh envelope from my back pocket, I placed two of the tenners into it and added a fiver. Returning to the office on the loading bay, I winked at my colleagues as I went inside. I placed the money on the table. He opened it up.

'What's this?' he said. It was without conviction.

'Half was too much, Bri. You were on the beach. Twenty-five's good. It'll get you a good drink. We've already spent the rest.'

You could see him weighing up what to do. It did not take long. He pocketed the cash. Another khazi, I thought. The world's full of them.

'Don't do anything without my say-so from now on,' he said. 'We'll forget this happened, and you can have a slice of it from now on. If you want to weigh in the lads, then it's up to you and out of your share. But it's my show from now on. Understand?'

Oh, I understood alright. I couldn't wait to shaft the fat Orange bastard. All I needed was time to come up with a plan.

It was easy, really. I talked a lot about Duke and my father to the lads on the loading bay, discussing their adventures, laughing at their misdemeanours and detailing their dubious achievements. Brian was a decade or more older than me and knew enough about clubland in the 1970s to feel apprehensive. I never directed any of the conversations towards him, but he was taking it all in. As well as that, I let him get the impression that I was active in hooliganism at away games, frequently mentioning "my mate Stanley" whenever we used craft knives to slice the binding on pallets. I set him up. I wanted him to think I was a bad bastard.

He took two weeks off over Christmas. This was someone who knew how to work the system. By adding bank holidays, he stretched those ten working days to nearly three weeks away from the office. It was the quietest period of the year, anyway.

It was also an expensive time. I was on the phone to the wastepaper people immediately. Again, they did not want to deal with me. I was explicit. There was another company I would call if they didn't send out their van. They did.

On the Friday I called the recycling firm. Their boss told me not to bother making the journey to their premises, he would come to the loading bay. That was fine by me.

I'd thought it through. It was the last working day before Christmas. The post room girls were leaving early and there was lots of drinking going on. Few staff were paying much attention to business, and the walkway outside the warehouse was busy with lunchtime activity. The wastepaper man turned up on the loading bay, expecting to have a conversation in the office. He did not anticipate my tactics.

'Shall we talk inside?' he said as the envelope stuffers and secretaries from upstairs poured in and out of the building.

'Nope, pay me my money first.' I was sensible, but intense.

'Brian said…'

This was the moment for a grandstanding gesture. I shrieked, the howl of anger echoing off the low ceiling and amplifying the roar out into the street. 'GIVE ME MY MONEY!' People turned to look. The lads on the bay, who I'd warned to expect a scene, scuttled inside the warehouse. 'How much money have you and that fat cunt scammed from this place?' I shouted. 'Give me my money!' I was spraying spit on to his flabby face. His blood pressure, to judge by his florid cheeks, was going through the roof. 'You want everyone to know how much you and Brian have stolen?' It was a calculated risk, and it worked. He produced a wad of cash from his trouser pocket and thrust it at me. Immediately I became calm, even solicitous.

'Thank you, I appreciate it. Let me buy you a Christmas drink.' I took his arm. He winced at the contact. 'Come on, we're going to be partners. Have a bevvy.' He shook his head and scuttled off. The performance was less Duke than a conglomeration of gangster films from Cagney to Mean Streets. As he disappeared, I called after him, erratic again: 'You pay me now. Brian's gone. He's dead. It's over.'

That was a good afternoon. The boys got their tenner each to go on the ale, and we all got drunk. On January 2nd, I would have to face Brian.

The hangover was serious. I'd been to Watford on New Year's Day and treated the trip as if it was a Saturday. When I woke up on the 2nd, I didn't want to go to work. I was not looking forward to the showdown.

It was mid-morning before Brian realised what had happened. This time there was no politeness, no request for me to come down to the office for a discussion. He walked up to me on the sixth floor and said: 'What the fuck are you playing at? You're finished here.'

I was ready. 'No. You're fucked, fatboy.' He was shocked. 'You've been robbing stuff from the security warehouse and selling paper. Let's get it all out there.' He stepped towards me but again I was prepared and thrust him up the corridor with a vicious double push with my palms.

'I will fucking kill you, you fat Orange cunt,' I said. 'This is how it's going to work.'

He cowered. I could not believe he was so craven. 'You can do what you like with the security warehouse, but the wastepaper is mine,' I said. 'If I get caught, for any reason, my people…' I left that vague, 'have been told you are responsible, and you will suffer. You fuck with me and I'll kill you, or have you killed! It's my show from now on. Understand?' I looked around. There was no one to be seen. So, to emphasise my point, I swatted his face with the back of my hand. 'Call the fucking cops. Go on.'

After that, he never spoke to me again. Before the ycar was over, he had a heart attack and died. He was horribly corpulent but, after the events of the next few months, I always wondered whether I scared him to death. On the other hand, Liverpool men die young. I'm sure even his wife thought he was no loss.

The stench of decay and defeat was everywhere in that grim spring of 1985. The miners' strike was broken, and the men marched back to work with their heads held high, their brass bands playing and their banners waving in the chill March wind. The defiance was superficial. Nothing would ever be the same for these people. Their defeat was greeted with national elation. Vulgarism was at its zenith. Its proponents had gained too much ground for Britain to ever claw back.

Kids still had fun. They were running wild. They took pleasure where they could, and confrontation was ingrained in everyday life. If the police thought they would get any respite after the rancour of the picket lines, they were mistaken. Ten days after the strikers returned to work, the sight of constables running for their lives once again horrified the nation.

Millwall went to Luton in the FA Cup and the south London fans burst out of the stands and terraces with a glee that was seductive. As the police fled for safety, the Millwall mob hugged each other like they'd scored a goal and bounced down the pitch with such joy it was hard not to be excited for them when you watched on TV. 'Sooner or later, something has to be done,' the commentator said. 'Dreadful scenes. Nobody seems to be able to control it.'

They were still trying to treat the symptoms, never addressing the years of neglect that allowed a generation to think pitched battles on streets and at matches were normal.

'Now you care about us, you bastards,' I thought, watching

the rioters hurl ripped-up seats. They were a multi-ethnic crew, black and white together, dressed in Fila tee-shirts and Sergio Tacchini tracksuit tops. They threw plastic missiles at the police and menaced the older generation. Youths from the depressed docklands of south-east London were tearing apart a crumbling Edwardian stadium under flimsy floodlights in a decaying, depressed Bedfordshire town. You did not have to travel far from the centres of wealth and power to feel the anger.

It felt natural to fight. News reports from South Armagh to South Yorkshire illustrated the anarchy. There was no consensus, only confrontation. You want knuckle? You'll get it. Britain wanted it badly.

No one was prepared to face the truth that we were living in a broken society where the breaches were being deliberately widened on a daily basis. It was easier and less frightening to fall back on tired ideas, to create folk devils to both scare and reassure the populace. A decade or so earlier, Mods and Rockers were the symbols of Britain's decay. The very people who had been demonised back then were happy to uncritically rage at football hooliganism, the latest manufactured crisis.

The myth of organised pandemonium was already taking hold. Police budgets were increased, and special units were formed to 'infiltrate' the gangs. It was insane. Paranoia ran wild. Groups of mock-heroic, boastful kids were transformed into another wing of the enemy within. Few saw it as an indicator of a more serious problem: there was no society, history was over. By government decree.

It was ugly. In April, Liverpool played Manchester United at Goodison Park in the semi-final of the FA Cup. Civilisation broke down that day.

We had been brought up to despise Mancs. The two cities were economic rivals and Manchester built the Ship Canal because it resented paying the port of Liverpool to transport its goods abroad. Football had become the main manifestation of this competition. Most people involved in the violence had no idea about the roots of the hatred. They just hated.

Outside the ground, pubs were wrecked. Their windows were shattered as if a bomb had exploded inside. On the streets, running battles took place. No one was safe.

The nastiness started early. The phone rang at 7.30am in my auntie's flat, two doors away. She came and got me. A mate was calling: 'The Yankee's open, it's rocking and we're expecting Mancs in town by eleven. Get down here.'

The Yankee was what we called the American Bar on Lime Street, the place where Liverpool's boys drank. I was inside before eight, crushed at the bar, having been admitted through the locked door only after repeated banging on the window. The fella next to me nodded. I knew him from away games. 'No civilians today,' he said. 'None.'

I shuddered. No Manc was safe. Women, children; anyone was fair game. The mood was… I want to say genocidal, but I would be accused of exaggeration. But that is how it was.

Just before eleven, the normal opening time, someone switched on the juke box. The first record to play was Psycho Killer by Talking Heads. Everyone joined in the chorus, bouncing as we sang, 'Oh, oh, oh, oh, aye-aye-aye!' Singing was normally a communal expression of pride. Yes, it often carried a threat, but the articulation of Scouse power and uniqueness was more important. That day it was a howl that cried out for blood.

A number of crazed individuals hammered six-inch nails through golf balls and threw them into crowded pens inside Goodison. Magnesium flares were fired at opposition fans from close range. Stanley knives were the weapon of choice when the two sets of supporters crossed paths outside the stadium.

Madness was in the air. There was a loss of perspective, of humanity. We all got sucked into it, God help us. Unrestrained fighting broke out in every part of the ground.

That night, about 9pm, the Yankee imploded, and a huge brawl broke out. By then the Mancs were long gone. The thirst for savagery remained.

The staff retired behind a door at the end of the bar and turned on an air-raid siren that was so loud most of the fighting stopped. We poured out into Lime Street and scattered in all directions. The flashing lights of Black Mariahs were converging from both ends of the road.

I lost my companions in the chaos and headed towards the Adelphi. Outside the hotel, I bumped into Billy. 'What the hell's gone on today?' he asked. 'They've cancelled the gig. There's been murder inside already.'

We went to the Newington and sat in the lounge. Insanity was in the air. A group of mates were arguing at the bar until, suddenly, one butted another on the bridge of the victim's nose. A short, untidy scuffle took place as the two antagonists were led outside through different entrances. I knew one of the group by sight and he acknowledged me as he passed. He shrugged. 'That sort of day, mate,' he said. I nodded. 'They're brothers. They'll make it up. Just one of those days…' He was very drunk and was dishevelled from the day's combat. 'Brothers shouldn't be scrapping,' he said. 'Not brothers.'

Billy shook his head. 'Always fighting with the wrong people,' he said. 'You've spent the day brawling with people who are the same as you but have different accents. We are at each other's throats. Society is breaking down.'

There was always something of the prophet about Billy. But I wasn't listening. It took me too many years to realise we were giving the vulgarists exactly what they wanted.

Things got worse rapidly. The European Cup final was looming. This time it was in Brussels. I had disposable cash because of the wastepaper fiddle. It should have been a fantastic trip. In Paris four years earlier, I was down to a tenner by the time I hit the City of Light. There was no other option but to steal food and wine. It is safer to run with the mob when you have to go on the rob. The downside is you attract the attentions of the police. The first time I was tear gassed was in the French capital. I was getting too old for that sort of behaviour.

With a pocketful of notes, you can get off the beaten track and enjoy a foreign city instead of gathering in a central area and risking the wrath of the local riot police.

There was a complication in Brussels. We were playing Juventus. Italians again. Memories of Rome twelve months earlier were still raw.

On the train coming back from Ipswich, the first game after we found out who our opponents would be in Belgium, my arse cheek throbbed. No Italian was going to do that to me again.

That was the refrain in the American Bar, too. We were aware that Turin was nearly twice as far away from Rome as we were from London, and that Torinese were very different from citizens of the Eternal City, but the fear lingered. History could not be allowed to repeat itself. As Psycho Killer played in the Yankee, you could feel the mood hardening. If Juve wanted it, they would get it.

There was a plan knocking around, but violence against Italians was not part of it. Loads of the boys were hiring transit vans and arranged to meet in Blankenberge, a dozen miles from Ostend. Part of me wanted in. I never found out who picked this sedate resort town as a destination – someone said it was Belgium's Eastbourne – but what transpired sounded like a cross between a Western movie and a horror film. In other words, pure comedy.

The affluent and mainly elderly residents were going about their business when a score or more transits appeared on the horizon, pausing a moment for effect and then disgorging squads of scallies to pillage the town. The local police were not prepared, and on that mad Tuesday a number of mild outrages were perpetrated.

The boys arrived in the Belgian capital the next day with their booty and tales of looting. It would have made national headlines in Britain, for sure, if events had not overshadowed it.

There were a number of factors at play in Brussels. After Rome, many of us were angry and suspicious. Normally we approached European away games in a relaxed mood. This time, many of us had hair-trigger tempers.

Then there was the drink. There was a myth at home that Continental beer was weak. Lads who were drinking 2.8 per cent pints of mild sank schooners of strong lager like it was water. There was a wild insolence about us that I had never seen before and never since. In some ways it was more frightening than the day at Goodison the previous month when it was a simple matter of people running amok. In Brussels, there was no hysteria. We were more like an occupying army: in full control and able to act without consequences.

I had money, but instead of heading away from the crowd, we were drawn to the Grand Place. The authorities did not impose control, and we were sucked to the centre of the vacuum where anarchy was strongest. The Juventus fans looked on in awe and fear. They were not targets initially, but we radiated threat. They could see how quickly we would turn.

It was hot. I found a flimsy, dirty Liverpool cap on the street. It did not do an effective job of blocking the sun. I decided to swap it for a thick, cotton Juventus sun hat. I picked a victim and approached, giving the illusion of friendship.

Fans often swapped scarfs and favours at these games, but I was offering damaged and worthless goods for a valued hat. The man, older than me, did not want to make the exchange, but I demanded it. It was bullying disguised as cultural interaction. He could smell the ale on me. I could smell his fear.

The bars began to shut as the ugly mood intensified. I ranged outside the Grand Place, looking for beer. A crew of boys I knew, fresh from Blankenberge, were sniggering on the street.

They called me over and pointed to a jeweller's window. It did not have a metal grille inside the glass. I joined in the chuckling. They told me there was a supermarket down the street where I could get beer. They were right. There was another lad I knew standing in the doorway of the shop handing out crates. 'Free to us today, la.'

By the time I got back to the jewellery shop, the window was shattered and ring trays were scattered all over the street. Riot police were standing on the spot the Scousers had vacated. I loved it. I didn't even need to spend the pocketful of Belgian francs I was carrying. We could not be stopped.

All the misplaced aggression, all the fury, came to the fore that day. It was the wrong place and the wrong time.

The football culture I'd been immersed in for almost a decade had been the opposite of what was projected into the popular imagination. It was not nihilistic. It was creative. Match going boys produced The End, the first of the football fanzines and the inadvertent father to the bastard lad's mags of a decade later. We were political, some only in the softest sense, but generally committed to socialism. Liverpool FC were the pride of the community. Everton, too, had emerged as one of Europe's best teams. Our benighted city had the two best sides on the continent. Football was a vehicle for our pride.

On a warm, hazy night in Brussels, we gave our enemies all the ammunition they needed. That was the least of it. Before the match, thirty-nine people were killed. I could go into all the reasons why it happened, and they would be valid. There was a Belgian government inquiry that apportioned blame. It would be cowardly of those who misbehaved to point anyone in that direction, though. Had we not been out of control, it is most likely no one would have died.

Unlike Rome, there were no stabbings and hardly any punches thrown but there was something worse, more insidious. There was mass terror that caused people to panic, run away, and crush against a weak, inadequate wall.

I was in the section where and when it happened; one of those young men who caused that fear; someone who spooked normal, harmless spectators at a football match into fleeing into an area where there was no space to escape.

They laid the bodies in a line outside the ground, out of sight from most of us, and the match was played. That was almost as astonishing as the way we acted. I had no idea anyone was dead until we were halfway across the English Channel. It put my throbbing arse into perspective.

It is hard to put into words my feelings after returning from Brussels. I felt bad, but not guilty. There was no murderous intent. You could convict most of us of being drunken dickheads, but that's about all. In the Yankee a fella I knew summed up the popular feeling: 'If the shitbags had stood and fought, no one would be dead,' he said. There was not much empathy.

Part of me can see why. We had been demonised and regarded as pariahs for so long that this was just another excuse to circle the wagons and ignore the invective that was being poured down upon us.

The most embarrassing thing was the attempts by people to deflect the blame. A Liverpool club official claimed it was Chelsea and National Front elements who started the trouble. That was ludicrous. If we'd seen the merest hint of fascists, they would have been punched back to the holes they came from long before the ale kicked in on the afternoon of the game. The dead were our responsibility. At least in part.

People looked at you differently. Brian was more terrified than ever. The other lads at work joined in the fun. 'Alright, Killer,' they would shout whenever I showed on the loading bay. I'd snigger and try to catch the warehouse manager's eye. If I walked past him in the corridor, I'd deliberately bump him. You could see the strain wearing him down.

On a wider level, the disaster spilt over into politics. Hardly anyone in the country had the remotest sympathy for the city. This little beauty was in the Sunday Times, filed from an

International Olympic Committee meeting in East Berlin: 'The facts are as yet imprecise, but there is grounding for belief that the quite clearly organised assault by alleged Liverpool supporters in the Heysel Stadium had financial and ideological backing from left-wing agencies outside Britain.'

Organised assault? It was a bunch of pissed-up morons with hair-trigger tempers after the previous year in Rome. They wanted to make us Cold War warriors. Even I wasn't up for that. The only financial support we got was from the friendly shopkeepers of Blankenberge and Brussels, who did not have the gumption to employ store detectives or install metal grilles.

Everton won the title and were expecting to compete in the European Cup in the new season. The Government demanded that English clubs be withdrawn from Continental competition and European football's ruling body followed up with a ban. It was unfair on Everton and the other teams, but we should have been banned for ever. No one felt sorry for our rivals, though.

At the end of July, Liverpool played their first match since Brussels. It was at Burnley. There were no more international adventures for us. The world was closing in again.

There was already a song for Everton, rattling around the train as it chugged across Lancashire. It was to the tune of 'The Laughing Policeman.'

'There was an Evertonian,
Just two months ago,
Who thought because they'd won the league,
To Europe, they would go.
They thought they'd go to Roma,
And maybe Munich too,
But they're not going anywhere cos we killed forty-two.
Ha, hahahaha, hahahaha, ha, hahahahaha, hahahaha, ha….'

It was only thirty-nine but the initial death toll had been overestimated on the night and the boys used a bit of poetic licence based on that miscalculation. It got sung quite a bit in the Yankee.

We had to change at Preston. As we waited for the local service to pull out into the woolyback hinterland, people on the platform stared at us in a way I'd never been looked at before. I said to my mate: 'Christ, see the way they're gawking at us?'

He shrugged. 'They've never seen mass murderers before.' He said it in a flat manner, without any boastfulness but without any hint of regret. I accepted the statement as the truth it was, reflecting that I couldn't add to Billy's tally of seven family killings, but I was at least vaguely culpable in too many avoidable deaths. When we disembarked at Burnley, there was a little mob of about fifty locals who wanted to see if we'd live up to our barbarous reputation. We did.

On the Monday, I went into work to hear the news of Brian's death. I did not mourn. Instead, I immediately thought that the security warehouse fiddle had been delivered into my hands by providence. The company would promote internally, and I was the most capable of the group. I strolled through the aisles full of marketable consumer goods with a great sense of satisfaction. I'd be wealthier than ever. By the end of the week, I was the new warehouse manager.

Like I said, 1985 really was a fucking ugly year. They don't come uglier.

It could not go on. The pressure was mounting. It was becoming increasingly clear that the Government had decided to crush our political will. The day of the picket line was over, but we still tried to make our presence felt. News At Ten showed film of a group of us outside Walworth Road abusing Neil Kinnock, the Labour leader. I spat at him. People congratulated me for weeks. Everyone was losing a sense of perspective. We were past caring.

You could smell defeat in the air, but losing did not matter. It was too late. The only thing that was important was to go down fighting. It was not the vulgarists that beat us; it was the people who should have been standing alongside us against the biggest threat to British society since Hitler.

Thatcher was changing the rules and withdrawing money from the city all the time. The council were clever, adapting to the developing circumstances and maintaining their promise to protect jobs and services and create new, liveable housing.

Then they made a fatal PR mistake. In an attempt to outmanoeuvre the Government, the council sent out redundancy notices to its employees. Laying people off was never an option but the effect – and the way the messages were conveyed to the workers, by taxi – was a fundamental error. At the Labour Party conference, Kinnock lambasted Liverpool's politicians, calling the tactic "grotesque chaos." That was the killer blow. It was not the Tories with their obscene world view who vanquished us but a pathetic Welshman who pandered to the foremen of the nation instead of fighting those who were committed to destroying decency for their own profit and prestige. Kinnock still disgusts me. I would not even spit on the man.

On the first Saturday in October, we played QPR. I was on the eight o'clock ordinary. The glory days of bouncing off the train and singing in support of the city council and the miners felt like a long time ago. Yet there was still tension and excitement growing as we passed the Roundhouse.

There were Tottenham and Chelsea at Euston, waiting to depart north. Arsenal would be lurking around, too, looking for easy victims. They would not be us.

Even before the train stopped, the boys were jumping off, hitting the ground, running, and roaring into the echoing emptiness of the station. As the carriages disembarked, the three-syllable guttural roar went up: "LHI-VER-POOL," starting slowly and increasing in pace as we got to the top of the ramp at the exit of the platform. Our commitment to being outcasts was as strong as ever, but there were fewer of us than I'd seen for years.

It was a depressing day. The Met were taking no chances with us, and it was difficult to avoid being corralled into an escort. Barmen in pubs were more suspicious than ever. One would not even accept a £10 note I tried to spend. Heysel made them fear us more, Kinnock made them hate us more.

We got beat, too. Walking down to Loftus Road, the local fans gave us the same unabashed stare that is normally reserved for zoos. They had never seen mass murderers before. It was getting tiresome.

London was difficult. In the past, we would range around the West End, mostly Soho, and get the midnight train home. We were never entirely welcome, but now the mood was actively hostile. We got the special back instead. This was not the way it was meant to be. No strut into the Yankee, no one asking if there'd been knuckle, no feeling of being elite. No adventures, either.

We were in the American Bar by nine. We started the usual route. Next up was the Great Charlotte Street wine lodge for a large dock of Bismarck to chase down a pint. From there we walked round the back alley by Lewis's to the little Newington with a view to heading to the Roscoe or the Roscoe Head. After that, the choice would be Streets, Plummers or Chaucer. A straightforward night. If it really went wrong, the final destination was the Casablanca, an arty but rough venue that was somewhere between a rundown nightclub and a house party. It was all predictable.

Then one of the company made a suggestion. 'Your cousin does the Bier Keller, right?' I nodded. 'Let's go there. It's a madhouse. Everyone dances on tables. The band do Genesis songs. Come'ed. You wanna see the birds they get in there?'

I groaned. It was the last place I wanted to go. We were still in the little Newington, round the corner from where Billy was playing. Everyone agreed. I was the only one to object. We diverted to the Beehive. Your Cheating Heart was on the jukebox when we arrived, and I blanched at the memories of the Big Club. As much as I loved Billy, I dreaded the thought of him running through a set of cover versions. He had charisma. I'd heard the thrilling vibration in his voice and felt the compulsion to listen to what he was saying or singing. He had sent spasms and shivers across my body when he sang. Not only would he be mouthing the words of others, he would be amplified in the large cellar. But the boys knew he was my cousin. It would have been cowardly to disappear to the kebab house.

We went in about 10:30, in three instalments, so the bouncers would not recognise a large group. I knew none of the doormen and I had always made it a point of pride to not parlay my family history into free entrance to clubs. There was more danger than value in being recognised as Duke's nephew – especially now he was dead.

The audience was younger than us. Me and my mates were twenty-four or twenty-five and were elder statesmen in this Scally world. I felt old among the table dancers.

I stood to the right of the stage, back to the wall, and waited. About 11:30pm the show began. It would continue until close to one, when the kicking out process began. Billy came on and the crowd clapped. He fiddled about clumsily with his tuning and amps for some minutes and attention began to waver. Just as everyone seemed to have lost interest in what was happening on stage, he played the first nine notes of Duelling Banjos on his beaten-up old Gretsch, and the audience was electrified. His bandmate answered the call on a real banjo, and the pair turned to face each other and slowly upped the tempo.

Girls leapt from the seats on the long, Bavarian-style benches, spilling watery beer that was anything but German. They climbed on to the tables and began to bounce up and down as the beat gained pace. They shrieked and yahooed as if it were a hoedown. I was impressed by the craft of the two musicians, but a whiff of stagnation was mixed with the cannabis and sweat. Billy should have been beyond this by the time he was twenty. I turned around and looked at my mates. They were elated. One was playing an imaginary stringed instrument and grinning with the excitement of recognition. I alone stood still.

Billy had not opened his mouth yet. He smiled at his banjo player and then turned to face the room with a blank, thousand-yard stare. It was as if he did not care that there were people paying to see him. This was what he did, and, for a moment, I recognised that cavalier joy he took from performing and the seductive insolence that talent carries. I wanted to shout to him: to encourage him and exhort him to subversively throw in one of his own songs to disrupt the set. But I said nothing. I had drunk too much all day. The Bismarck was exerting its influence. As the duel finished, my mate came back from the bar with a Guinness and a large Bushmills. He sensed my skittishness and fed it with strong drink. Some mate, eh? Billy would have done the same.

Without any interaction with the crowd, the band went straight into Peter Gabriel's Solsbury Hill. Billy had always been a good mimic. During his showband days he had been able to comfortably impersonate the recognisable celebrities of the day. This was something different. He sounded just like Gabriel. The most shocking thing was it appeared that by disguising his voice, the electronic equipment was fooled. There was something there, something that never made it on to his studio tapes. A substantial amount of his aura remained and pumped out through the speakers. When he became someone else, he retained some of the presence that was so often lost when he was amplified. His charisma surfed the electronic pulses rather than drowning in the static.

The place was going wild, but I struggled to keep my composure. When Billy bawled out the words 'Boom! Boom! Boom!' almost everyone in the long cellar chanted and stamped their feet. My heart was racing. This was not how it was supposed to be.

It was becoming too much. He began The Sound of Silence and I closed my eyes in despair. It could have been Paul Simon on the stage. It certainly wasn't Billy. I forced my heavy eyelids open and saw it was him; but the noises coming out of his mouth were disembodied and fake. There was no truth in this building, in the sound waves that clogged the air.

He sang the line about the words of the prophet being written on tenement walls, and I understood. All those years ago, in the cool nook of the concrete, inner city staircase, I thought I'd heard the voice of the future. It turned out to be the sound of putrefaction, of a dying tradition. Billy was not a precursor of the future, but a symbol of a past that barely existed. His words were a summer's-day snapshot of optimism that was unwarranted. He was a false prophet. Now the scale of the deception was exposed.

I rushed out of the place, shoving the dancers aside. In the fresh air, I went to the small access road behind the club where the bins were kept and puked so badly, I thought I'd ripped stomach muscles. The world was sick, and so was I.

NO MORE HEROES

Demons come in different shapes. I had been determined not to become like the generation that preceded me. It was happening organically. In the security warehouse, I started each day assessing what I could sell. The fiddle was becoming the focus of life. It was lucrative. All the lads got their share. We did not consider it a crime.

My working methods were significantly more relaxed than the late warehouse manager's regime. When tasks needed to be done, they had to be completed quickly. If it was quiet, the boys could go the pub. We rotated manning the office in fifteen-minute spells, so no one missed out on the drinking.

We were drunk most days. The Dolphin had a rarely used downstairs function room that opened on to the loading bay and the pub's boss let us drink there. If management suddenly appeared, it would look as if we were in the back warehouse.

Money rolled in. The company was charged with accepting returned goods from catalogues and magazine promotions. Some were faulty and broken. Others had been delivered to the wrong address and were in perfect condition. Even the pristine returns were eventually sent to the dump. It was such a waste.

I was in the recycling business. Any goods with resale value – inexpensive multigyms, Capodimonte porcelain figurines, Guinness beer promotions where a single broken bottle had compromised the package – were money in the bank for me. My take-home wages from the company were £130 per week. On good weeks – after paying off all the staff – I was leaving on Fridays with £600 in my pocket.

It could not last for ever. In January 1987, I had an epiphany. The boys were in the pub, and I was taking my turn watching the office. It was important never to pull rank.

It was quiet. No wagons were on the bay. In five minutes, we would switch and there would be a pint on the table when I went back to the boozer. It was about 3.30pm and getting dark. I looked up the bay and there was a policeman coming towards me. For a moment, I was frozen. Running would be a mistake. I glanced around and then looked back at the officer. It was not a Busie.

It was one of the engineers that worked in the building. He wore blue one-piece overalls and no one rational could mistake him for a constable. My subconscious had projected my worst fears down the loading bay, and it shook me. It was the moment that I realised the fiddle had crossed the line into larceny. When I was caught – which was surely inevitable – there would be a court case and probably a custodial sentence. I knew I had to leave.

Norman Tebbit, one of the worst vulgarian politicians, sneered at us as lazy. He told a story about his unemployed father in the 1930s. The old man didn't riot, Tebbit said, he got on his bike and looked for work. Of course, this was in Hertfordshire, on the fringe of London, where a multitude of jobs were within cycling distance. There was nowhere to ride to in Liverpool. My bike would have to be a train or plane. I'd been postponing the moment I had to leave the city since I left school. That terrifying vision told me it was time to get out of the place.

Luckily, there had been a magazine sales push on BMX bikes. They were difficult to ship, and plenty were sent back. So I got on them. Over the next month, I sold every workable cycle in the warehouse, plus numerous other returns and – literally – tons of wastepaper. Over four weeks, the spree generated nearly £5,000.

Once you left a job of your own volition, you could not claim social security for six months. I'd built up enough cash to go to America and ride out half a year. Jimmy, Billy's brother, offered to set me up with a job in Manhattan. I turned him down. I would stay with him for a couple of weeks, but I had schoolfriends who had relocated to the West Coast. The plan was to go to Los Angeles.

From the moment I knew I had to work; it was clear I had to leave Liverpool. I'd put it off for too long.

The most seductive thing about America? When you spoke, you weren't criminalised for your accent. Not only that, but people were interested in you. Women, especially, would ask you to repeat what you had said. Being Scouse made you a pariah in England, but in LA, it made you fascinating.

Work was not a problem. There was an underground network of Scouse, Irish and British illegal immigrants that operated out of Santa Monica. Any newcomer could pick up a job quickly and, if they put in any effort, other opportunities would arrive. At least that's what everyone told you.

The obvious place to start was on the building. Construction was rampant all over Southern California and British trained craftsmen made a very good living. They always needed labourers. A mate introduced me to a finish carpenter from Yorkshire on my first Saturday night in the King's Head, and on Monday morning I was doing the heavy lifting for him. It was easy work at $50 per day. Sometimes it was largely watching him install exquisite wood interiors for ranch houses in Agoura Hills. On other occasions, it was simply fitting factory-made kitchen cabinets in cheap apartment complexes in Reseda. On the bigger building sites, almost everyone else was Hispanic. They laughed when the lunchtime roach coach – it was perfectly clean, but its horn played La Cucaracha to herald its arrival – served up tamales and we tried to eat them before removing the corn husk. Otherwise, they largely ignored us gringos. There was no nastiness. We were all illegals together.

It was fun for a while. Henry, the chippy, had a fondness for exotic dancers and would use any excuse to finish early and head to a strip bar. It was in these seedy but completely unappealing surroundings that I began to understand American culture. It was pornographic rather than erotic. It was about mass consumption and Henry consumed greedily, without discrimination. Quantity was all.

It applied to a number of aspects of life on the West Coast. A recommendation for a restaurant would invariably be based upon huge portions. Was the food any good? Who cared? There was a lot of it.

The favoured beers were 'light' – tasteless but with fewer calories than the more established brands. By British standards, they were high in alcohol. The main selling point seemed to be they got you pissed without getting you fat. They were bland, lacked bitterness, and never challenged the tastebuds. It was the flipside of puritanism. A society that lauded sobriety, heath and virtue had a behind-curtains, under-the-surface appetite for gluttony of all sorts.

This was Ronald Reagan's Promised Land, the template for Britain to follow. Vulgarism was at the heart of American vigour. It would do for a while. Once six months passed and I could go on the dole, it would be time to return home and find a direction. Hammering fence posts into the rock-hard earth one day – goodness knows why Henry had taken a job that involved stuff like this – I reflected that this was fine for now and wasn't the worst place to be for a tanned, lean, muscular Scouser in his late twenties. It was impossible to envisage being here when I was fifty.

Generally, newcomers graduated from building jobs after a few months. To open a bank account, you needed a social security card, but it was issued to foreigners with a warning across it saying it was not valid for working purposes. Luckily, within the expat community were a couple of forgers who were adept at taking the restrictive words off the document. If you knew the card had been tampered with, you could see it had been done. But most employers did not care to look too hard. With that and a CA driving licence, you could start applying for real jobs. Small businesses tended not to ask for Green cards. That was the route off the building site for most British and Irish illegals.

Then, on the Wednesday before Thanksgiving in the King's Head while waiting for a mate, I saw a face I recognised. The Gasman. He caught my eye, did a double take, tapped the man he was with on the shoulder, whispered in his ear, and then came across to where I was standing.

'Joey's lad?' he asked tentatively.

'Yeah.' I grinned. The last person I expected to bump into was the Ga… Neither of us knew each other's names.

'Gazza,' he said quickly. 'They call me that over here. They think it's an offshoot of Gary.'

There was a warning in there, but I laughed. 'Still in the import-export business?'

He chuckled. 'Sort of. But not quite in the way Billy took it to mean all those years ago. You seen him lately?'

I told him about the Bierkeller, the covers band and the waste of talent. 'He's making a few quid, right?' the Gasman said by way of rebuke. 'Better than struggling.'

He looked back across the room to his mate. 'This is not a good time. Fancy a beer tomorrow?' There was no work and no turkey dinner for me, so I said yes. 'Meet you at the Daily Pint on Pico. I've a place quite near there. Shall we say one? We can get something to eat after?'

'Yeah.'

'We can reminisce about the old days.' He smiled. 'Not much good about them, but I loved your uncle Duke.'

I hadn't been to this part of Pico. Too often drinking sessions were a tour of expatriate bars – the King's Head and King George in Santa Monica, Bangers in Reseda, Ireland's thirty-two in Van Nuys. Occasionally we'd go down to the Oarhouse in Venice to pick up gloriously dopey students. The Daily Pint was not on the Billy Brit pub crawl route.

It was empty when I got there – apart from the Gasman. It had a horseshoe-shaped bar that split into two rooms. One had a long shuffleboard table. Gazza was playing alone. I was still unsure what to call him.

He signalled the barmaid for another drink. 'Guinness,' I said. The floorboards were wooden. Bowls of unshucked peanuts sat on the bar. Signs around the place encouraged patrons to eat them, throw the shells on the floor, and grind them underfoot to feed oils into the wood.

We played. And talked. 'You here on business?' I asked warily. 'Yeah,' he said. 'You like the Beatles?'

Everyone did as far as I knew. It was a strange question.

'I'm here for a Beatles festival. It's at a hotel by the airport.'

I was surprised. He had come all this way because he was a fan? He chuckled.

'You thought import-export meant drugs,' he said. 'Billy did. He wasn't quite right. There was a little bit of that when I first went to Holland, but it wasn't my game. It was dangerous.'

This was candid. So was my response. 'I thought you were an armed robber?'

Again, he smiled. 'I was a daft kid, skint, stupid, and desperate. Amsterdam was the best thing that happened to me. I learnt so much living in a foreign country. Most of all, I learnt to stay away from guns, crime, and the possibility of being locked up. Duke tried to warn me. But you only learn on your own.'

It was time for another drink. I moved towards the bar, but he stopped me. 'I get the ale, alright?' It reminded me of my uncle. This was not a subject for discussion. He was buying.

We sat down as people began to come in. He asked: 'What are you doing?'

'I'm on the building,' I said. 'It's alright. I was bred for manual labour…' I left it a moment, '… and battle.'

He spat his beer all over the table. 'Very good,' he said, composing himself. 'How much they pay you? Work weekends?'

'Fifty per day. Generally no.'

'I've got a couple of days for you this weekend. Two hundred a day?'

He looked at me and saw my thought process. 'No crime involved.'

He explained. The Gasman had a stall at the Beatles fest and sold rare records. They were bootlegs, he admitted, but they were produced by a company – in which he had an interest – just across the Dutch border in Germany where the copyright laws made reproduction of live albums and the like legal. At least that was his story. It was convincing.

'I'd like you to come and man my stall,' he said. 'Mainly to talk to people. The accent sells a lot of vinyl. I had a lad who did it for me here and he's gone home. He was skimming from the takings, so I gave him a little shove. Let's see how he enjoys being back in Garston when he's signing on. Do it this weekend. It could turn into something.'

It seemed reasonable. I'd been to enough record fairs to know that they were relatively civilised. Back in Liverpool, I had a pile of Jam bootlegs. No one was getting hurt. It was barely a crime.

'I also sell collectibles,' he said. 'Memorabilia. Autographs, rare releases. People pay huge money.'

'Forgeries? Blag shit.'

He was amused. 'No, no need for that. There's lots of real stuff around. It's the opposite. You keep your reputation by making sure you don't sell fakes. I'm here this weekend to try to get one of the real rarities. The fella who's selling it doesn't like me, though.'

'Money talks?'

'Not in the world of obsessives.'

What he wanted was a Beatles album I'd never even heard about. It was a compilation released in 1966 in the US, but the tracks were the least interesting part of it. Called Yesterday And today, there was very little exciting about the content. The cover made it special.

The lovable Fab Four were frustrated by fame and Beatlemania. They hated their cuddly image. At a conceptual photoshoot in 1966 with a snapper called Robert Whitaker, the group donned butcher's white coats and clutched a number of decapitated baby dolls and joints of meat. McCartney loved the pictures. One became the cover of the album, but the retail reaction caused the record company to recall the release and pulp many of the sleeves. They were replaced by a softer, Moptop cover.

Some versions had the new photo pasted over the original sleeve as Capitol, the record company, tried to cut costs. It was known as a 'slick'. Fans peeled off the new cover and the 'Butcher' sleeve became one of the most desirable rarities for collectors. Very few slicks were on the market. The original, shrinkwrapped, unopened covers were almost impossible to buy.

My attention drifted. He was explaining now about the differences between stereo and mono versions of the record. It was too much geekery. Then the Gasman got to the point. He had heard through the collector grapevine that the son of a former record company executive was preparing to sell a boxload of twenty-four authentic, unopened Butcher originals at the festival.

'I'd give him five grand for one,' he said. 'I've got a buyer in Japan who'll give me fifteen. But we had an incident a couple of years ago. Over a girl. He won't sell to me.

'Anyway, that's got nothing to do with you. Come and schmooze Yank obsessives, sell a few records and I'll give you a few quid and we'll have a laugh.'

'On one condition,' I said, feeling bold. 'Tell me why you're The Gasman.'

He guffawed. 'Seriously,' I said. 'It's a frightening name. People were terrified of you.'

Auschwitz and its associations hung around the nickname. It gave this man the whiff of a killer. He shook his head.

'My first earner? Emptying gas meters of shillings with a screwdriver. You remember when you'd put a bob in the meter in rented houses? I was an expert in breaking open gas and leccy meters. So that was my nickname when I was about twelve. 'Gas-meter Peter.' It turned into The Gasman later.'

I gawped in surprise. 'Here, with civilians, I'm Gazza. At home, I like to have an aura. Don't be telling anyone I told you this. Or you'll feel the wrath of The Gasman.' He was smiling and there was no hint of threat.

'I'm not the only one,' he continued. 'You know John the Dog? Another of Duke's mob? How he got that name? He was drunk one night, was desperate to have a crap, but there was nowhere open, so he ended up shitting in the street like a mongrel. He turned it around by telling everyone it was because he bit some fella's nose off when he was in the army.'

With that, Gazza launched into a series of tales about clubland Liverpool. It was not a bad way to pass Thanksgiving afternoon.

I liked the Gasman. They said there was opportunity in America. They were right. It just arrived in an unexpected manner.

A hotel near LAX was the venue for the convention. It was packed with people whose lives were consumed by the Beatles and, sure enough, Gazza's bootleg LPs were in high demand. It was easy work. With me was a young American lad who could answer the arcane queries posed by buyers and deal quickly with payments and change. I was largely ornamental. After humping boxes of records in and helping to set up the stand, my role was to be Scouse. People were queuing just to hear me speak. Lots of customers asked whether I knew John, Paul, George, or Ringo. The best I could do was tell them that one of my dad's first jobs was on the door of the Blue Angel, Alan Williams's club. Williams was an inveterate drunk who called himself 'the Welsh Bard' because he had been barred out of so many Liverpool pubs. He was 'the man who gave the Beatles away,' their first hapless manager. The Americans looked at me like I was speaking a different language. Then they asked me to say it all again. They just wanted the accent.

The Gasman was tense. The buzz was that the son of the Capitol Records' former president was about to arrive with his twenty-four sealed Butchers. In the event, it was only five. That was sensational enough. A crowd surrounded him. It was like Beatlemania until people realised it was only someone with expensive records to sell.

Some of the collectors started arguing with the man about the provenance of the records. Were they fake? Two traders from the Pacific Northwest took a punt and paid $1,000 each for a mono version and Gazza offered $2,500 for a stereo copy. The seller laughed in his face.

A small huddle of hagglers wanted more proof. They demanded the seller call his father to back up the story. The American headed out of the dealer room to the lobby to use a pay phone, followed by a small knot of interested parties. The Gasman drifted away, frustration and anger radiating from him. For a moment, I thought he was going to turn back, break into the cluster of people, and beat his rival to death. Then I had an idea.

'Give me some cash, mate,' I said. 'Just give it to me.' He glanced sideways and passed a wad. 'Go on,' he said. I peeled off $1,000 in fifties and gave him the rest. 'Let's give it a go.'

I strode over to the group, pushed a couple of people out of the way, fronted up to the man with the vinyl and said loudly: 'You stole my cousin's records. Paul wants them back.'

Why I said this, I don't know. He stepped back in response to my voice, but he was constrained by the phone booth. 'Paul who?'

I hurled myself at him and shrieked. 'Which Paul do you think, you cunt? He's my cousin. Give me the records!'

It was a similar technique to the one that had worked on the loading bay. My irrational maniac act had gone international. The other dealers took a step back. The fury created a cordon I could work within.

The man looked stunned. I put my hands on the records and pulled them towards me. When he resisted, I butted him. As he slumped to the floor, I grabbed at the precious discs, getting hold of one. Then I threw the twenty $50 bills in the air and screamed: 'He's stolen my money! Get my money!'

I did my best, big-eyed McCartney impression and gently prised the precious album from his hands. There was little resistance. The confidence and authority – and violence – of my approach left everyone speechless.

Backing away, I did a double thumbs-up gesture in true Macca style, turned around, and walked with certainty straight out of the hotel. Gazza came running after me. 'Christ, you got one.'

'Yeah. I should have taken the fucking lot. Let me get out of here before they realise what we've done. You should go back and say you couldn't catch me. I'll be in the Pint by yours in an hour.'

I grabbed a taxi and told the driver to drop me by the San Francisco Saloon, further up Pico, just in case anyone was following. A bit of paranoia crept in. It took twenty-five minutes to walk to the agreed meeting place. The Gasman was waiting, and the relief showed on his face. 'I thought you'd fucked off,' he said.

'Nah, just being careful. What about the lad on the stall?'

'He'll cope.' He stared at the cover. 'This is like… have you ever wanted something but never believed you could get it?' I shrugged. 'This is something I never thought would happen.' He was a fan. It got in the way of business.

'Sorry about the grand,' I said. 'I was worried one of the other dealers would try and stop me. I needed a distraction.'

'Shit,' he said. 'I would have gone five times higher. More. Paul's cousin? You've got some nerve.'

'He'll be after you. People saw me at your stall. They'll link us.'

'Nah, you were just a Scouse fella working the day for $50 who saw an opportunity. Anyway, I'll be on a flight out tonight. We'll worry about comeback later. He won't go to the cops.'

He took me to a run-down bungalow near the intersection of Venice Way and Andalusia. He let himself in and said, 'I keep this place for when I'm in town.' Inside it was modern, swish with high-quality electrical equipment everywhere. There was a safe in the bedroom. He put the precious record into it. It looked like a very sophisticated piece of machinery.

Noticing my stare, he said, 'I deal in cash. And things like this LP.' He patted the metal box. 'This will scare off a junkie. They can take the record player and telly, but the stuff that matters stays in here. I make a lot of money. You want a job? You're too bright for the building site. I have things you can do.'

'And don't worry. You won't end up in jail unless you pull stunts like today regularly. I won't let that happen. Duke's ghost would kill me.'

There was a bottle of champagne in the fridge. Not cheap Californian fizz, but Laurent Perrier. 'Why shouldn't a working-class man drink champagne?' he said. So we did. Then he continued his pep talk-cum-job offer.

'The way you carry on, you're less likely to get into trouble in LA. If you go home where there's no work, you'll soon be running wild. Stay awhile over here. It's a different place when you've got a car and a few quid.'

He threw me a set of keys. 'My car's at the hotel. It'll be parked out front here tomorrow. Use it until I come back. You're on my payroll. Wait.'

He went to the safe and came back with more cash. 'Here's two grand. A month's money. Don't blow it. I'll be back in a couple of weeks.

'Some advice. Avoid the English bars for a while. People might come looking for you. Drink where the Brits don't go. Better still, drink at home for a week or so.'

'What do I do for the money?'

'Lie low. That's all I need from you in the short term.'

It was no hardship avoiding the King's Head. I'd had enough of Britishness, anyway, with the Union Jacks and pictures of the bloody Queen.

Gazza thought again and produced another thousand. 'When you pick up the car, get on the ten and head off to Vegas for a few days. Have a bit of fun.

'Now go get a cab to your place. If things go well, I know people who can sort your documentation, so you won't be illegal. Lawyers, I mean, not forgers. Start slowly and get some experience, and you can turn this into a good career.'

So, on the basis of a single blag, I was in the record business. Well, at least on the outer margins of it.

There was never any physical relationship between Missy and Gazza. It was all business. She never asked where he was from, who he knew, or why he was in Amsterdam. He was still low down the pecking order in the bootlegging world at the point they met, and she gave him the opportunity to climb the ladder. He had only become involved because Liverpudlian drug money bankrolled the pressing plant. Meeting Missy changed his life.

She supplied tapes from contemporary acts – live shows at first – that allowed the bootleggers to step outside the narrow Beatles world. His knowledge of the Fab Four had made him initially attractive to the money men, but Missy's recordings gave the business another dimension. Gazza became an important piece of the operation. His bosses were sceptical when he proposed paying some woman in London for material. When they listened to how good it was, he was given his head. As trust built, she began supplying studio outtakes. By the late 1980s the company – and it was legitimate in the Netherlands and Germany – was paying Missy enormous amounts. Because of this contact, the Gasman was effectively CEO. Their relationship was one-to-one. No middle men. Payments were originally in cash, but soon accounts were set up in the Channel Islands. It amused Missy when the Hitman raged against bootleggers for taking food out of the artists' mouths. She saw it as cross-promotion – especially as it promoted her.

Things were tough for Billy. He looked youthful enough, but the mayhem of the covers band had faded by the end of the 1980s. It was back to playing pubs and, although the scally following remained and landlords thought the group well worth their fee, it was a return to scratching a living.

He met and married, an attractive and ambitious woman from Childwall. She was a bank manager and although initially excited by Billy's musical performances and status, she quickly soured on the showbiz world when she checked her prospective husband's income.

Billy had enough cash tucked away to pay his share of a deposit on a house in Waterloo, but as he turned forty, life became a struggle. Lisa, his wife, had a baby boy in 1992 and the pressure mounted on the new father. The child made him think of the kids he did not know. The Lartys. His own flesh and blood brought up by another man. It was hard to suppress a shudder of shame and disappointment when he held his newborn son.

The grind was eased in the late 1990s when Billy was offered teaching work at the new institute for performing arts. He was still something of a local celebrity, which irked his wife. Luckily, her career was not halted by motherhood. They lived an affluent life. When the first series of Charisma hit the TV screens, he told his classes that shows like this were a temporary aberration. There were no shortcuts to fame. Status had to be earned. It was great advice but the youngsters sitting listening thought he was an anachronism. Many of the students had one eye on the fast-track.

In the early years of the new century, Billy was comfortable, henpecked, and respectable. He was now past fifty. His forties had not been exciting, but he was glad to leave behind some of the adventures of his first four decades. Looking towards the final third of his existence – as he saw it – he imagined few alarms. He had survived life's booby-traps. So he thought.

The 1990s were good for me. My new boss initially paid me $500 per week, but it quickly went up. The Gasman was as much a visionary as anyone in the music industry. Within weeks of me starting to work for him, he was back in LA talking about compact discs. They were, he said, the way forward. All the Beatles bootlegs were now on CD. The plant on the Rhine was producing more shiny discs than records. Soon, I began to get a sense of what he was about.

'How much did you get for the Butcher album?' I said. He blushed.

'I could not sell it. It's framed on my wall in Holland. I had a special cabinet thing made so I can take it out and hold it. Daft, eh?'

Then he surprised me. 'There'll be a consignment of AC/DC live albums coming in.' There was a garage next to the house on Andalusia and, every couple of weeks, I was required to oversee a delivery there or a pickup of stock. 'I want you to take them to record shops from the Valley to San Diego.' He put $1,000 on the table. 'Buy a car. Nothing flash. Something to get around in.'

Over the next few months, CDs and vinyl featuring numerous bands arrived and were dispatched to sellers. It meant I frequently had handfuls of cash, which I left in the safe in Venice. Over the course of twelve months, Gazza's trust in me grew. More and more responsibility was coming my way – and that meant more money.

By 1991 I had three people working for me and was shifting loads of units at events like Lollapalooza and record fairs across

California where the stock ranged from Led Zeppelin to Elvis Costello CDs. A Mod festival? Jam boots aplenty and even an acoustic version of Paul Weller's Wildwood album. Not only was Gazza getting mixing-desk tapes from live acts, but people in some of the UK's most prestigious studios were leaking out-takes. It must have cost a lot of money, but it was generating even more. I was soon flying to New York, Chicago, Philly to make sure the independent stores in the distribution network were getting their merchandise. At the fairs it was cash and carry. It was good business.

It did strike me that it was, no matter what the Gasman said, illegal activity. In my darkest hours there were nightmares where the bastard busie who abused me on the night of the Divvy's murder came back to haunt me. 'You'll end up in jail,' he would leer. 'It's in the Moran blood. Destined for jail from the moment you're born.'

I would jump. The beautiful, unerotic, enthusiastic, sexually athletic, interchangeable, and ultimately forgettable Californian girl lying next to me would flinch. 'Bad dream?' she would invariably ask.

'Flashback,' I'd reply. 'A flashback.'

Gazza was convincing. 'You work for a German company,' he said. 'The laws in Germany allow us to produce these records. The laws here are, well, vague. Plus, we have friends and business partners in the States who will protect our interests if there's any trouble.'

I had the card of a high-octane lawyer from Studio City to call in case of any problems. It felt like a reasonable safety net.

Things were going well. I was earning so much money that when each one of the itinerant Brits moved out of our Santa Monica apartment; I picked up their share of the rent. Eventually, they all left. None were replaced.

I was able to make the apartment comfortable. After five years of working for the business, I was taking home $2,500 a week. It wasn't Brentwood money, but it wasn't bad. The company had sorted, somehow, a Green Card and life was pretty good. I was saving, however, waiting for the inevitable time when I would have to go home.

Home. An emotionally charged word. In truth, nowhere felt like home.

Billy never watched the first series of Charisma. He avoided shows like this as a matter of principle. Then the phone calls started early in the second season. 'Is that your Julie on the telly?' A dozen people asked the same question and more repeated it in person on Monday. They all knew the answer.

The Saturday night show was repeated on Wednesday. He tuned in. The first shock was the judge. He recognised her, and the nickname he had given her, immediately. More than thirty years on, he still dreamt about how his life might have been different had their love affair been allowed to develop naturally. In his fantasies he had become a pop star and the young girl his manager, wife and lover. There was no regret for the killing, only the consequences.

Now he watched with horror. The two women with whom he had fantasised about being reunited were in the same room, on the television screen, on one of the nation's most popular shows.

There was no question that the girl was his daughter. The family resemblance was so strong that it was like looking at photos of his mother. Her performance was embarrassing. Like her father, her voice did not lend itself to electronic transmission. Objectively, despite all the emotion, he could see no reason why Julie would proceed to the next round. Unless something else was going on.

When the camera went on Missy, he stared at her. It lingered while she made a decision and he knew that look so well. Finally, she spoke. 'I can see something. I can see something…

Yes, there's something I recognise.'

He froze. She knew. Missy knew that this was his daughter. This was her revenge.

Were they colluding? Had they plotted this together? Two women whose lives he should have known intimately, but to whom he was just a sour memory? He shook with pain. He rose from his chair, went to the toilet, and vomitted repeatedly. It was so painful, so racking, that he thought he was having a heart attack. His wife found him on the floor of the bathroom, whey-faced and breathing in shallow gasps. He passed out. An ambulance was called. The quiet days were over. Billy's life was taking another turn.

His partner in murder really was a brilliant man. The Gasman realised CDs were the way forward and his production line was cranking out the discs when his competitors were still certain that vinyl was forever. By the mid-1990s he realised something new was happening.

We were in New York. It was yet another Fest in New Jersey. 'We need to do something different,' he said. 'Things are changing. CD sales are dropping. The companies are going to put pressure on people like us. Before long, they won't want us at conventions. But that's just the beginning of it.'

From a briefcase, he produced a small computer. 'It's a PowerBook,' he said. 'Cost me nearly five grand.'

Technology had always been one of his hobbies. His place was full of the newest gadgets. He sensed my indifference.

'You have a computer, right?' He knew I had a Power Mac. You could get the football results and reports on CompuServe. It was a useful word processor, and it was fun to play games on the screen.

'Well, technology geeks are making bootlegs available through computers. There are ways of listening to almost anything through things like this.' He patted the clunky but portable machine.

'Next year, or the year after, these devices will have CD players. And recorders. Then the business will be in trouble.'

'How do you know all this?'

'I pay people to tell me. There will always be a market for CDs and vinyl, but science is catching up with us. They're even selling boots through the computer. There's people holding auctions for bootlegs where the highest bidder wins. The buyer sends cash in the post and then the records and CDs get mailed out. I'm looking into it. This computer stuff is only going to get bigger. At our end, it's getting harder. The BPI and RIAA are leaning on the authorities to crack down.'

He was right. The industry associations of the British and American recording companies were flexing their muscles.

It was an ominous conversation. Dangerous times lay ahead.

A matter of days after the conversation about the future with the Gasman, the next phase of life arrived. Unexpectedly. After a long day in the dealers' room, I returned to the hotel to freshen up. The festival had finished, the boys working for me had packed up the van and were on the road, and I was ready for a beer.

In my room there were about fifteen trays of CDs and a dozen or so boxes of records that had been delivered to me at the hotel but we hadn't needed. They were being picked up the next morning to be distributed to Manhattan's record shops. It was a normal night.

As soon as the lift door opened on my floor, I knew I was in trouble. A dozen men were screaming, pointing guns at my head. It was obvious they were police. They were rough, but not too brutal. They cuffed and searched me, ran through my rights, and took me into my open room.

I remembered Duke's advice. Silence was my only weapon. They were getting no answers.

They were taking a very rough inventory of the recordings. 'My, my,' one said, 'there must be $30,000's worth at least here. You're going to jail, dickhead.'

My main concern was that the lads in Jersey and the van had got away. They had the stock and about $100,000 in cash.

That vision on the loading bay at Canning Place had finally materialised. It was not a good feeling. On the way downtown, I started to feel a bit better. They didn't have much. Six months, I reckoned, maximum, and then deportation. It could be much worse. And maybe with a good lawyer, who knows?

I can recall the journey to the Metropolitan Correction Center. The next thing I remember was eight days later. My dad always threatened to knock me into the middle of next week. The horsemen at Orgreave tried it but fell a few days short, so I never thought it could really happen. It did.

Julie's progression on Charisma made Billy's problems worse. It was a minor heart attack, but it scared him badly. The doctors told him to avoid stress. Every time he thought about the two women he had loved and walked away from, he shuddered.

For the first time since he was a teenager, there was no solace in music. His guitar lay untouched. In the past, the chords had acted like a balm. The rhythm used to cleanse his mind and dissipate tension. Now the notes were jarring, discordant.

It seemed everything had been stripped away from him: his children, his great love, and now the art that had saved him and propelled him onwards was soured. He tried to avoid the show, and friends kept away from the subject, but it was impossible to ignore. It was the biggest sensation on TV. The papers were full of it – he flinched at that thought. What if…?

In a deranged dream during the cardiac arrest he had seen the Divvy, the man he murdered, laughing. The spectre's torn throat gargled and spluttered blood as he tried to speak, and Billy shivered in terror. So this was death. Then the spirit pointed. Billy followed the finger and saw Missy and Julie together, giggling. No, it was not the end, it was not death. This was something different. It was the past holding him to account. The fatal consequences of a moment of fury had followed him down the decades, unnoticed, hiding around corners, lurking in recesses, waiting for the moment to ambush him and exact revenge.

When he emerged from his blackout wired up to a battery of machines, he understood that this was just the beginning.

Duke had taken on the guilt, but that did not absolve his cousin. For Billy, the consequences of the killing had been felt keenly. He had suffered. He had come to see himself as the real victim of that unhappy new year. In this hospital bed, for the first time, he considered the man he killed; how he had taken away everything that man ever had and everything he could ever have. Then Billy had another epiphany. He was not experiencing real emotions but repeating a line from a film. It was nonsense. 'The cunt deserved it. Fuck him,' he said aloud, startling a nurse. Another thought struck him. He needed to kill another man himself.

There were tubes everywhere. In the arm, up the nose. Machines bleeped. It was a hospital. It came as a surprise. I lifted my right hand to try to find out what the problem was. Had I been shot? Stabbed? A heart attack? The arm jerked back. I was handcuffed to the bed.

At that point, the last thing I remembered was eating in Castaway in Burbank, looking down on the lights of the Valley with a very attractive graduate student from the Midwest. She was new in town. Very bright in a limited way. I always thought it interesting that Liverpool women hated me. They saw through me immediately. The more distant in class and location the girls were from urban Merseyside, the more likely they were to be attracted to me. The women from my own background recognised a waster when they saw one.

What the hell was I thinking? I tried to focus on the situation. Had I crashed coming down from the restaurant? Is that why I was in handcuffs? There was a disembodied groan. It was my sound. I hoped I hadn't killed the girl or anyone else. Trying to think hard, I reached the conclusion that I hadn't. After an early scare on Coldwater Canyon in the 1980s, I never drank alcohol when I was driving and had scrupulously avoided drugs for a decade. No, not a car crash. At least not in the literal sense.

The best thing was to act mute. I might not have remembered what happened, but I'd never forget Duke's advice. When the nurses and doctors came, I didn't even ask them where I was. The staff were professional but detached. They had a New York brusqueness about them. It took a day or so before I came to the conclusion that I was in the Big Apple. How? Why? No one told me.

Two men came to talk to me. They were wearing cheap suits and were like cartoon detectives. They seemed a little sheepish at first, asking how I was. The silence made them rattier. They wanted to know who I worked for, where I got the merchandise, and who my New York contacts were. I would have loved to tell them that I barely remembered my name. But seeing the angst they suffered at my silence gave me pleasure. Things were coming back. By now, I knew I'd been in Jersey for the Beatle Fest. I'd been busted for bootlegging. So why was I in hospital? The cops weren't telling.

The next day, a visitor arrived in a different kind of suit. It must have cost $10,000. Unlike my previous visitors, he had no intention of eliciting information. 'I'm your attorney,' he said.

My jaw dropped open. In shock. He misinterpreted the reaction. 'Don't speak,' he snapped. 'I'm here to talk. You're here to listen.'

'In three hours, you will be released. Bail will be posted. Some time in the next week the charges will be dropped. Can you walk?'

I nodded. 'You will be met outside the facility by a car. It will drive you to the airport, where you are booked on a flight to San Diego. You will be met there by another car which will take you over the border to the best hotel in Tijuana. Your suite will be booked for a month. Rest, recuperate, and then go back to LA and carry on as usual. Do you understand? Nod.'

I understood. And was a little scared. It did not seem like the Gasman had sent him. He reeked of the mob.

Sure enough, a black-windowed limo was waiting for me. The driver opened the door. There was someone in the back seat. My weak knees wobbled a little more.

'Get in, softlad,' a voice said. It was Scouse with a longstanding transatlantic twang. Ducking my head, I saw with relief that it was my cousin Jimmy - Billy's brother who had taken the jailbird's seaman ticket back in the sixties and jumped ship in

New York. He was laughing and holding a bottle of whisky. 'You'll be needing a stiffener.'

'Christ, Jim, I thought I was going for one of those rides where you don't come back.'

He chuckled. 'You've seen too many mafia movies. How are you, la?'

'Better for seeing you,' I said. 'What happened?'

He told me. The arrest at the hotel had been straightforward. I'd been booked and placed in the cells. Someone in law enforcement, he reckoned, had thought it would be a good idea to rattle me a bit. They were irritated by my silence and put me in a cell with a drug dealer who'd swallowed half his supply of PCP minutes before his arrest. It seems a confrontation happened quickly, but the screws were inclined to ignore the sounds of anarchy coming from the lock-up. The fight rumbled on for a while and, it seems, I got a number of good blows in. At some point, the junkie got on top. 'You must have slipped or something,' Jimmy said kindly.

'He bit your ear off...' My hand instinctively went to the organ. 'They sewed it back on,' Jimmy said. 'And then he banged your head against the door until they realised there was only one voice shouting. They thought you were dead when they finally got to you.'

No wonder my short-term memory was gone. 'It turned out that this dealer had been running wild, anyway. He'd cut up his wife before he was arrested. It looks bad. They're shitting themselves that you'll sue. They'll drop the case.'

'Will I be alright in Tijuana?' I was still a bit nervous.

'Who do you think we're dealing with? Gangsters?'

It had crossed my mind. 'We're family,' he said. 'We go a long way back. I knew Gas-Meter Peter even before Billy's thing. I've been working with him for a long time. To be in a business like we're in, you need local connections. I have friends in this city. They are your friends, too. They were impressed that you never said a word when you were arrested.'

'I didn't know anything.'

'You knew enough for the Feds to join the dots. You could have mentioned Gazza. Or some of the shops you supply. Our local partners appreciate the way you handled things. It seems you didn't even shout for help. That's what the busies wanted.'

I laughed. Scouse slang seemed so incongruous here. We reached La Guadia. The ticket was first class.

Jimmy hugged me. He then put a hand in his pocket and produced a small package. 'This is for you. Don't open it here. It's a few quid to tide you over from our friends. The Gasman will probably want to give you a bonus, too. Oh, and you'll need a little plastic surgery. The stitching isn't great. As it happens, we have a friend south of the border who's very good but can't practise in the States. Here's his address.' He handed me a card. 'Give him a call. You'll be a priority. He's been told that you are fully insured. He'll know where to send the bill. You take care, la.'

As I went through to airside, he called after me. 'One more thing. Stay out of New York for five years. Not a big problem, but our friends would feel better if you did. If you need to come, call me. But don't need to come.'

What do you say to that? In the toilet on the plane, I opened the envelope. It seemed I was always sitting on bogs, ripping open sealed packages. I thought of the loading bay at Canning Place and the fiddles of more than a decade before. How the hell did I get here?

The little packet was chunky. It was three inches or so thick and; I assumed, feeling its size and weight, contained about five grand in unused tens. A little sweetener and some walking around cash that could easily be spent unobtrusively in Baja Norte. Then I shit myself.

The top note was a $100 bill. So were the other 499. There's a lesson for you. When you sit on a toilet, drop your pants just in case. It's easier to clean up afterwards. At least I'd have plenty of cash to buy a new pair of underpants.

The fifty grand was a turning point. I had saved almost that amount over the years. I'd stayed in the same rent-control apartment and did not need roommates. I had driven a Honda Accord even though I could afford a Porsche. There had always been a deep concern that the job would attract the attention of the police. It was best to be unobtrusive. And I figured I would have to run for home one day and would need a cushion when I landed back beside the Mersey. I was never going to be skint again.

When I got back to LA, I called Henry, the chippy. We still drank together. I made a proposal. Find a property that we could buy with my money, we could work on it at weekends and on slow days – no tit bars, I told him – and share the profit when we sold it. His work would enable him to locate somewhere suitable. He had twenty grand to put into the pot from an endowment he'd taken in the 80s and added that to the bankroll.

It worked beautifully. In 1996, the prices were low. They went mad from there. Starting with one ramshackle house in Upland, we made half a million in two years. Each. Initially, we did all the renovation ourselves. It didn't take long before we were able to pay other people to do the work.

Jimmy in New York was right about Gazza. He gave me a hefty bonus and a pay rise. The job was now hands off. He was paying me to do nothing. Others did the conventions, gigs, and went to the stores. It was time to move on.

The Gasman was now a rare visitor. He turned up at my apartment one night and we went to the King's Head. He reminisced. This felt like the prelude to us parting company. Our relationship started here. I was expecting it to finish in the same place.

'It's time to get out,' he said. 'People are making boots available on computers like I said they would. It'll hurt us. I like what you're doing. Getting into property.'

I was a bit surprised because I hadn't mentioned my new direction to him. He continued. 'Why don't I get some money brought over to you and you can pay cash for houses? Put the profits in the bank. We'll work out a split.'

It seemed reasonable and was at least on the road to legitimacy. 'You'll have to be a bit careful, because you've been noticed, but your joiner mate can help. And let's think about investing in some property at home. All those terraces around Anfield are dirt cheap. And you can buy half of Manchester for about fifty quid.'

I grimaced. 'Once a hooligan.' he laughed. 'It'll take two years, but everything we do will be totally legal.' It sounded good.

'How long will you be in town?'

'A week or so,' he said. 'You can buy my house in Venice real cheap, tart it up and sell at a huge gain. That'll give us a good start.'

I laughed when I heard the reason for his visit. 'One of our potential business partners, a Mexican with a ton of dough, is having a blowout in Disneyland. I'll go. It'll help me formulate our exit strategy. Maybe I can sell some of our assets. That's if I can drag him away from the booze and whores he's promised.'

'Didn't think they allowed alcohol in the Magic Kingdom,' I said. 'I went out with a girl who worked there. Squeaky clean. The place, not her.'

'He's got that much money he's block booked the hotel. Said it's going to be wild.'

It was the Gasman's biggest blunder. The 'business partner' was the FBI, and it was a brilliantly set-up sting. Poor Gazza got six months and was deported as soon as his jail term finished. He was now on the radar of the British authorities. Luckily, no one knew about the place in Venice, the almost unbreakable safe, and his offshore accounts.

We pumped cash into property on both sides of the Atlantic. Some houses we sold, many we kept and rented. Every day that went by, we got more legit and prices rose.

As the millennium turned, it was time to move back home. Gazza could not bear to leave Amsterdam. He had a flat in Chelsea and rarely made more than a flying visit to Liverpool. I was looking for more cheap houses in the north-west and mulling over whether to buy a flat in the Albert Dock. I liked being close to the river and so near town. It amused me that it was within spitting distance of Canning Place, where the loading bay had once stood.

All the time in America I'd believed that, philosophically, I was still in Liverpool 3. Back in the area; it became clear that the place had left me. The Albert Dock, in particular, was horrible. It was full of footballers, gangsters, and dubious entrepreneurs who could smell a region on the rise.

It would take an intellectual leap that I could not perform to move there; like voting Tory. You can travel the world, but parochial biases never leave you. But what if the parish has shifted in a different direction? I concluded that home had moved away from me as much as vice versa.

What shocked me was the political mood. Growing up, everyone I knew was politicised, if only in the loosest sense. They cared. Socialism was a way of life.

That attitude seemed to have faded. The sort of kids who once sold Militant newspapers on Saturday mornings were now selling drugs. Gangs across the city battled for turf. They all wanted to be the next Curtis Warren – an acquaintance of Gazza's in Amsterdam. Everyone was looking for shortcuts to wealth and fame.

I'd listened to my black friends in LA and sniggered when they talked about Whitey deliberately sending drugs into their neighbourhoods to foster crime and addiction and leave African Americans in a state of dazed, unpoliticised compliance. The best evidence they could cite was a scene from The Godfather. It was laughable paranoia. Then I went home and saw the city that fought Thatcherism neutered.

Superficially, there was little resistance as vulgarism continued its advance into the twenty-first century. It made me sick to see Tony Blair's sneakily delivered Toryism hailed as Labour success.

No, the new base camp would have to be London. In the capital, I would always be an outsider, the enemy within. It was just a place to live. In Liverpool, the cultural moorings had shifted. There were even England flags in the pubs and in the windows of houses around Scottie during the European championships. The city and I had drifted in different directions. It was no longer possible to bridge the gap.

I trawled around my old haunts for a week, getting increasingly maudlin. One evening, I took a cab from town to the Glass House. The driver was a bald, talkative fella of around sixty. He tuned in to my transatlantic twang and said: 'What brings you to these parts?' We were turning onto Vauxhall Road.

'Been living away,' I said.

'Where you from?'

'Burly.'

He nodded. 'I had some great mates from Burly. Used to drink with a lovely fella, a singer. Billy Green. He was talented. Haven't seen him in years.' He mulled over the thought. 'Did you know him?'

'Yeah.'

'Lovely man.' The driver was in his own interior monologue until we reached Leeds Street. Then he went off at a tangent. 'It was a hard place, though. Some wrong'uns round here.' We were approaching the roundabout at the bottom of Blackstone Street and I interrupted him and asked him to drop me at the recently erected memorial to those who died in the bomb shelter on the day Duke was born.

'Knew lots of people from the Gardens,' the driver said as I paid him. 'Some good people and some bad characters.'

I waited for my change. 'There were two brothers, vicious bastards. I think they were relatives of Billy's but he wasn't like them. The Morans. Both dead now, thank god. Duke Moran was a flash get. Loved himself. His brother Joey was evil. They'd be before your time.'

'Not really.'

He looked up with a grin. 'So you remember that beaut, Duke?' He laughed. 'How did you know him?'

'He was my uncle.' The bare pate went white, and he stuttered, groping for words. I thought he was going to cry.

'Don't worry,' I said. 'There's nothing I don't know about what they were.'

He scrambled in his money pouch and tried to give me some cash back. 'Joey's lad?' There was panic in his voice. 'Oh, Jesus.'

'No offence taken.' I shook my head at the offer of the note.

'No, no, no,' he said, his voice ascending in thirds. Billy would have turned it into a song. 'It's a pleasure bringing you here. This one's on me.' He threw a £20 note out of the window. I'd paid him with a tenner and already had the change in my hand.

I nodded. 'Thanks.' He stared for a moment to see if I was sincere and then shot off in case I changed my mind. The past ambushes you when you least expect it.

It did it again two days later. I'd rung Billy and arranged to have a drink. We had last met eleven years before in the Hamlet on the corner of Scotland Road and Boundary Street – not the one on Kirkdale Road, forty yards away – on a sunny Saturday evening in April. He had been at Villa Park, and I was just back from Sheffield. It was a horrible, emotional day. It is not a time I wish to recall. On the Monday I took a plane back to the States. I'd barely visited Britain since and had been home just once for a funeral. I never came back for a football match again. Billy was shocked to hear my voice when I rang him. I sensed he was hurt by the lack of contact.

I suggested meeting in the Queens on Williamson Square. It was a place with no associations for us. Both of us had drank there plenty of times, but it was never one of our haunts. Why did I want the most neutral place I could think of in town? I don't know. If the cab driver had not mentioned his name, then maybe I would have headed back to London without ringing him.

I was early so went into the Richmond around the corner. The last time I had been in there was with Duke. There were a gang of young fellas at the bar. They were loud, surly, and threatening. The barman gave me a pint of Guinness, and I sat down with my back to the window. Looking up, I caught the eye of one of the lads at the bar. We locked gazes. Instantly, I knew he was Duke's son.

It was strange to see him after so many years. He had not grown up in that time.

Kevin was short, barely five-foot-three. It was not unusual to see undersized men when I was growing up. The desperate diets of the pre-war era had produced a stunted generation. Rationing, and the lean post-conflict years, meant the next crop of people were barely any taller. We were bigger from the 60s onwards as nutritional standards rose, but six-footers were still rare. Living in America felt like being among giants.

By the 80s, kids were gaining height. There were more calories available to consume. Many of them were empty, but the growth hormone was being triggered. Not Kevin's.

He looked like a throwback to another period. He was stubby, just slightly plump, and appeared half a decade younger than his age. On a superficial glance, he could pass for sixteen, an impression reinforced by the youth of his companions. Closer inspection revealed a disturbing agelessness about his face. He could have been in his 30s. In America, he would have been carded at every bar he visited.

There was no freshness about him. Anger radiated from his being. He had inherited all of the family belligerence, but none of his dad's charm.

He took longer to realise who I was. Deep in the recesses of his mind, he must have had an image of me playing football in the garden on the evening before the funeral. I was forty now, but still recognisable. You could almost see the thought processes. Is it a busie? Where do I know him from? Is he a threat?

He was clearly the leader of the little group at the bar. The rest were in their mid-teens and had a similar disturbed, violent aura. We engaged in a short, dangerous flirtation. Egged on by his mates, he walked across.

'Do I know you?' he asked with insolence.

'No, Kevin, but I know you.' He drew himself up to his full, inadequate height and his mates stiffened. 'I'm your cousin.'

It took him a moment to compute the information and then he kicked a chair away from the table and sat down on it, even though it had skidded into an awkward position where he had to twist his head to look at me. 'Yeah,' he said. 'Yeah. The funeral. Jail. You came with us to the jail, too.'

I nodded. 'Your dad was a great man.'

He gestured to his acolytes. They were all wearing variations of tracksuit tops and jeans. My cousin was in a full tracksuit. Very Reservoir Dogs. His swagger was unconvincing, but it was unpredictably skittish. His knuckles were misshapen, suggesting a familiarity with violence. He leaned forward, trying to intimidate me. 'I heard you were in the States. What are you doing here?'

'Visiting. It's good to see you.'

'You didn't come to my mum's funeral.' That was true. I'd been in Tijuana. It was not the time to pay respects to the dead. Disobeying the instructions could have led to me joining her.

'It was impossible, I'm afraid.'

'You hear that?' he called to his gang. 'He's afraid.' They were enjoying the scene.

His mate came across with two large whiskies. 'I'd like to get this,' I said benignly. 'This is my pub. I get them,' he snarled. He was either slightly stoned or vaguely drunk,: capable of any outrage. And fucking stupid.

'So,' I continued sweetly, 'how are things and what do you do with yourself?'

'I'm a businessman,' he said. 'Import-export. International trade.' He smirked a grin of such stupid venality that I almost laughed.

'And what do you do? In America.'

Property, I told him. 'You're respectable,' he said. Turning to his mates, he shouted: 'This is my cousin. He's respectable.' They laughed. 'You sure you're part of the family? You're not the milkman's, are you?'

He leaned in close. 'If you'd have been a proper Moran, you would have sorted the Divvy yourself, wouldn't you? You were old enough. My arl man wouldn't have got sent down.'

This little kid who had his father taken away was still angry. I could see that. Part of me felt sorry for the little fool. But I wasn't being taken for a prick. I leant in and spoke softly.

'Your dad put family first,' I said. He snorted. 'And he taught me many lessons.' The slight gear change of tone brought his attention back. 'He told me never to let anyone make a dickhead of me.' I looked him in the eye. 'So, you'd better have a fucking gun if you're going to start with me. A knife won't be good enough. If you want to try, go ahead. That's if you want your mates to see you embarrassed.'

Our faces were about seven inches apart. I stared, unblinking, waiting for the slightest flinch. In my hand was a dimpled pint mug, still full of stout. If he moved more than a blink, I would twat him.

Finally, he did a realistic assessment. I was dressed in expensive clothes – not designer wear but garments that nodded to the scally look of the 80s. I was lean and tanned, but not soft. The muscles had been kept taut in the gym. He was a bit flabby. Fleshy. He had never done any manual labour, and it showed.

'Unny jokin' man,' he bellowed. 'We're family.' He punched my shoulder softly in the bravest, passive aggressive manner that he judged would not provoke a reaction. I did not smile. 'Gerrus, another scotch,' he slurred. 'For my long-lost Yankee cousin.'

I stood, downed the spirit in my glass. 'I've got to go, I'm afraid.' I went to the bar and produced a thick roll of cash. The lads were impressed. Peeling off five fifties, I gave them to the barman. 'Give my kid cousin and his mates a bevvy and keep them coming. Make sure they have a good night and keep one of those fifties for yourself.' It was far too much, but it underlined my point.

I walked out, patting the little shit on the face as I passed. 'Seeya, Cuz,' I said.

The little twat needed a father figure in his life. Circumstances had taken his role model away. It was too late now, though if he'd shown a little intelligence and humility, I might have tried to help. I could have given him a job. But how many drug dealers want regular employment? Then it struck me: if he harboured so much resentment about me, how must he feel about Billy?

At least it gave Billy and me something to talk about. He was aghast and amused at the same time.

'It's my fault,' he said. 'I used to go and see him and his mum all the time, but when he became a teenager, it was obvious he hated me.'

Then he guffawed. 'You told him he needed a gun?'

Now I went red. 'I know it sounds stupid, but it's because of America.'

He gave a sceptical look. I tried to explain. 'Occasionally, in the sort of places I'd drink, you'd get dickhead Yanks who can't take their ale.'

He wasn't buying it, so I carried on. 'So, they act the hard man. I face them down. One of the things I always say to them is: 'Have you got a gun?"

'What if they have?'

'They're white boys at Newport Beach or somewhere like that. They're wearing tee-shirts and shorts. Chinos in winter. If they're packing heat, it'd have to be in their undies!'

'OK, so what happens, then?'

'They are not expecting the question. It confuses them. When they don't answer, I say: 'No gun? Then you're well and truly fucked.' Never had one have a go after that.'

'And what if one produces a pistol?'

'Then I'm fucked!'

The one thing I could not understand is why Duke's son was oblivious to the signals that should have alerted him to danger. Billy explained his theory.

'The city's changed. Once, we travelled the world. I was the last of that generation, but you grew up with people like me coming home and going away.

'Your generation left for work. Most went to London. They didn't see the world, but they lived elsewhere. It gives you a different viewpoint.

'And even those who didn't live away went the match. Now, football's expensive. You need a letter from the Pope to get a ticket and you have to book a train months in advance. The kids never leave the city anymore.'

He mulled over his pint. 'They are more insular. Fella's like Kev can only relate to the things they know. I reckon he didn't even see a threat. To him, you're a knobhead because you're not like him and his mates. By the time he realises you're not to be fucked with, it's too late.'

Billy's grasp of the city's mood was spot-on. Why, I asked, did he not get into politics? His charisma was more suited to the spoken word. He had no urge to be a demagogue. 'I just wanted to sing. I just wanted to make people happy.'

It never made Billy happy, but we had a brilliant night. He was as carefree as I'd seen him. He was writing songs, teaching and there was none of the covers band nonsense. For the first time, I could remember he felt content. The shock of Charisma was still months away. If only I'd been the last ghost from the past to surface.

Even before Julie was crowned Charisma winner, it was inevitable that Billy would be caught up in the wave of publicity. Earlier in the series, the girl had confided in her mentor that she had not seen her natural father since she was a child. Missy immediately passed on the information to her national scandal-sheet contact. By the time the contest reached its semi-finals, the local newspaper was keen to claim proprietorial rights to the potential star. An estranged father was collateral damage in the quest for publicity.

It wasn't the biggest story. The News of the World ran it across pages 22 and 23 on a spread heavy with advertising. 'Charisma girl's dead-beat dad wanted to be a pop star,' the headline said. There was a hastily snapped picture of Billy, but it was blurry and furtive. The piece was a hatchet job. '… deserted young family… jailed for beating up stepfather… failed rock career…' It was hugely embarrassing and set back Billy's recovery.

Public sympathy swung behind Julie. On the following Saturday night, her phone votes spiked. It was the highest volume of texts in the season. All at £1 per vote. The girl's down-to-earth nature, her residual niceness and unthreatening low-key attractiveness made the nation take her to its bosom. Your father may not have loved you, but we do, the voters said. Her co-competitors were appalled. Cinderella had suddenly become a threat. The producers led the contestants to believe sass and swagger would win the day. Mr Charisma himself was dumbfounded. He began plotting out a career for Julie, much to Missy's amusement.

In Liverpool, Kevin Moran read the story. It made him angry. He had grown up hearing about how wonderful his father was, how Duke had been a stand-up guy. Wellwishers had told the boy about how his dad took responsibility and went to jail for his mates. The tales were meant to illustrate Duke's character, but his son was never able to grasp the context. All he could see is that two other people ran away and left his parent to stew in prison. He could never comprehend why everyone – even his mother – was so well disposed towards Billy. Why, he often speculated, didn't the actual killer hold up his hands and accept the blame? To him, he was Billy the Bastard, the man who stole his father. The resentment festered throughout his teenage years and into his early twenties.

He liked having a murderer for a father. It gave him status. It made people fear him. It was one of the key reasons Kevin's little mob of wannabe gangsters gathered around him. They were all younger than him – his contemporaries had seen through his bluster long ago – and lived in Dovecot, just across East Prescot Road from the Moran house. The sixteen and seventeen-year-olds in his crew were feral. They had been born on the other side of the great watershed in British society and grown up in the post-Thatcher world where the bonds of community had been stretched to the point where they began to fray. They cared nothing for politics. Their ambitions were to gather quick, ugly wealth by whatever means possible.

The older hard-cases around town laughed at Kevin Moran. He was 'King of the Kids' and it was only in deference to his father's memory that the bouncers on the doors showed him the bare minimum of respect. When he heard someone call him 'the King,' he took it in its most unironic sense and adopted it. The kids fell into line and used the nickname, but it soon morphed into the less grandiose 'Kingy'. The teenagers aspired to be like him, and Kevin's court was populated by retainers who were amoral and irrationally violent. They dabbled in drugs and sparred with equally unprincipled youths from Page Moss. Dovey Edz and Mossy Edz were at war and the tit-for-tat attacks were growing more dangerous by the month. Kingy imagined himself a godfather, the heir to an empire that was destroyed when his dad went to jail. He was determined to become one of the city's most feared gangsters and make all his enemies shake with terror.

It was Kevin who was shaking as the Charisma publicity unfolded. He stared at the local newspaper and felt hate surge through him. There must be something he could do, he thought, to make Billy the Bastard and his bitch of a daughter suffer.

'Now you're a star, you can do anything,' Missy said over a glass of champagne at the Charisma final afterparty. She looked Julie, the show's winner, in the eye. 'Men can't grab your pussy any more. If you fancy them, grab their cock. They'll queue up to fuck you. You become a hundred times more fanciable when you're famous. Live out all your fantasies.'

Now in her early forties, Missy's carnal appetite was increasing. The wild antics of the 1980s had been largely traditional rock'n'roll behaviour with all the usual twists: bondage, S&M, group sex. These activities were fuelled by drugs and drink and were relatively harmless.

When she began putting groups together, things took another twist. Power and control turned her on. The young boys who auditioned were fair game for sexual bullying. She would demand the desperate wannabees drop their trousers. She particularly enjoyed trying to tease erections out of young gay men. 'Look at your little acorn,' she would say, plucking at the victim's hapless penis. 'Isn't it going to grow into a big oak so you can stick it into mommy?' She would make straight boys kiss each other for her pleasure and, when the mood took her, would make use of her casting couch. Few men in the industry were more predatory than Missy. She was determined to be sleazier than the sleaziest male.

There was no sense of sisterhood. When fame-hungry young songstresses came in front of her, the starmaker would humiliate them as part of the process of readying them for a life in showbusiness. Any poor girls who were a pound or two overweight would have their flesh pinched painfully. They would be stripped off and made to stand on scales while Missy grasped a handful of pubic hair and yanked it hard. 'Shave it, fatso; no one wants to see your welcome mat.' The older woman relished the sexual bullying. It turned her on. 'I've got bigger balls than any man,' she would say. And she was acting like the worst sort of macho executive.

Inside the industry, people talked. The rumours were never going to make it into the Sunday papers, though. Too many tabloid reporters had enjoyed the benefits of Missy's information. She kept the best stories, the ones that could not have her fingerprints anywhere near, for the News of the World, but she was always careful to spread the largesse about. She made sure she had friends on the showbiz desks of every newspaper. The coverage of her was sycophantic and helped cement the image of the talent-show judge as the kindly auntie of British television. The youngsters she humiliated and abused were cowed by her popularity. The Labour government, still suffering from the 'Cool Britannia' delusion, appointed her OBE. Missy's rise seemed inexorable. Proposals for game shows and chat shows landed on her desk and publishers queued up to offer her the chance to write an autobiography. She felt invulnerable.

'Something's come in that might interest you,' the voice on the other end of the phone said. The call was from a reporter. 'It's about your winner.'

Missy waited. What could Julie have done? Drink? Drugs? A resentful boyfriend with naked photos or even a sex tape? 'Go on,' she said.

'It's her old man.' The woman almost laughed.

'What's he done? Had an affair? Been caught cottaging?' She chuckled. 'This is what you're down to? You've got to do better than this.'

'No, it's a good tale. It's not the man she calls dad. It's her real father. It's the one who deserted the family.'

'Go on.'

'Some piece of shit from Liverpool says that dear old pater killed a man. But that's not all. The kid claims that your Julie's real father framed his dad for the murder.'

It was true. The King of the Kids had brooded for weeks about Julie's success. One night he was watching a TV programme about kiss-and-tells and he was struck by a thought. Perhaps that would be a way he could hit back.

On Sunday, he bought all the papers. He scoured the pages and found what he was looking for. A little box that said: 'Have you got a story? Call the newsdesk on…'

The first number he tried picked up. He gave a very brief synopsis, left contact details, and waited. The next day, he received a call. The man was interested. 'I want five grand,'

Kevin said. The journalist snorted.

'Take it elsewhere. Good luck.'

'No, wait,' he said desperately. 'What can you pay?'

'A grand.'

After a moment of wavering, he cracked. 'OK.'

'And it needs to stack up. No proof, no money.'

Kingy was worried. He could not imagine how to furnish evidence. The reporter was confident. The newspaperman knew how he could stand this up. A couple of calls would get the ball rolling. First, he wanted to make sure Missy was onside.

Missy hung up. She thought for a moment or two and then made a call. The News of the World reporter picked up after a single ring. 'One of your rivals has a good tale about one of my girls,' she said. 'She's in the studio this afternoon. I'll leave a message on her voicemail about the call I've just taken and ask her to ring me back. I'll tell her I'm on a train and to leave a message. Then, at 8pm tonight I'll ring her and talk to her. You know what to do.'

He did. It was a simple matter of hacking the voicemails. Most people did not change the default access code on their remote message system. As long as he had Julie's number, he could listen to her messages. Missy made sure she was hacked, too. If the scam was ever exposed she could claim she was a victim.

Fame had not been everything that Julie expected. Like most people, she wanted the benefits but struggled with the downsides. Anonymity has its positives and sometimes she yearned for the pre-Charisma era. Days were now regimented. She was ushered from studios to personal appearances. The trappings of wealth and success surrounded the girl, but the effects did not filter through to her bank account. The long-term contract she had signed generated cash for the Charisma conglomerate and required her to sing other people's songs. Effectively, she was on a wage. It was a good stipend, but she noted with some concern that the previous year's winner had already dropped from public view. None of this was how she imagined it.

Instinctively, she was aware that this could be a fleeting

experience. At the moment, it felt gruelling. She did not want it to end, but it could not continue this way. Being recognised everywhere was intrusive. Everything she had dreamt about had happened. She was unprepared for the change. Events left her disoriented. It was like being transplanted into an alien world. The culture shock left her bewildered.

The phone call made things worse. Two different newspapers had called the company's PR people with allegations that her father – not the person she considered her real dad but the biological one – had murdered a man and framed someone else for the crime. The accusations had the ring of truth. Over the years, her mother had made a number of suggestions that her natural father was a violent thug who consorted with hoodlums. She was terrified of telling her mum. Suddenly, old wounds were being torn apart. None of this would have happened if she had not entered the stupid competition.

There was only one person to turn to: Missy. Her mentor left a message shortly after the PR people dropped the bombshell. Julie called back, as requested, and poured her heart out into the void of Missy's voicemail. Finally, the two women spoke. Missy had just one piece of advice. She suggested that it was worth Julie talking to one of the reporters. He was a friend – 'if leeches can ever be friends,' Missy said – and it would at least allow the girl to frame the story on her own terms. Julie flinched at the thought of the headline: 'My father the killer.'

After putting the phone down, she wept for an hour. Then, gathering all her strength, she called home and relayed the situation to her mother. 'That cunt,' the older woman said with feeling. It was a word she never used. 'Will we ever be rid of him?'

Back in Liverpool, Billy was beginning to get his life back together. The embarrassment of seeing his estranged daughter become a ubiquitous presence on television and in the newspapers had faded. If he had learnt anything in his fifty-odd years, it was that you get used to anything.

He had even begun to feel small stirrings of pride. After the initial shock, it was nice to see his child, even if it was only in the media. She looked so much like his mother, and the voice, for all its flaws, reminded him of his grandma. It was untutored and, at times, toneless, but it evoked Burlington Street in another age. It was a bizarre feeling. Completely irrational.

The sight of Missy dredged up different emotions. It healed him in a sense. For more than two decades, the idea of his lost love acted like an anchor for his happiness. He thought about her numerous times a day. The guilt that a more rational man might have felt for taking a life was alchemised into a sense of grief for his own loss. The dead man's desperate, gurgling face did not haunt his dreams; a soft, desperate craving stalked his nights. In sleep, he held an idealised image of his perfect woman. On waking, he felt a yearning that he could not shake. Until, that is, the bitch used his daughter to gain some sort of sick revenge.

It meant that he looked at his wife with fresh eyes. Suddenly, she was no longer second best. Yes, the spectre of Julie caused tension in the marriage, but things were settling down. That was, until a cameraman loosed off a series of photographs with his motordrive as Billy emerged from work one Thursday afternoon. It might as well have been shots from a machinegun rather than a camera.

Later that night, a reporter knocked at the house and gave a brief outline of the story the paper would be running on Sunday. Billy slammed the door, but the man continued to shout through the letterbox. That was what caused him to snap. He went to his toolbox under the stairs and took out a hammer. Shrugging off his screaming wife, he opened the front door and hurtled down the path. Luckily, the reporter was young, impervious to embarrassment, and quick on his feet. The newspaperman fled down the street at speed. Unfortunately, the photographer was stationed across the road. The paper had the money shot.

With his £1,000, Kingy had a party with his crew. They smoked weed, drank sweet, sugary alcopops and vodka, and talked about killing the Page Moss Edz. Then their leader showed them his pride and joy. It was a battered Smith & Wesson.455 revolver and a handful of bullets. It was nearly one hundred years old, and he had spent almost half of his newspaper cheque on it, paying the cash to a drug dealer in town, a man who had got his first break in the business of crime from Duke two decades earlier. Now he could not wait to use it. The pistol would give the Dovey Edz the edge in their ongoing war with their rivals.

Missy's assistant delivered the stack of Sunday papers. The tabloid that had originally brought the story to her had gone big on it. Billy, waving a hammer, rushed out of the front page. 'Charisma star's 'killer' dad runs wild,' the headline said. 'Hammer wielding maniac framed mate for murder,' the subhead claimed. A small, circular picture of a pensive Julie completed the package.

Inside, the interview with my cousin laid down the allegations. The paper went hard on the accusations. Too hard. They knew too much. They had, of course, hacked Missy, Julie, Billy, and even me. Kingy had supplied the numbers of friends and family that might have got a call from Billy. There were a dozen people he could have got my contact details from.

I was on a plane, so Billy left a long, rambling message. 'Call me when you get this. A paper's running a story about the Divvy, saying I set Duke up. Your mam will probably be mentioned. How can we stop it? Do you know anyone who can stop it? That little twat Kevin's sold us out. His dad will be turning in his grave. The cunt deserved to die. We don't deserve this.'

After hearing this, and other messages, the red-top editors knew they were on safe ground.

It was a satisfying read for Missy. Now she turned to the News of the World to see how they had approached the tale. Julie's involvement would ensure she got a sympathetic ear from the paper. Her picture was on the front page with a small headline. 'Star shocked by killer dad's past.'

Missy opened to the spread and ran a practised eye over the

pages. There was no need to read the copy. Poor deserted girl shamed by dead-beat killer dad. Yet something bothered her. She looked harder at the package.

It took a moment to realise what unnerved her. Julie had provided the wedding picture in exchange for the promise of an even easier ride. It was the photograph with me in it. Missy stared at the gawky seventeen-year-old groom, and there was a germ of recognition. I've seen something, she thought. Her glance flicked across the other photos, and she froze. The picture department had rooted out an amateurish publicity picture from the Scouse Pie years. This time Julie's father had long hair, and she recognised him instantly. A numbness spread across her mind. It was him. Him. It suddenly became clear. The girl, Julie, was the image of her parent. What Missy had seen in those auditions was not talent. It was something else.

She had barely thought of him over the years except as a touchstone for her contempt for men. His features quickly faded from her memory. They had posed for a few Polaroid snapshots during their relationship, but she had thrown them away within a month of his disappearance. The face, the body, the walk, his smell, had dissolved in her mind and only a residual anger remained. Now everything came flooding back.

Had the girl and her father plotted together to humiliate and destroy her? Then she thought rationally. They were the people hurt by this story. Missy did not know what to think. For the first time in years, she felt helpless and lost.

THE LAUGHTER OF
OUR CHILDREN

The firestorm of publicity blew over quickly. Julie got sympathy. It feels like the world is imploding when you are at the centre of a media storm, but attention spans are short. The initial burst of infamy, the brief encounter with notoriety, passed. Soon even the stardom began to recede into something approaching normality. The girl got enough work to be comfortable without the everyday mania that can make existence difficult.

Things moved on. A new series of Charisma was already in the early stages of production by the time the newspaper story hit the streets. Missy's focus switched to other things, other people. Her fame did not diminish. The ratings for the programme remained on an upward curve.

Only Billy suffered. He had another heart attack about a month after the unwelcome eruption of media scrutiny. I was back in the city so went to visit him in the Royal. His voice, once so strong, was a croak. Listeners used to lean into him to hear his thoughts and hung on every sentence. Now you had to shuffle forward to make out his words.

He thought he was dying. He wasn't, but he was giving up. The only thing he wanted to talk about was the past. Even that was negative.

'I've been thinking about everything,' he said. 'I thought we had opportunities. I thought we were the generation that could break out of the slums and actually change things. I was wrong.'

'I dunno,' I said, trying to introduce some levity. 'You live in a nice semi and were a pop star. I'm a Rachman-style property magnate.'

There was no smile. 'There's no escape. Did I ever tell you about my mate Jimmy B?' He hadn't.

'It was when I first came back from sea. I was desperate for money and worked on the building wherever I could. I got a scaffolding job knocking down a place on Cheapside. No cards, cash in hand, no safety equipment. Company was owned by a millionaire. He lives on the Isle of Man.'

I waited. The effort was exhausting him. 'Jimmy fell and was killed. At the inquest, the boss denied all knowledge of him and said he'd been up there robbing lead. That's our lives.'

It was a strange allegory. 'His brother fell off a building while working, too. It was six weeks before. Or later. I can't remember. It doesn't matter. We're all just waiting for the fall.'

The gloom hung over him. 'I've been seeing a girl in London,' I said. 'I was telling her about you. She's desperate to see you play. I've told her what it's like when you sing.' A bit of flattery might cheer the patient, I thought.

'Why?' he said. 'I have no voice. I never had.'

I left and walked down London Road. It used to be a vibrant place. TJ Hughes's was one of the family's favourite department stores and the shops all around were busy and bustling. The area was dead now, shabby and boarded up.

Further into town, new buildings were sprouting up. It was mainly student accommodation. The nature of the city was changing in front of our eyes. Suddenly I felt as maudlin as Billy.

On a whim, I went into the Lord Warden. I'd been in there with Duke nearly three decades earlier. It hadn't changed. The manager, Jim, had been a friend of my dad and uncle. He had left his nickname, the Panther, back in the 1980s. He winced these days when it was used. I was going to niggle him for old time's sake. There was no sign of him, so I sat down and nursed a Guinness. It tasted sour. When, I wondered, was the beer revolution going to hit Britain? Small breweries had been popping up all over California for a decade and were producing superb ale. There and then I realised what my next project would be: a brewery.

It was an exciting thought. The Gasman would want in. This was not the sort of place where it felt appropriate to use a mobile phone, so I left the dregs of the curdled stout and headed for the door. Coming the other way was my cousin, Kevin.

We stood for a moment, weighing each other up again. 'You've been busy,' I said. He had not emerged from the sale of the story completely unscathed. His Page Moss enemies had taken to spraypainting 'Kingy is a grass' all around Prescot Road. They had even crept into Dovecot to graffiti the area.

'What the fuck is it to you?' he said.

'I've just been to see Billy in the Royal. His heart. You happy now?'

He moved on to his tiptoes, straining his neck to get the height. I leaned in and his upturned nose came close to mine.

'Last time you asked me if I had a gun,' he snarled. 'I've got one now. You need to watch yourself.'

I backhanded the little fucker as he rocked back on to his heels. He crumpled, and I punched him as he tried to regroup. The barman came running over and wavered about intervening. He knew my cousin. 'Kingy,' he said, 'are you alright?' He turned to me. 'You better get out of here. You're fucked, mate. Don't know who you think you are, but you're in trouble.'

Ignoring him, I turned to Kevin. He was bleeding from his lip and still on one knee. 'You bring your gun and come and see me.' I looked at the barman. 'I'm his cousin,' I said. 'It's a family get-together. Now fuck off back the bar before I slap you.'

With that, I punched Kevin once more on the top of his head and went back on to London Road, walking slowly in case the shortarse came out after me. He stayed inside.

After crossing Commutation Row, I went to St. John's Gardens and sat on a bench. What the fuck would Duke think? I wondered. He'd be fuming at me, I thought. He always told me not to punch jaws or heads, and instructed me not to pound my knuckles into anything hard, like a skull. Slam your fist into their solar plexus, he always said. Use knuckle dusters or a cosh for faces and heads.

I held out my hand, and it was swelling up already. I'd broken the bloody thing. My uncle would not have been impressed. You were supposed to break other people's bones, not your own.

The Gasman rang me the next day. 'How old are you?' he said, an equal mix of laughter and disapproval in his voice.

'The little twat threatened to shoot me.'

'He's just stupid enough to try it,' he said. The chuckle had gone. 'Or get one of his rats to do it for him. Have you seen what's going on out there?'

I had. There had been a handful of shooting incidents in the previous couple of weeks. Gun prices had shot up on the black market.

'It's not like in our day,' Gazza continued. I felt a spasm of irritation that he was including me in his age group. 'We'd have a straightener. Fists only. Now these little bastards don't care. They'd shoot you as soon as look at you. They've no fear. It's fourteen-year-old's running round like Billy the Kid.'

'Well, he's old enough to know better.'

'Listen,' the Gasman said. 'I'll go see him when I'm home. I'll have a word. Duke wouldn't like this shit. Nor would your dad. Jesus, you're cousins.'

That meant nothing to me. Him neither.

'Anyway, I've got a new business for us,' I said, changing the subject. 'Beer.'

'I like the sound of that,' he said. 'I'm in Amsterdam. Come over and tell me about it. Belgium's the best beer country in the world. We get loads of their stuff here. Let's drive down and go to Antwerp. I've got some business there.'

I knew what he was doing. He was getting me out of town just in case my cousin was crazy enough to exact revenge. It made sense. All it needed was one of the little scumbags to get stoned or drunk and decide to make a name for themselves. In all those years in the States, I'd seen no gunplay – except from the police. What the hell had happened to the city while I'd been away?

Gazza couldn't let the bootlegging business go. We had enough property income to live well. But he was still involved. He saw catastrophe on the horizon and had talked me into taking a different direction, but he could not walk away. On the plus side, it meant there was still plenty of cash sloshing around. Producing beer would be another way of making it clean. He liked the idea.

We were in Kulminator in Antwerp, drinking Orval, dazzled by its taste. The Gasman loved the chaos of the place, the variety of shining glasses around the bar, and the bewildering selection of bottled beers on display. His pager interrupted us.

He had a mobile phone, but there were safer ways of communicating. We always carried international pre-paid calling cards and used public telephones for any conversations that could attract the attention of the authorities. The message gave him a phone box number in Liverpool, but no indication of who was making contact or why they wanted to speak. With a shrug, he took a swig of beer, said 'get us another one' and went off to find somewhere to make the call.

He came back after about twenty minutes. 'Your fucking mate's gone and done it,' he said grimly. 'He's shot someone. He needs to get out.'

'Eh?'

'Your cousin. He told you he had a gun. It wasn't blag. He phoned the Panther. Said he needs to leave the country.'

'Who's he shot?'

'Probably some rat from Page Moss. They've been trying to

kill each other for a couple of years.' For a moment, the Gasman was pensive. Then he switched to anger. 'What's wrong with the little fuckers? It's not like it's about money.'

It was worse than we thought. The King and his followers had been gathered in an unoccupied house, playing video games, drinking and smoking weed when one of the younger kids came charging in demanding action. 'The Moss Edz are in the Kentucky Fried Chicken.' The schoolboy had spotted a couple of rival gang members in the fast-food outlet and cycled the half mile to the house to alert the rest of the crew. This was an insult. They spilled out of the property and leapt onto the BMX bikes that were strewn across the overgrown garden. Whooping like apaches, they rode west towards their prey. Their leader had his pistol tucked into his belt. He felt like a warrior.

By the time they reached the restaurant, their quarry had either gone, or it had been a false alarm. They mooched about for a while and then slowly made their way back towards their den. At the edge of the park, they spotted a couple of young lads they did not recognise sitting on the swings in the playground. 'There they are,' Kingy shouted, and the entire mob turned in the direction of the two interlopers.

The strangers started running towards the centre of the fan-shaped park, staying away from the paths and forcing the cyclists to negotiate the bumpy grass. They switched direction and hooked towards the trees and bus stop on Pilch Lane. There were six-foot high metal railings there. They were trapped.

Fear gives people strength. The two boys scampered up the barrier and flung themselves over the top, oblivious to the pain inflicted by the blunt spikes. They each landed with a thud by the bus stop, bounced up, and ran across the road. Kingy sprung off his bike, reached for his gun and shouted after the lads. One turned around as he crossed the street and gave his pursuers the finger. His face froze when he saw the pistol.

Four shots rang out before the young man's legs started

working again. He fled towards his mate, who was already around the corner and past the off licence.

The Dovey Edz scattered. The police would be on their way soon. At the opposite corner of the park, Kingy stopped. He gave the gun to a fifteen-year-old who lived about one hundred yards away and would be home first. The boy was quite nervous and on the periphery of the crew. He had a slight stutter and was visibly terrified of the gang's leader. Best of all, he had never even been cautioned by the police. His parents believed he was a good kid going through a rebellious phase. They were probably right. That made him the perfect fella for the job. 'Hide this,' Kingy said. 'Keep it safe. I'll see you at the den tonight.'

It was 7.30pm, still light. At the bus stop, unnoticed by any of the gang, a 12-year-old girl was bleeding to death. No one spotted her in the mayhem. A bullet hit her in the back as she turned to watch the boys running across the road. She was dead before an ambulance arrived.

As far as the group of wannabe gangsters were concerned, it was just another jape. They knew the shots would increase police attention but figured that things would calm down if they lay low for a day or two. They went back to the abandoned house, smoked some draw, drank cheap cider, and their leader drifted off into a satisfied doze. He'd sent Page Moss a message.

A ten-year-old woke him at 9.30pm. 'Kingy, Kingy. The busies are everywhere. There's someone dead by the Park.'

His first thought was that the Moss Edz had hit back. 'They shot one of ours? I'll fucking kill them all.'

'I don't know, Kingy,' the child said in his high-pitched voice. 'Someone said it's a girl.'

This sent Kevin into apoplexy. 'They try to shag our women and now they're killing them! Let's destroy the twats.'

He went out into the garden. One of his older lieutenants, a ragged scally in his late teens, was coming down the street at a fast clip. 'Mate,' he said, 'you gorra get out of here. The busies are after you. They think you killed the girl. You have to hide.'

Kingy was stunned. 'I didn't shoot any girl.' Then anger kicked in again. 'Some other fucker shot a girl. I wouldn't shoot no fucking girl.'

'I'd get out of here. They'll be coming soon. Everyone knows we're here. Don't go home.'

Kevin got on his bike and rode quickly out of the area. He pedalled down into West Derby, past rows of semis with their well-tended gardens. This was the world he had grown up in, where boys and girls went to good schools, and were expected to go to University. It was a huge moment for Duke when he bought a house in the district. West Derby was the dream move for many of Scotland Road's poor.

Duke's son had been offered the sort of education that the aspirational lower classes crave, at St Edward's College. The purple blazer set him apart from the rougher kids, whose approval Kevin sought. He sorted that out when he was expelled.

It wasn't until he got close to his old school that he stopped. He took out his phone and rang a former classmate who had kept in contact. 'I've had a bit of trouble,' he said. 'Can I dump my bike at yours?'

The next call he made was to the Lord Warden. This time the Panther was in. Kingy did not go into specifics. 'I need to get out of the country,' he said. 'I need the Gasman to help. He owes me.'

Jim was appalled. He had left all this madness behind long ago. There had been reports of a shooting on the radio earlier, but he had thought little about it. The kids were playing cowboys and indians for real across the city. He was well out of it. Now he assumed the call, and the gunplay were connected.

'Are you fucking stupid calling me on this phone?' he told Kevin. 'You're not on your fucking mobile, are you?' The silence provided the answer. 'Christ,' Jim spat. 'Go somewhere safe. Don't call here again. And throw away that fucking mobile phone. Get someone to get you a pay as you go. Get someone to come in here tomorrow at 7pm and leave a number. Then, after we've spoken, throw the new fucking phone away, too. Now fuck off.'

The Panther had always been careful. After thinking for a moment, he nodded to the barman. 'Got to go out for half an hour. I'll be back before closing.'

It was dark on London Road and few people were about. He walked down Pudsey Street. It was gloomy. The huge, brick cliff at the rear of the Empire Theatre loomed over him as he strode towards Lime Street station. Inside, he headed to the bank of public phones and called Gazza's pager, giving his friend a number. The usual agreement was that the return call would happen in twenty minutes or, if that was impossible, three hours later.

Jim rang a mate who worked on the Echo to find out who had been shot. He'd had no success when the other phone rang. The Gasman was on the line.

The city was in a state of shock. The twelve-year-old had been to an Irish dancing class with a schoolfriend at a nearby church club. The classmate lived locally. The victim was getting the bus home and, when it appeared in the distance, the other girl bade goodbye to her mate and crossed the road to walk the two hundred yards or so to her house. The bus driver, seeing no one standing at the stop, never noticed the body lying on the floor. The friend did not realise anything was untoward until the dead girl's parents phoned to ask whether their daughter was still in Dovecot. The worried father had waited at Huyton bus station to take his only child home to one of the new-build semis in Huyton Village. The only thing that arrived to join the man that night was a lifetime's misery.

The parents were a media dream. The father was a middle-ranking civil servant and the mother a primary school teacher. They were articulate in their agony and photogenically presentable. They gave the sickeningly compelling case an added piquancy: the beautiful, only daughter of a loving, lower middle-class home, snatched away by a feral gang culture. A dysfunctional society had stepped into the homes of ordinary, decent people and brought evil and pain. The killing made national headlines.

The shooter left his bike at his mate's house in Norris Green and used the landline in the living room to call one of his cousins on his mother's side of the family to ask whether he could stay the night. When the relative agreed, Kingy walked to Broadway and took the 17 bus to St. Domingo Road, where he got off and ambled downhill to Marwood Towers.

By the time he reached the eighth-floor flat, the news bulletins were reporting the full extent of the horror in Dovecot. The cousins sat and smoked a joint while they listened to the radio.

As the gravity of the situation became clear, they formulated a plan. The cousin walked down to the garage on Scotland Road and bought a can of petrol, telling the man behind the counter that his car had run out of fuel. While he was away, Kingy took off all his clothes and packed them into a plastic bag.

Somewhere in the past, Kingy had been told that washing with gasoline was a good method of removing gunshot residue. He rubbed the petrol into his body. Once he finished, the pair poured the last of the flammable liquid on the clothes in the bag and dropped his mobile phone on top. The cousin went downstairs and set the package alight in the communal bin. Everyone would blame local kids.

The house stank of petrol fumes, but the pair lit another joint and drank some beer. Kingy crashed out in the early hours. It had been a long day. He was exhausted. He was too drunk and stoned to feel fear. Plus, he knew people that would help him. They would get him out of the country. They owed it to his dad. It was just an unlucky shot, anyway. Next time, he would get the bastard he was aiming at.

The next morning, the Gasman left the hotel to make a long phone call. When he came back, he looked ill. We sat in the lobby and spoke quietly, murmuring in Scouse.

'He's killed a girl. A schoolgirl.'

There was nothing to say. It was a case of waiting for him to continue. 'She was just an innocent bystander. He was aiming at someone else. The girl was at a bus stop. Wrong place, wrong time. The poor family…'

There was silence for a full minute. It felt much longer.

'He expects me to get him out. His dad did it for me.'

I sensed that my input would not help, so sat mute. 'It's moral blackmail. I have to do it, don't I?'

It was not a question I was prepared to answer. Did he owe any debt to Duke? And was it recoverable by his dead friend's son? And did I have a familial obligation to my cousin? He had effectively lost his father because of the threat to my mother and us kids.

'I think a lot about that night,' the Gasman said. 'I was young and wild. It just went out of control quickly. Fucking Billy went mad with the bottle.'

Two Americans came and sat down in adjacent seats. 'Let's take a walk,' he said. We headed north, towards the docks. It was appropriate. 'I always thought I was going to become a docker,' Gazza said. 'I never thought I'd travel. Not like Billy. I got seasick on the ferry. There were no jobs, though.

'My heroes were dockers. When I was at school, if we were

describing a big, strong, tough fella, we'd say 'he's a docker,' no matter what he did for a living. It was shorthand for being a hero; a compliment, a description of someone you could rely on.

'My ambition was to become one, but the docks shrunk. I didn't want much from life, really. I was forced to live abroad; forced to live like a mercenary. I made a mistake, but never imagined that would happen.'

The monologue was about something else. He said: 'What should I do about Kevin?'

What, indeed? The more I thought about him, the less kinship I felt.

'I didn't kill anyone,' Gazza said. 'I was holding him, hitting him, so that makes me guilty. But I didn't kill him.'

'It felt like we'd done the right thing. That fella was a threat to everyone around him. You know we were going to run him over the next week?'

I nodded. 'That's how we were brought up. It was social justice. I mean, people rarely ended up dead, but we tried to deal with anyone who was out of control. Drunks who misbehaved in town would get a slap, but civilians didn't get it. Not like this...'

There was some rewriting of history going on. I remembered someone telling me a story about my dad firing a gun on Lime Street when members of the Kray's crew came to town and tried to muscle in. Stray bullets must have flown everywhere. He was no marksman. Recklessness was nothing new.

But Kingy's disregard for neighbours and people around him transcended accidental shootings. The kid was psychotic.

Gazza read my mind. 'He might be Duke's son, but he's a lost cause. I'm not helping him get out. He belongs in jail or in a coffin. Am I wrong?'

No. He wasn't. 'I'll get the number and call him later. I'll tell him myself.'

The decision had been made. Neither of us could bring ourselves to help a child killer.

Kingy put down the phone. He tried to think. It was twenty-four hours since the shooting, and there was no evidence to link him to the crime apart from the word of his retinue of adolescents. There was only one way out. He picked up the receiver again and rang the police headquarters in Canning Place. 'I know who killed that girl in Dovey,' he told the man who answered. 'Write this down.' He gave a Dovecot address. 'The gun's there. You'll find the lad who shot her there, too. He's one of the Dovey Edz.'

He hung up and went back to the flat. Fuck it, he thought. I'll give every cunt up to get a deal. He began to write notes about everyone he knew who was committing crimes. He had plenty he could sell to the police. He wasn't going down for thirty years for that stupid cow who walked into his line of fire.

Billy was recovering from his heart attack at home when the phone rang. His wife answered, pulled an uncertain, disturbed face and said: 'I'm not sure. He's not been well.'

He sat up. 'Who is it?'

'It's your daughter.' He gestured for the phone.

'It's Julie,' the voice on the line said. 'Julie…' There was a moment's hesitation. '… Larty.'

'I saw you on telly,' he said. 'You were very good.'

She grunted. Neither knew what to say. 'Why did you never contact me?' There was an edge in her voice, as if ready for a row.

'I did.' he sighed. 'There wasn't a day that went by that I didn't think about you.'

She began to speak but stopped. The plaintive tone in his voice had the ring of truth.

'I'd like to talk to you face to face,' she said.

'Just you?' There was an element of alarm in his response. He wondered if her mentor was putting her up to it.

'Yes. Just me.'

'Where? Do you want to come here?'

'No,' she said with certainty. 'No. Somewhere public. The Adelphi?'

He chortled. 'It feels like we're in a spy movie. OK, when?'

'I'm doing a radio interview tomorrow morning,' she said. 'It's short notice…'

'I'll be there. What time?'

'One.'

'OK.' The line went dead. Billy turned to his wife. She looked so sad. 'Is this a good idea?' she said.

He shook his head. 'The worst. But it has to be done.'

There was a mound of flowers at the bus stop. The murdered girl's friends left heartrending, incoherent notes expressing their loss. Strangers laid down bouquets with messages of love and sorrow. The police rounded up the Dovey Edz and their Page Moss enemies. Boys and men aged between twelve and twenty-eight were dragged in for questioning. Detectives were appalled by the snarly attitude of the younger suspects. They laughed in the face of the police.

In the door-to-door inquiries, one name kept cropping up: Kevin Moran. He was from a bad family; a venomous little runt who preyed on younger kids; a modern day Fagan with his troupe of dangerous urchins. He was nowhere to be found. Within the first forty-eight hours, the authorities resigned themselves to the idea that Moran had skipped the country. They rousted all the gang's known hideouts and looked into the leader's background. He had very few friends. His life was centred around the crew.

A hotline was set up. A significant number of callers gave the same name. There was one exception. On the third day of the investigation, someone rang in and provided information that electrified the office. They were given a tip-off about the killer and the murder weapon's whereabouts. The gunman was a fifteen-year-old boy who lived a couple of hundred yards from the crime scene.

An hour later, two dozen armed police descended on the house close to Dovecot Park. The mother was stunned. There was no way her son could be involved. Then a detective came down the stairs with a revolver in a plastic bag. They handcuffed the teenager and bundled him out to a van. A small knot of neighbours jeered the prisoner.

'Did you hear the shot that night?' a policewoman asked the distraught mother.

'We thought it was a car backfiring,' she said, fighting the urge to cry.

'That was no car. That was the sound of your child taking a little girl's life. You must be proud.'

Horror had arrived at another house.

The meeting did not go well. The Adelphi, the most famous hotel in the city, was once ornate but had suffered neglect. Its grandeur was blunted by a film of grime. It had been glorious in the age of the transatlantic liners when my grandfather had hauled rich men's cases from the river to reception. Now it was just old and faded. Billy felt the same.

He sat in the corner of the bar and waited. It was nearly half an hour after the appointed time when his daughter arrived. He asked what she wanted to drink, and she turned down the offer, saying that she wasn't staying.

There were no niceties. 'Did you kill someone like the paper said?' she asked.

Billy nodded. 'I'm not surprised,' Julie said. 'You nearly killed my dad.'

'Do you know why?'

'I don't care.'

'And that's why they'd never let me see you kids. They wanted me out of your lives.'

'No wonder,' she said.

'I was the one who was wronged…' She cut him off. It was not what she wanted to hear.

'No, we were wronged. You never even remembered our birthdays.'

Billy was furious. 'I sent presents and money every birthday and Christmas. So did your nan. And lots of members of the family. They were always sending you a few quid.'

'We got none of it,' she said bitterly.

'You need to ask your mum where it all went.'

Julie bit back. 'Are you saying she's a liar? Are you saying she stole money off us?

'You walked out. You never came to see us. You're a murderer. You expect me to believe a word you say?'

It was, he thought to himself, a difficult argument to rebut. After a moment's silence, he took a new tack. 'How is your career going?'

'Why? want a story to sell to the newspapers?'

He dipped his head and spoke sadly. 'No one suffered more than me from the publicity.'

She snorted.

'Did your… did Eileen… I mean Missy, ever mention me?'

'You!' Julie declaimed theatrically, turning every head in the bar. 'You? Why on earth would she mention you?'

'I knew her. I was… we were… we knew each other when we were young.'

'You are insane,' the girl said. 'You're a fantasist. You probably never killed anyone either. You're making all this stuff up. This has been a mistake. Goodbye.'

She rose and walked out of the room. 'I love you,' he said weakly. 'I really do.'

He was alone again. He sat still for almost an hour, leaving his drink untouched, until the barman came and asked if he was OK.

'No,' he said, rising to his feet. 'No. Not OK.' Unsteadily, he walked out on to Lime Street. It would be easier if he never saw his daughter again.

The ability to compartmentalise people and relationships was a knack he had developed early, and it had been useful when he was away at sea, on tour, or in jail. It was impossible to block out Julie, though. He would see her on posters, screens, and newspapers on a regular basis. Radios and televisions would project her voice, penetrating the void of his consciousness. There was no escape from what he had done, nor what he had become.

News of Boy P's arrest was all over the airwaves. His identity could not be publicised because he was still fifteen. Kingy was confident that the youngster would be too scared to name the real gunman. P's silence was crucial to the next part of the scheme.

He and his cousin concocted a plan. First, he needed an alibi. The cousin was sleeping with a girl who was so high most of the time that she could barely remember what day it was. With a mix of threats, a cache of drugs and financial inducements, they encouraged her to say that she had been having sex with both of them on the night of the shooting. The idea of a threesome was just scandalous enough to make it believable.

Once she agreed, they plied her with cheap vodka and wraps of heroin. She slipped into unconsciousness and the pair celebrated by raping the comatose woman. When they sold their story to the police, it would not be a complete lie. And anyway, it was just a night's fun for them. The next day, content that there was no real evidence to tie him to the murder, Kingy went home and resumed his life as normal. It was superficial. He was waiting to be arrested and ready with his strategy.

Boy P's arrest was followed by Boy A's and Boy M's. The media started calling it the Alphabet Murder. The underage youths had been in thrall to stories of Duke and the gangster days of old – all told by Kevin Moran. In those tales, no one ever spoke to the police. Silence was the best weapon against the busies, they were led to believe. It worked to a degree. A and M were back on the streets within three days and even cockier for their experience. They were shocked to find that Kingy was hanging round Dovecot. He had a new bike – the old BMX had been retrieved from his former schoolmate and stripped down. The parts were dumped all over the city.

He went round to each of A and M's houses and spoke briefly with them. The conversation was the same. 'They've got the shooter. He did it. It was his gun. Everyone knows it. It had nothing to do with any of us. He was trying to prove he was a big, hard gangster. He bought the gun off me.'

That was the story they were to stick with, whatever pressure might be applied.

The police picked Kevin up later that day. His tactic was different from his father's. Kingy Moran did not shut up.

'I want to help,' he said. 'I was going to come and see you, anyway. I was thinking about that poor girl's family. The killer needs to be off the streets forever.'

The detectives were wrong-footed. 'My dad was framed,' he continued. 'I barely saw him growing up. I want the right murderer jailed this time.'

So began a preposterous but compelling tale. He bought the gun and then sold the firearm on to the accused. Kingy gave the seller's name immediately and suggested that the man was a regular vendor of weapons.

He had realised in the past few days, he said, that he was too old to be running around with a gang. The war with Page Moss was silly. It was two sets of working class kids killing each other. He had become politicised and had abdicated his position as boss of the Dovey Edz. Boy P's gunplay was part of a leadership gambit.

The policemen were stunned. They could smell the bullshit, but it kept coming.

Kingy was beginning to think about settling down, he claimed. He had met a girl. He had seen firsthand the destruction a life of crime could inflict on a family. There was no possibility that he would put a child through it.

When he gave them the girlfriend's identity, the detectives guffawed. She was a well-known crackhead. And guess what? This was his alibi. He had, he said, been engaged in group sex on Netherfield Road when the poor schoolgirl was shot. It was embarrassing, but loads of couples like to swing a bit. 'We love each other even though she likes double cock,' he said, grinning.

He was reformed, he told his interrogators. Because of this, he was happy to help the authorities. His offer was simple. He would name all his criminal contacts: the dealers, the robbers, the gangbangers and the fences, and provide the sort of information that would lead to convictions.

They waited to hear his demands. There were none. He had done nothing, he said. He did not need to bargain. They held him for forty-eight hours and then kicked him loose.

Nothing in the story added up.

Boy P was suffering more fear at the thought of Kingy's vindictiveness than he was at being convicted for a murder that he did not commit. The schoolboy was timid and tearful. He shook and stammered. There was never a possibility that this kid was leadership material.

This was the biggest case on Merseyside for a decade. Reporters descended on the city from all over the world and the publicity machine showed no sign of slowing down. The police looked more stupid by the day.

'Why did you never tell me you knew my father?' Julie spent a week working herself up for this confrontation. Missy stared her down.

'I don't. I didn't.'

'You never knew him twenty years ago?'

'I knew a lot of men. So many I can't remember.'

'You remember this one? I saw him. In Liverpool. Then he wrote me a letter. He thinks you used me to get revenge.'

Missy snorted. 'He should be so fucking lucky,' she said, turning the laugh to a snarl so seamlessly it was sinister. 'Yes, I knew someone like him. He vanished. Didn't he do the same with you?'

The girl nodded. 'So why the fuck are you coming in on the bounce to me? No, I didn't know you had anything to do with him until I saw that paper and recognised him when he was young. And if I'd known you were connected with him, I'd have fucked you off at that first audition.'

Rage suddenly swept over Missy. She wasn't entirely sure why, but she exploded. 'And you come here and talk to me like this? I made you, you cheap bitch. I can send you back to whatever shithole you came from if you fuck with me. Get out of my fucking office before I end your poxy career.'

Julie scuttled out. The showdown was a serious miscalculation. Missy waited until her breathing settled, took a bottle from a tray of drinks in the corner of the room, and poured herself a shot of tequila. She drank it and smiled. That would teach the silly little cow.

Part of her was intrigued by the fate of her former beau. His disappearance had been a watershed for Missy's relationships. After that, she never fell for any man so completely again. She had no interest in rekindling any kind of relationship, but there was one thing she rued ever so slightly. He was a murderer. That turned her on. It would have really got her going when she was young. She wondered if it was evil she saw in him. Over the years, she had learnt that evil excited her as much as power.

Over the next few days, Kingy became more brazen. People feared him. The gang, so arrogant in front of the police, were deferential to the killer in their midst.

He was pleased with his work in the interrogation room. It was an opportunity to pass on information about everyone who had ever crossed him – and some of his allies. In his warped mind, he saw this as a chance to take rivals off the streets. If he could create a void or two, he could fill it. It was easy for him to imagine that he could gain advantage and build an empire outside Dovecot.

There was another strand of logic in his scheme. Even if the cops managed to put together a case against him, he had been cooperative enough to engineer a deal. There were plenty of details that he held back. They would come in handy if the crisis escalated.

There was a flaw in his thought process. He had not taken into account the effect the case had nationally. The girl's parents made heartbreaking appeals for information. Reconstructions were staged and filmed using a petite policewoman to play the role of the victim. There were repeated raids on houses of gang members across the city. The case was a cause célèbre. Kingy was watched wherever he went. It was something he enjoyed at first, dragging plainclothes policemen across town.

What he did not know is that the authorities were also eavesdropping. A listening device was installed in Boy M's bedroom.

With the police following him everywhere, Kingy took to going to the houses of his young acolytes. In the privacy of their homes, they spoke freely. The microphone in Boy M's room picked up everything Kevin said. 'No fucking grassing,' he threatened. 'Just say it was the kid's gun, and he fired it. They can't pin it on me. None of us will do any time. He'll take the blame, the little twat. I never liked him. I should have shot him and not her.'

They all laughed. Kingy would not have found it funny had he known who was listening.

Over the course of a month, the police compiled enough instances of Kevin alluding to himself as a killer for them to act. In a series of dawn raids, the murderer and many of his accomplices were swept into custody.

At first, the gang's leader had the same relaxed attitude that he displayed during his previous period under questioning. Then he heard the tapes. His demeanour changed immediately.

He spilt the whole story. Everyone who had helped him cover his tracks was implicated as he turned from swaggering hard man to a whimpering mess. Desperate to deflect justice away from himself, he asked to cut a deal for a lesser sentence. 'You've been watching too many films, mate,' a detective said. 'You'll go down for longer than your old man. Well, Kingy, you'll be changing your name to Queenie when you get to the nick.'

Things initially moved fast. He was remanded in custody the following day and moved to HMP Woodhill, some 170 miles to the south. He was placed under close supervision. Other inmates hissed at him and shouted 'little girl killer' whenever they got a glimpse of the newcomer. The prison officers were barely more welcoming. Tough times lay ahead.

The trial was predictable, but sensational. Kevin Michael Moran pleaded not guilty but was convicted of murder by a jury whose deliberation period was little more than a tea break. He was jailed for life with a minimum tariff of twenty-two years.

The boys P, M and A were given between two and three years in youth custody. Another six people, including the killer's cousin and fake girlfriend, were imprisoned for aiding and abetting the murderer. Justice was done and seen to be done.

The newspapers pored over every aspect of the guilty man's life. Duke's conviction was dredged up and the obvious links between the murderous father and son were emphasised. It made it sound as if their lives were part of a single, unseemly narrative: that Duke and his child were cast from the same mould.

It was infuriating to read. My uncle was always part of the community from which he emerged; his son only ever had contempt for those around him. Kingy wasn't the only one. All his feral little crew had disdain for their parents and their neighbours, and came to think of anyone outside their clique as potential victims. They despised and terrorised adults, and preyed on their contemporaries. There was no society in their minds. They wanted instant gratification and did not care about those who got in their way. They paid lip service to the idea of brotherhood, but only the youngest maintained that ethos under pressure. Their leader – and his lieutenants, who had reached adulthood – sold out the rest of the cohort in a moment.

Duke stood on for his friends. His son junked any notion of

fidelity when the crisis came.

The newspapers made difficult reading for Billy. His name was rehashed again in sidebars, and the unprovable allegations that he framed Duke had a second airing. It was cheap, easy copy and gave editors a chance to get a picture of Julie Larty on a spread that otherwise featured photographs of shaven headed thugs or hoodied adolescents.

By the time the case began to fade from the collective consciousness, it was well into the new millennium. It had been a rough time for Billy. He looked older than his fifty-four years. We met in the Beehive on Paradise Street, close to where I'd worked in Canning Place. The big, 1970s hotel across the road had been demolished. Soon, older buildings would follow. A huge new development was beginning in the area.

'It's not the city we knew,' I said.

Billy misconstrued the statement. 'It's changing. It's becoming less distinct every year that goes by. It's becoming an English city. The attitude has changed.'

I laughed. 'I meant the redevelopment. Every time I come home, there's a new building going up. I get lost in town now.'

'That's part of it,' he said. 'You used to know you were in Liverpool when you went into a pub. You couldn't be anywhere else. I travelled the world when I was at sea. In the best cities you know, you couldn't be anywhere else. This was one of the best places.'

It was too negative an analysis, but he went on. 'It's both physical and metaphysical. I've said this to you before. When people stopped travelling, things became different. Less cosmopolitan. Scousers always travelled, Milltowners stayed put. We were a global people. Now we're local again.'

I was not in the mood for Billy's maudlin observations. 'I'm thinking of moving back,' I said. 'Spending most of my time here again.'

It was true. Something had changed. The connection with the city that I thought had been broken was being renewed. It was football that kick-started the process.

I was going to Stamford Bridge for a game – in the corporate section, of course – and was drinking at the Butcher's Hook on the Fulham Road. It was a terrible bar with awful beer but my host was meeting another two guests there. We stood outside and watched the crowds drift up towards the stadium. I was regaling my companion with tales of how dangerous this area used to be on matchdays in the 1980s. His middle-class eyes were glazing over. He would have been an infant when we were running the gauntlet two decades previously.

There was a rumble of chanting from down the street. 'Here's your lot,' my host said. It was a couple of hundred away fans, corralled by nearly as many police. The escort had almost man-to-man marking.

They were chanting, and the words stunned me: 'We're not English, we are Scouse.'

The Londoners looked at them with real contempt. They could not compute the logic of the song. The home supporters were shaking their heads and catcalling our boys. They must have thought the chant was an affectation, but I understood. The spirit of Scouse particularism had survived. I thought it was gone. Clearly, I'd been away too long.

I found out later that there was an underground movement among Liverpool fans determined to maintain the Scouse identity. A group called Keep Flags Scouse targeted Crosses of St George and Union Flags at matches and covered them with red Liver Bird banners with the words of the song written on them. They politely requested the owners of the offending flags to remove their symbols of England and the British State and, if the unacceptable banners were not taken down, they were confiscated. This was eye-opening. It was glorious.

There was even a mythological codification of what was and wasn't acceptable to display at Liverpool games. The Boss Wednesday agreement – it was a play on Northern Ireland's Good Friday agreement – did not exist but it would be gleefully cited to those foolish enough to put the name of a Middle English town on a banner and take it to a Liverpool game. If someone had the temerity to display, say, a Union Jack with Essex Reds written across the horizontal band, they would be told that it contravened section six, subsection two of the Boss Wednesday Agreement, a clause that expressly forbade the use of non-Liverpool district names on banners. It messed with woolyback minds.

There was a general consensus that our flags should be red, should feature Liver Birds and only the place names of Liverpool neighbourhoods or the contiguous towns outside the city's limits, like Bootle.

It was half jokey, half real. KFS hit squads prowled our ends at away games. This was great. I became a matchgoer again.

Going to the games made me aware that there was also a renewal of political awareness among young people. It was not as widespread as it was in the militant 1980s, but it was still vehement. The resistance was still there, planted deep and waiting for the right conditions to grow. As in my youth, football and politics were still intertwined. Kids like my fucking stupid cousin got the headlines. But for every Kingy and his crew of rats, there were tens of others who were committed to social justice and eager to express their disparate sense of identity. Once I saw it that day in west London, I was in thrall to it again. Liverpool was crawling with students, and that gave the city a youthful feel, but it was the inventiveness and quirky compassion of the locals that was resurfacing. At least that's the way it felt to me, and it was drawing me back. The siren call of Scouse might have been a foghorn, but for nearly two decades the word 'home' was just shorthand for a physical place. Now it meant something again. The connection had been restored.

Billy was talking while I thought about all this. I'd tuned out. It was no use explaining it to him. I realised he was talking to me, giving that eyebrows raised, are-you-ignoring-me look. He tried again. 'Will you go to visit him?'

I spat out a mouthful of Guinness.

'No chance. Why would I visit that little shit?'

Kingy regularly made the news. He was not as famous as the Moors murderers or the Bulger killers, but he was in the next strata of notoriety. According to the most recent burst of publicity, he had beaten another prisoner with some sort of cosh. Before that, he was said to have begged to be put in solitary after being attacked by other felons. Next, I suspected he would knife someone or be stabbed himself. I rather hoped it would be the latter.

'Not him, you soft get, Gazza.'

The previous year, the law had caught up with the Gasman. He could not leave bootlegging alone. He had continued to dabble in the business. It had to end sometime and, after the Disneyland debacle and his deportation from the States, the UK authorities were always going to catch up. They did in 2002.

The trial was another sexy media story. The judge said he had 'caused significant potential losses to recording companies, performers and artists.' David Bowie, Michael Jackson and Prince were just a few of the superstars named by the court as victims of the Gasman.

He was given a four-year sentence. Well, as Duke said all those years ago, he had that coming. The kicker was more painful. The judge ruled he had to pay back assets of nearly £2 million or face another five years in jail. At least he had the money.

We chuckled about the statement made by the British Phonographic Industry's anti-piracy unit outside court. 'We are delighted to see this man in jail,' the spokesman said. 'We have been pursuing him for more than a decade. He was one of the major figures in a global criminal enterprise and his very nickname, the Gasman, spread fear throughout the world.'

Gas-Meter Peter had made the big time. You had to laugh.

'He's out soon,' Billy said.

'He'll go back to Amsterdam. And hopefully retire. He's had to sell his cars, his flat in Chelsea and a couple of houses down south. He'll appear skint. He'll be fine. He's got enough money hidden away. The property and brewery are all in my name. I'll give him a job in this beer business when he gets out. After all, he owns most of it.'

It was going well. We produced a West Coast pale ale, in the northern Californian style, a very hoppy and resiny drink. It was beginning to get noticed. Once again, Gazza's instincts had paid off. It made little money, but it was legal.

'What about you?'

'I'm well out of the bootlegging business,' I said. It was true. 'I own a lot of property and have been diversifying. I do OK.' We had reached the awkward part.

'You doing alright for money?' I asked. He grimaced. 'If you…' The sentence got no further. He cut me off with an open palm and a fierce look on his face. There was no way he could bring himself to take my cash. The teaching job had disappeared after one bout of publicity too many. Rock'n'roll was supposed to be full of outlaws, but it wasn't quite working out this way for Billy. His wife could finance the family, but it must have hurt his pride.

Charisma had spawned an entire generation of reality shows that churned out identikit celebrities who rode a swell of fame for a year or so and disappeared back into obscurity. Billy hated the way the entertainment world had developed – after all, it was personal to him – and access to instant stardom rankled. It had been a depressing few years. He kept returning to the subject after a few beers.

'You have to pay your dues. You have to earn success; it's like doing an apprenticeship. It never works if you're thrown in at the deep end. You can't cope.'

The anger was mixed with an undercurrent of concern for his daughter. He needn't have worried. She was a sensible girl who would wring every bit of long-term stability out of this short time in the spotlight. And she had a likeability factor that radiated out of the television screen.

At that point, I realised something. She had some strange, unquantifiable form of charisma. And where technology greyed out her father's vibrancy, it exacerbated and enhanced Julie's niceness.

At least the show gave her a chance. Increasingly, it seemed that the majority of people who were having success in the entertainment industry were from privileged backgrounds. Old Etonians were getting top billing on TV and in Hollywood. Pop stars were the sons and daughters of Lords and Ladies or City bankers. The shrinking welfare state did not provide any sort of safety net for those who needed time to fulfil their ambitions in art. The opportunities that Billy had spoken of so thrillingly all those years ago had been blocked off. Escape routes had been sealed. Venues were shutting down everywhere, and only those who could treat music and acting as an affordable hobby were progressing in the business. That's the way it seemed, at least.

The sad thing is that the talent shows were just another form of patronage. Ability had little to do with success. Most of those entering the contests were of a similar level. The winners were generally the ones that were pre-selected by producers like Missy on the basis of them being the most potentially profitable. An industry of exploitative freakshows had sprung up that gave the illusion of giving a chance to those who otherwise would not have had any hope. Not much of a chance, though.

With a start, I realised Billy had asked me another question. I had not been listening again. He could no longer hold even the captive audience of his biggest fan.

The King of the Kids was now catcalled as Kidkiller everywhere he went. After the conviction, he was shunted around a handful of prisons, and an air of chaos followed him around the system. The local paper kept everyone up to date with his movements. Flicking through it one night, I noticed that his latest home was Wakefield, where his father had spent the majority of his sentence.

It was ironic. This is where the toddler had experienced his only interaction with his dad. I wondered whether visiting now was similar to when I went to see Duke. And I wondered who visited his son. It was hard to imagine a queue forming to see him.

The week before Christmas, he made the headlines. A fellow inmate stabbed him. It was a huge story for a few days and then faded off the news pages. He died on Boxing Day, just after the tsunami hit the Indian Ocean. The cataclysmic event pushed Kevin Michael Moran's death down the agenda. I missed it. Billy rang me with the news three days later. He sounded relieved. No one in our circle felt any sense of loss.

Duke was born in the cacophony of catastrophe and made his mark. His son disappeared unnoticed in the swell of bigger issues.

Neither of us would attend the funeral. It was over. He had no children and there was very little possibility of me reproducing. I was the last of that branch of the family. It was probably just as well.

Against all predictions, Julie Larty proved to be a more enduring celebrity than most of her talent or reality-show contemporaries. When her five-year contract with Stevenson's company ended, she broke off all ties with Missy and the Charisma star-making machine. She thrived under new management, popping up in television dramas, West End shows and inheriting the sort of reassuring, affable, northern female role once filled by the likes of Gracie Fields and that Tory bitch Cilla Black, a traitor who came from Scotland Road.

The occasional story cropped up in the redtops reworking the break-up of Julie's family and the murder allegations, but she assumed it was just Missy making trouble. The women never spoke again after she moved on.

There were other, more urgent tabloid scandals to be read. The Charisma merry-go-round prospered on the backstories of its participants, and potential stars were increasingly chosen for their unimaginable backgrounds as ratings slowly slipped. A contestant's drug-dealing brother, a sister forced into prostitution, a terminally ill family member these were the sort of tales that excited viewers and readers. Missy made sure her contact at the paper was fed with sensational information.

Things were changing, though. Her favourite reporter retired suddenly, and his phone number stopped working. There was no showbiz send-off at the Fortress and no tributes in his paper. He just disappeared. Yes, she had other contacts in the media, but no one with nearly the same level of trust. That turned out to be another stroke of luck for Missy. It soon became clear why the writer had left. The first stirrings of the phone-hacking scandal were leaking out.

For a short while, Missy was nervous. She had been complicit in hacking many of the artists under her charge – and numerous other public figures – by supplying phone numbers and ensuring the victims' lines were occupied by calling them, allowing the hacker to get access to recorded messages. Instead, things worked in her favour. There was no evidence that she was involved, and the investigation showed that Missy's own mailbox had been illicitly accessed. She knew that, of course. The question was whether the reporter involved would confess the full extent of his transgressions.

It was a genuine concern for Missy. After months of silence, the journalist rang her. They arranged a meeting in Soho at the Groucho Club. She was expecting a clumsy attempt at blackmail. Instead, her contact dropped a different sort of bombshell. He had cancer and was not expecting to live too long. Missy managed to hide her relief. She offered any help needed and, in front of the man, wrote out a cheque for £20,000, unsolicited, to see him through those last tough months. It could not have worked out any better.

In the end, the news organisation involved paid Missy £750,000 in an out-of-court settlement for being hacked. Yet again, she had taken a slice of the profits at both ends. When the News of the World closed, the last lingering fears she would be unmasked for her part in myriad exposes disappeared.

She was aware that she had narrowly escaped a scandal, but it added to the sense that she was indestructible. As the first decade of the new millennium ended, she had everything going for her. She was a national treasure; it looked like she was in line to become a Dame, and she had the financial power to do anything and buy anyone she wanted. Was she happy? It didn't matter. She could sate any desire that came to mind.

116

Things began to turn for Billy. The negative publicity caught the eye of several people. One of them was a chancer who was trying to make a career as a promoter. The notoriety generated by Julie's rise to fame, and the associated clamour, had the knock-on effect of reminding people about Scouse Pie and the covers band that drew 1,000 people a night in their heyday. The entrepreneur was on to something. The twentysomethings of the 1980s were approaching their fifties. They were ripe for nostalgia. He approached Billy, who was not interested initially. Over a beer, I convinced him it was worth a try.

It was remarkable. The scallies of thirty years earlier had got jobs, careers, houses. Enough of them had disposable income that they were willing to spend recapturing moments from their youth. Suddenly – again – Billy was an overnight, local sensation. Yes, he was billed as 'Charisma Winner's Dad' at first, but soon it became 'Liverpool's own…'

His health returned. Success, even on this minor level, made him glow. For a man who had given up, it was a massive change. And a positive one. I even went to see him. For the first time, I could listen to that pliable voice and accept that he was justified singing other people's words for a living.

The internet gave his original compositions a new life. The songs were popular on local radio, and a very well-respected combo covered Pursuit on their album. Enough cheques arrived to make Billy's self-esteem bloom again.

I met him in the Glass House on Vauxhall Road, just

two hundred yards or so from where his words on the stairs thrilled a young boy. What he had to say was almost as exciting. He was going to sea again. He would sing to a captive, cruise-ship audience full of ageing baby-boomers. It was the perfect environment for Billy. His mixture of songs and old showband patter served him well. The booking was for a seven-day Mediterranean trip, but there was potential for future engagements. The thought of being on the high seas again excited him. 'It's like Butlins for coffin dodgers,' he said, grinning, 'but I've got a bit of life in me yet.' The money was good, but his wife was not happy.

'It'll work out,' he said. 'It'll give her a break. I've been sitting at home moping for too long. It's great to be an entertainer again.'

We were joined by some of his old mates. A few of the kids who squatted in the cool, concrete turn in the stairs all those years ago now sat around a table laughing and playing cards. I went up to order a round and, after handing out the beers to the group, moved back to the bar to collect my pint. For a while I watched. Billy was telling them a story about his days in the showband. They'd most likely heard it a hundred times – I had – but each retelling brought a different wrinkle, a new gag, a slight twist of direction. They were hanging on his every word.

Yes, he still had something. It probably was never enough to have got him to where he wanted to be, but it was better than nothing.

At last, things had worked out for him. I had not seen him so happy in a long time. He became wrapped up in the game and the conversation and, on a whim, I finished my ale and left without saying goodbye. I walked along Vauxhall Road back towards town, feeling like a little kid again.

117

Every now and then, Julie Larty would pop up on TV or in the papers. She seemed to be doing fine. The six-week wonder was still charming the public more than a decade after Charisma. The most remarkable thing about her career was that people seemed to have forgotten that she had come to prominence in a reality show.

Missy was not as ubiquitous as she was in the early years of the millennium, but she still maintained a high profile. Disturbing rumours circulated about her behaviour. There were a couple of incidents where she was seen at a public event in a dishevelled state. There were suggestions she was drinking or that her cocaine use was spinning out of control. She did not seem to have as many friends in the media's new generation.

When Jimmy Savile died, Missy was effusive in her tributes. 'He was a great man,' she said. 'He did exactly what he wanted to do. He was in control. I loved his attitude and approach. I didn't know him very well, but I met him once and think I got to the bottom of the man. He inspired me.'

It was an open secret in the industry that there were certain expectations that came with involvement in the agency created by Missy and Stevenson. He retained the Mr Charisma nickname, although both sexes in showbusiness referred to him increasingly as 'Blow-job-or-no-job.' Sexually pliable boys and girls tended to get promoted more fiercely by their mentors. Missy always had a young, ostensibly homosexual man on her arm. There was talk that she liked gay couples to perform for and on her.

She was prone to bouts of rage, too. Those close to her put it down to years of substance abuse. Her fascination with Aleister Crowley continued, and effigies of her enemies hung skewered around her office. Julie's name was on one.

When allegations about Savile's predatory behaviour surfaced, and hundreds of victims reported countless sexual assaults, several famous personalities faced investigation into abusive behaviour in their past. Missy was amused by the arrests of ageing celebrities. The scandal centred on the BBC and her associations with the national broadcaster were scant. Apart from attending recordings of Top of the Pops back in the 1980s and appearances on talk shows, once Charisma turned her into a star, she had barely set foot on BBC premises. It tickled her she had carried out a sexual assault at Television Centre. On Savile.

It never crossed her mind that anyone would complain about her conduct over the years. Women did not get accused of this sort of depraved activity.

The last thing Missy expected was the police turning up on the doorstep of her Belgravia townhouse. No one tipped her off. Detectives took her, a number of computers and boxes of books on the occult, to the station. To make it worse, a BBC reporter found out that an arrest was about to take place. He agreed to a deal with the Met, and the broadcaster was able to film the entire scene from a helicopter.

The story made the front pages of every paper the next day. Even the broadsheets used her picture. A man in his early thirties alleged Missy had groped him in the mid-90s when he was part of a failed boy band. In the wake of the publicity, another dozen people – of both sexes – made similar allegations. One man claimed Missy forced him to commit homosexual acts with another youngster while she looked on. A number of girls said she demanded they strip naked and then slapped them with a riding crop. The most damaging accusation came from a former member of a pop band who asserted that the woman had convinced him to participate in a black magic ritual at her house in the 1980s when he was fifteen. The detail he supplied was compelling. She ordered him to strip naked, wash in a bath of salty water, dry off and don a gold, silk shirt and stand in a pentacle made of candles while she chanted strange words. The charade ended with her performing oral sex on the terrified teenager.

With each wave of allegations, more victims came forward. Her partner in the rise to fame, Stevenson, did not exactly rush to help her. When reporters doorstepped him, his comments were ambiguous at best. 'She was always wild, but I thought it was just sort of…' he groped for a word, '… flirty. You know, a bit Carry On. It's a very sexual industry. Most people seemed to enjoy her company and find it a bit saucy. I know I did. I never saw anything that overstepped the boundaries.' He failed to mention that his lawyers were working their way through his contact book and approaching 'conquests' of both sexes with a pile of cash and a wad of non-disclosure agreements.

The journey from national treasure to pariah was short. The majority of Missy's showbusiness friends blanked her. Too many of her relationships had been built on ambition and fear. The aspirational looked for another avenue to help satisfy their desires. The fearful gained their revenge by spreading gossip about the nefarious carnal activities of the accused.

The trial kept the nation captivated. Missy maintained her innocence right up until the doors of the court. On day three, she sensationally changed her plea on three counts of indecent assault. The judge noted that there was an element of grooming in the crimes and pointed out the breach of trust that her behaviour represented. She was, he said, an opportunistic predator who used her position to abuse vulnerable young people.

She was motionless in the dock when the fifteen-month sentence was handed down. There was a gasp in court and an outcry in the media. Her OBE was rescinded. It was, most believed, a light punishment.

Julie was forced to put out a statement after the conviction. 'I was new to the world of entertainment,' it said. 'Some of her behaviour shocked me, but I thought it was normal in showbusiness. A lot of people seemed to have looser sexual morals than I was used to. I never saw any crimes, but she could be outrageous. None of us had any idea she overstepped the mark in her private life.'

The prosecution appealed. The sentence was doubled. The celebrity who was once feted across London's ritziest venues was sent to HMP Holloway. She served her time in the same cells where suffragettes were held for fighting for women's rights. Missy never had a sense of sisterhood. Prison did nothing to encourage a rethink.

She was released after serving half her sentence, one of the last felons to do time in the historic jail. Then she disappeared from public life. Her wealth remained intact. Rumours said that she was spending a lot of time in Thailand to sate her perverse desires. A couple of papers sent reporters to check out the situation, but if she was up to no good in the Far East, there was no evidence to be found. She went back to the name on her birth certificate and, even though it was used in the trial, few recognised it. Missy would always be a creation of a certain time that existed only during a period when culture lost its way. That character was a product of an era of greed and an epoch where people were encouraged only to have responsibility to themselves and profit. It was good that she was gone from day-to-day British life. Too many like her remained in the public eye.

118

Gazza was in town. The brewery we set up was going nicely, and the property business had grown over the years. We called it Duke Brewing, and the flagship pale ale was named after my uncle. Gasman lager was its companion beer. It was highly necarbonated. Hair Of The Dog was a brown ale that nodded to his friend John. Panther IPA crept up on you.

The courts stripped almost all of my partner's visible assets, but our legitimate businesses had long been established and he had money and property on the Continent. He was enjoying semi-retirement.

We went to the Mitre – now renamed the Ship and Mitre and restyled as a craft beer and real ale pub. It stocked our produce. A man in front of us asked for two Dukes, a Gasman and a Panther. 'Some crew, that,' I said. Billy was going to join us. The pair had not seen each other for more than a decade.

The changes to the pub's décor had not materially altered the nature of the place my drinking companions knew from the sixties. We sat in the back room, up on a small raised area of seating, and reminisced.

'We used to have a drink here before going the Hotsy Totsy,' Gazza said. 'All the characters used to come in. Loads from Gerrard Gardens and the Crescent, the Foneyhoy boys and youse from all along Vauxy. Bad mob.' He shook his head, recalling a more rugged clientele.

There were students and beer hipsters at the bar. 'They would have scared this lot senseless,' he said. He turned to Billy.

'Wasn't it in here that you…?'

'Yeah, I was walking in with Duke, and he was coming out. He legged it.' Billy spoke about the attack on his children's stepfather as if he had seen it in a movie. 'I threw him over the tunnel wall.'

'Where were you away?'

'Walton,' Billy said. 'Now that was a rough place.'

'I only got an open prison,' the Gasman said. 'White collar crime. You know me, never got involved in any of that rough stuff. What was the fella's name?'

'Larty.'

The Gasman made the connection. 'Yeah, Julie,' he said. 'Should have remembered. You see her?'

'No, unfortunately.'

'I'd love to know what she thought about that judge on the show, the one who was her mentor.'

Billy's ears pricked up. 'She was a weird one, that Missy,' Gazza said. 'I paid her quite a lot of cash over the years. Got my money's worth, mind you.'

Both of us were shocked. The Gasman had no idea that Billy had a relationship with her. The connections were getting stranger.

'How did you know her?' I asked.

'Who do you think got us all those studio tapes in the early days?' You always hear about jaws dropping, but never believe it happens. Billy's was gaping. I guess mine was, too.

'I met her in the Dam. She was with a band. All in leather. Jeez, she looked horny and…'

'You fuck her?' Billy interjected a little too fast. Christ, I thought, there's still jealousy there.

'No,' Gazza laughed. 'I was big-shotting with her in a bar, trying to impress and thought I was in. All I got was humiliated and a business proposition. She fed me tapes for about fifteen years. Until she got big on telly. I heard rumours about the weird shit. She was into the occult. Someone told me she liked Thailand. She could buy anything there. The hard-core stuff in the Dam wasn't enough for her. Don't want to think about what she got up to in the Far East.'

I wondered whether Billy would say something, but he moved the conversation on. 'I just hope Julie wasn't exposed to any of it,' he said.

'She seems a sensible girl,' the Gasman replied.

'She is. Anyway, how long you home for?' It was time for a different subject.

After an hour or so, Gazza left. He had a number of people to see, and it was a short trip. We hugged as he departed. I whispered in his ear: 'You learn your lesson. Stay retired.'

I went the bar and returned with two more Dukes. We both sighed as one.

'Well?'

'Small world,' Billy said lightly.

'Don't give me that. I heard it in your voice. You were worried he'd shagged her.'

'No, not really…'

'You still imagining about how your life could have turned out? After all that's come out about her? She's a sick individual. That was the luckiest escape you've ever had!'

'You didn't know her,' he said. 'It was different. Had things not happened… had I not been forced to go away, then it all might have been different. There was a nice, caring side to her, you know, and I seemed to bring that out.'

'It might have been the other way round. She might have sucked you into the shit she was involved in.'

'No one's evil,' he said. 'It just happens. We let it in. This society we live in encourages it slyly. You know what the worst thing is?'

There was no point in hazarding a guess.

'Believing that you are the most important person in the world, the only one that matters. She wasn't like that when I knew her. People weren't like that back then.'

People have always been like that, but maybe he had a point. Less of them were self-absorbed in the time he was talking about. It wasn't a golden age, but there was more than nostalgia that made people look back with regret.

I walked along Dale Street after putting Billy in a taxi. On a whim, I carried on down Water Street to the Lanny.

No one called it the Lanny anymore. It was the Pier Head. It was where the liners docked and somewhere near here my grandfather was pecked in the eye. A seagull flew above and squawked on cue. It was a comforting sound, the voice of home.

I sat and looked at the Mersey and reflected on the night – or it might have been more than that. Powerful people have always taken advantage of those with less leverage. Class, wealth, and patronage dominated the world I grew up in. We wanted to change it. We dreamt of equal opportunity, of no longer kowtowing to others because of an accident of birth. It seemed a reasonable expectation.

Vulgarism was off the leash, though. The 80s created opportunity, but not for everyone. The worst people, the most selfish and callous, were encouraged to run wild. More often than not, they were starting from a standpoint of privilege, anyway. They wanted to replace the traditional Old Boy Networks with their own cliques. They did not want to open up possibilities to different communities. They cared only about acquiring wealth and power. Screw everyone else.

Superficially, men like Duke were outlaws. He stole and had no respect for the law. What help could he get from the authorities if he needed it? But there was another aspect to his character. He understood his position in the world and his relationship to those around him. When the moment of crisis came, he realised he had placed Billy and the Gasman in an invidious situation and that the murder was his responsibility. He could have squirmed out, named the other two, and tried to bargain for years of freedom. Instead, he chose to take the punishment.

I smiled. I almost heard him say: 'I had five years coming.' There was some truth in what he said, but he knew what he was sacrificing.

Duke was part of a network, a community, and his belief system was rooted in decency. Some would call him a gangster, but he was concerned about those around him. In reality, he hurt very few and helped a large number of individuals.

He was a greater symbol of Britishness than the respected paragons of virtue who wrote off swathes of the populace and inflicted acts of political vindictiveness. There was nothing vulgar about Duke. His son grew up on the other side of Britain's great social watershed. Kingy was the essence of vulgarity.

It was bigger than Kevin and his singular circumstances, though. The Divvy was an aberration who turned out to be a forerunner. The drug dealer Billy killed was unusual in his utter contempt for everyone else in the neighbourhood. Vulgarism released thousands of Divvies. Kingy was one of them, a predator who cannibalised his own community.

The Dovey Edz and their ilk were nihilistic. Thatcher said there was no society and the kids of the underclass were living proof that she was right. The short life of Duke's son had been played out against a backdrop of politics designed to destroy the bonds that tied people together.

I'd seen it close up. The Governments of Kevin's lifetime had no moral compass.

They talked about the 'managed decline' of this city, contemplating creating an economic famine regardless of the consequences for the populace. They pulverised the mining industry in a rolling act of ideological savagery. My elbow ached at the memories, but not as badly as the hearts of those poor bloody pitmen and their women and dispossessed children whose villages were wiped off the map through deliberate neglect. The latest buzzword was 'austerity', a euphemism for policies that caused misery for millions.

The will to resist had been destroyed across much of the country. The idea of community was derided and Trades Unions destroyed. Anywhere people stuck together was a target for the vulgarists. No wonder the subsequent generation were only out for themselves.

Duke's son was a child of his age. It was terrible that he was deprived of a father, but that was not unusual in our background. Liverpool men died young. They went away to sea and didn't return. If anything, young Kevin was lavished with more affection than had his dad still been around. Yet during his formative years, the message put forth by the most powerful people in the land told him the only person he had any responsibility to was himself. Drugs made the situation worse. It was heartening to see a growing backlash against his kind of behaviour in the city.

Missy was a strange case. I had only seen her on television. Her fame and stardom gave her a different kind of power. She could open doors for aspiring young entertainers and grant them unimaginable opportunities. It was the purest patronage, and she used the position to humiliate and sexually demean those who came begging for her favour. Perhaps something in her background sparked the vulturine carnal desires; maybe Billy's sudden disappearance, which she could have taken as a cruel rejection, had a destructive effect. It was hard to know. The Gasman's view was that she was driven by money and abnormal sexuality. That might have been his bitterness at being one of the few of her business partners who didn't get to share her bed.

Julie Larty was one of the desperate thousands who pleaded

for a shot at the big time. Missy granted her it. Why? Did she see Billy in the girl? If the show was about pure talent, surely Julie would not have made it through the first interview. But maybe not. You did not need Missy's uncanny knack to see that the girl had something that the public found compelling. Julie had it, Missy could see it, and the reason did not really matter. It wasn't talent – or not much of it, anyway – but Julie had enough personality to succeed within the narrow boundaries of the TV show. It would take a redefinition of the word charisma to justify her victory, but what she had was close enough. She was quaint, old-fashioned. Julie evoked a different time when people were nice and cared.

Could she have made it in the traditional way, starting off in pubs and clubs and working her way up through the business? That's doubtful. Her father had paid his dues, learnt his trade, and become a slick performer. At each step up the ladder, he had enough appeal to succeed – until the summit was almost in sight. That was beyond him.

Julie could only have been presented to the public fully formed. What they saw was all she had. She could not have negotiated years of improvement.

Charisma, and shows like it, sent out ugly lessons for generations of teenagers. It told them that there was a route to instant celebrity and fortune. They would line up to beg and plead before people like Missy for decades to come, humiliating themselves on and off camera for that million-to-one chance. It was the showbiz version of playing the lottery, only most paid with their integrity.

It would go on. The rewards were so great and the poverty of opportunity so pronounced. Being financially poor is awful; believing there is no potential to change and improve your life is devastating. The show created irrational hope. Except for Julie, the finalists and winners were more or less pre-determined. Maybe she was too, in a way.

I did not want to become a career criminal. Was that predestined, too, like the policeman told me on the night of the Divvy's murder? Of course not. All I know is that being born into poverty is a political act. It is the first act of resistance and the first defeat.

There was never a good time to be poor, but I cannot blame Billy for misunderstanding. The high water mark of the working class had already passed and he could not see the tide was running against him.

Between then and now, there had been a revolution in the nation's culture and belief system. We were close to the beginning of a decades-long struggle when he spoke on the stairs, but we misunderstood what the conflict was about.

The realignment of the psyche of a nation was in progress. We thought we were engaged in a simple class struggle, but it was much bigger than that. The vulgarists selected the battleground, and the good guys were fighting the wrong war.

No wonder we lost.

Standing looking at the Mersey, the enormity of our failure hit me. So, with a deep breath of salty, damp air, I understood that defeat was our destiny, but resistance defined us. At least it was an identity. And I was back at home, a place that had more fight in it than most. I was ready for the next phase of the unwinnable conflict. Scouse power, la, Scouse power.

Acknowledgements

The songs in this book are real. They were created by Kevin McFarlane. When I started thinking about basing a story around a singer, there was a ready-made body of work available. That was a massive help. Kevin's ability needs a greater showcase than this.

Albert Boniface has provided invaluable help and support. Not in the literary sense but in real-life matters. An irreplaceable friend.

Tony Coleman suffered by having to listen to the tortuous development of this work, taking solace in his pint while I vented frustrations at my progress. Thankfully Peter, Martin, Glenn and all the crew at Cask Pub and Kitchen in Pimlico made sure we had the best beer available to dull any creative pain. Peter and Martin's generosity has been boundless.

Michael von Herff and Zach Osterman provided a perspective from across the Atlantic while Rae Singh and Jan Gorski-Mescir gave a view from Europe. Their positive response – and criticism – helped enormously.

Ian Prowse's reaction to the novel was a delight, which was satisfying because he is close to the epicenter of the action as well as being one of the best singer-songwriters that Merseyside has produced.

Thanks to all at Northodox, especially Ted and James. Their mission to bring northern writers to the forefront is one that needs to be backed, give them your support.

Finally, I owe much to family and friends, many of whom are no longer with us. Part of me hates this book because it accentuates some of the negative features of my background. The reality was much more nuanced and happier. Yes, the streets around Vauxhall and Scotland Roads were poor in wealth. But they were rich in love and community support.

SUBMISSIONS ARE OPEN!

WRITER &
DEBUT AUTHOR   [ ]

NOVELS &
SHORT FICTION   [ ]

FROM OR LIVING
IN THE NORTH   [ ]

UNDER THE BRIDGE

A LIVERPOOL MYSTERY

JACK BYRNE

**WHEN SECRETS
RESURFACE**

**THE PAST
REACHES OUT**

THE

HONEY

TALKER

BE CAREFUL WHICH RABBIT HOLES YOU FALL DOWN

MALCOLM HAVARD

THE SILENT
BROTHER

SIMON VAN DER VELDE

Printed in Great Britain
by Amazon

23722345R00225